forever
starts now

forever
starts now

USA TODAY BESTSELLING AUTHOR

STEFANIE LONDON

Entangled Publishing, LLC
10940 S Parker Road
Suite 327
Parker, CO 80134
Visit our website at www.entangledpublishing.com.

Amara is an imprint of Entangled Publishing, LLC.

Edited by Liz Pelletier and Lydia Sharp
Cover design and illustration by Elizabeth Turner Stokes
Photo of umbrella © dilyaz/Shutterstock
Photo of boots © Antonsoz85/Shutterstock
Photo of boots © HelenaQueen/Shutterstock
Interior design by Toni Kerr

Print ISBN 978-1-64937-023-5
ebook ISBN 978-1-64937-036-5

Manufactured in the United States of America

First Edition July 2021

AMARA

ALSO BY STEFANIE LONDON

KISSING CREEK SERIES

Kissing Lessons

THE PATTERSON'S BLUFF SERIES

The Aussie Next Door
Her Aussie Holiday

THE BEHIND THE BAR SERIES

The Rules According to Gracie
Pretend It's Love
Betting the Bad Boy

OTHER ROMANTIC COMEDIES

How To Win a Fiancé
How to Lose a Fiancé
Trouble Next Door
Loving the Odds
Millionaire Under the Mistletoe
Taken By the CEO

Forever Starts Now is a sweet, small-town romance that is full of hope and heart, but there are images and themes that might be triggering to some readers. Divorce, infidelity in a character's backstory, death, and cancer are discussed in the novel. There is no death shown on the page and there is no cheating in the romance. However, readers who may be sensitive to any of these elements, please take note.

*To all the people who've found the
courage to try again.*

CHAPTER ONE

Monroe Roberts stood in the kitchen of the Sunshine Diner, hands on her hips, mouth open in disbelief. There were some days she was sure the universe was testing her, like she was a big ol' goldfish and the almighty was tapping a finger against the glass to see what she'd do next.

"What do you mean Jackson quit?" she asked, shaking her head.

A young server named Rai sighed and repeated herself, "He said that he could get paid more for working less at McDonald's."

"He said those exact words?"

Rai looked down, her cheeks red. "Actually, he said he could get paid more for taking less shit at McDonald's."

Monroe looked over to the cook, Big Frank, for support. The older man, who'd earned his name for his towering stature and barrel-like chest, simply turned to the stovetop so he could flip the French toast he was currently cooking, an amused smirk quirking his lips.

"And by 'taking less shit' he means doing the job I pay him to do instead of slacking off?" Monroe sucked in a deep breath to take her frustration down a notch. There was no sense blowing a fuse over the small stuff.

Hadn't her father always told her that when she was younger? Apparently Monroe lived a little too closely to the stereotype for her bright red hair—too argumentative, too fiery. Too *difficult*.

She was pretty sure her ex would agree with that one.

"Thanks for passing it on." Monroe reached out and touched the teen's shoulder. "Don't worry, I'm not going to shoot the messenger. I don't suppose you want an extra shift or two while I find a replacement?"

"Sure thing." Rai nodded, looking relieved to be extracting herself from the awkward conversation. She grabbed the plate that sat on the warming shelf and headed out of the kitchen, her long black braid swinging behind her.

Over at the stove, Frank chuckled to himself.

"Don't you start," Monroe said. "That's the fifth resignation this month."

Frank slid a spatula under the French toast and carefully placed it on a plate. Then he drizzled syrup over the top and added a gentle dusting of powdered sugar and a spoonful of his incredible berry compote. Using a pair of tweezers, he carefully placed paper-thin curls of orange rind on top.

For a dude who looked like he could be a member of a motorcycle gang, Big Frank had a surprisingly deft touch when it came to plating food.

"Can you blame them?" he said.

Monroe frowned. "What's that supposed to mean?"

"Look out there." Frank gestured to the diner's main area, which could be seen over the top of the warming shelf. "What do you see?"

Monroe sucked on the inside of her cheek. What she saw was a sad sight. The Sunshine Diner, once a thriving local business, was eerily quiet. Only one table was occupied. An older gentleman sat with a newspaper in his hands, which he lowered as Rai brought his toast and eggs to the table. It was a familiar scene. The same man came in morning after morning to buy the same plate of eggs and toast and to drink his body weight in coffee.

Some days he was the only person they'd see for the first three hours of opening.

Granted, winter had only recently passed and tourism season wouldn't begin for a little while yet. But this year, more than any before it, the diner had felt frighteningly empty. Her staff often hovered nervously around where she posted the work schedule, as though they were waiting for some kind of hammer to fall.

"What do you see?" Frank asked again.

"Empty tables," she replied, scrubbing a hand over her face. She'd tried everything—breakfast specials, lunch specials, an afternoon "happy hour" for coffee and cake. Nothing seemed to work. "Empty...everything."

"You think young kids want to work here when you're ordering them to clean, clean, clean and yet nobody is coming in?" Frank put the plate of French toast in front of Monroe on the prep table, but she'd completely lost her appetite.

"If they're turning up for a shift, then they're expected to work even if the place is empty." Monroe folded her arms across her chest. "That's no excuse."

She liked everything to be done properly. But for the last few years she'd come to the realization that not everyone cared about rules or promises or commitments. Even if no one else seemed to honor those things, wasn't it her duty to keep a high standard?

"What are you still doing here?" he asked her, shaking

his head. "I remember some plucky redhead telling me a few years back that if she was still working here when she turned thirty that I officially had permission to shove her out the front door and lock it behind her."

"You don't want me to quit." She rolled her eyes. "I'm an amazing manager."

"You're grumpy as shit." The edge of his lips tugged up into a smirk. "And you fired my last sous chef."

"Okay, *firstly*," Monroe said, holding up a finger. "I'm only grumpy when people are lazy. Secondly, Dax was a dishwasher, *not* your sous chef, and I fired him because he was incapable of turning up to work on time. I gave him triple the amount of chances I would give a regular employee because you liked him, but if the guy can't tell the difference between a.m. and p.m. on his schedule, then…"

She threw her hands up in the air.

"Fine," Frank conceded. "But I think you're grumpy because you know this isn't what you're supposed to be doing."

Monroe swallowed down the sick feeling that always came up whenever she thought about the dreams she'd once harbored. God, how was she so naive to *ever* think she'd be anything more than a diner manager? She visualized the cupboard in her kitchen that held the remnants of those dreams—cake tins and specialty decorating tools and expensive dyes and gold leaf and every kind of piping nozzle known to man.

She'd even kept the obnoxious trophy from the nationally televised baking competition she'd won there. It was shoved way in the back, behind a stack of nested round tins and her electric hand mixer.

"What I'm supposed to be doing is making rent and taking care of my dad. That's it." She waved her hand as if shooing a fly. "Sorry I don't buy into the whole #bossbabe bullshit."

"You don't think it's a good idea to have ambitions?" Frank frowned. "I tell Adrienne all the time that she has to dream, because that's the whole point of life. Why get out of bed in the morning if you're not working toward something?"

"It's different for Adrienne," Monroe said, shaking her head. "She's sixteen. You *should* be telling her to dream, because she has her whole life ahead of her. But for me, I'm governed by reality and the reality is that I have responsibilities and people who rely on me."

"Your sisters can help take care of your dad."

"Loren has the girls." Four of them, all under ten and each one more mischievous than the last. "And Taylor has the tattoo parlor. That takes up a lot of her time and she's growing her business."

"When is *your* turn?"

"You think life is so fair that we can all get a turn?" Monroe scoffed. "Come now."

"It's like talking to a brick wall sometimes," Frank muttered.

"At least I'm consistent." She grinned.

"If you're not going to eat this, I will," he said, gesturing to the French Toast. "It would be a crime for such art to go to waste."

"Have at it. I need to go over yesterday's numbers anyway." Monroe pulled off her apron and smiled as she watched Big Frank scoop up the plate and head out into the diner to take a break. They might butt heads on the regular, but he was as standup a guy as she'd ever met.

Even if he did like to constantly poke her sore spots.

She was glad he pushed his daughter to excel, but that wasn't what Monroe needed. Sometimes dreams crashed and burned. That was life. Why the hell would she put her heart in the crosshairs by striking out on her own when she had a steady, reliable life already? Staying here was the low risk, *smart* move.

At that moment, the staff entrance at the back of the kitchen swung open and Monroe's boss, the owner of the diner, walked in.

"Mr. Sullivan." She instinctively perked up. "I didn't know you were coming in today."

"Monroe." He nodded and walked forward a little stiffly. She knew better than to offer her arm to him for support. Because woe to anyone who assumed the man was fragile—Jacob Sullivan was sharp as a tack and had the kind of steely disposition of someone who'd lived through tough times. Not only that, he was surprisingly quick to clip your ear if he felt like you were encroaching on his space. For as far back as Monroe could remember, he'd been like a third grandfather to her. He was a family friend as well as her employer, and she held endless quantities of love and respect for him.

"Empty again?" he asked with a sigh.

"I'm afraid so."

He headed into the storage room, which doubled as an office, since that's where they kept the internet modem and the printer. Mr. Sullivan frowned and looked over the sales report from the last week. "I see we hired yet another dishwasher. Jackson something?"

"Uh, about that…he quit."

He cut her a sharp look. "Why?"

"Long story."

"Well, don't take too long. I'm eighty-one, and I don't want to die listening to you tell a story about how my business is failing," her boss groused.

"Your birthday isn't for another three months, so technically you're only eighty," Monroe fired back. "No sense giving up those months before they happen."

"*Only* eighty." He snorted. "Live a couple more decades before you tell me it's 'only' anything."

"You didn't want to focus on the part where I remembered your birthday?" she asked, folding her arms across her chest and fighting an amused smile.

"Remembering won't keep you in my good graces, girlie. Gifts will. You know the whiskey I like."

Monroe already had a bottle of it sitting in a royal blue gift bag at home. The liquor store had a discount the previous week, so she'd planned ahead. He wanted the same thing every year—a bottle of the good stuff and a boozy chocolate cake, which she always took pleasure in making for him.

She was certain the man would live until he was a hundred, not because he'd lived a healthy lifestyle but because he'd pickled his insides.

"Nice job at dodging my question anyway," Mr. Sullivan said. He sighed and for a moment, he looked every bit of his eighty, almost eighty-one, years. "Look, I've known this was coming for some time."

Monroe's throat suddenly felt tight. "What do you mean?"

"Ingredients cost more, but people expect to pay less because of all these damn fast food places. The winters seem to be getting longer and we can't keep any of the young hires for more than five minutes."

Monroe bit down on her lip. Sure, they'd had a bit of a turnover issue recently, but that was par for the course in food service. And yes, the profit had taken a hit, but Monroe had been trying to get creative with the menu. Problem was, the Sunshine Diner *wasn't* as cheap as the fast food outlets and not as quirky as the hipster places, so they slipped through the cracks of people's attention.

Like that wasn't a sad trend for every damn thing in her life.

"What are you trying to say?" she asked warily.

"I'm thinking of selling."

The words were like a fist to her solar plexus. "You can't sell."

She expected Mr. Sullivan to have some crabby comeback or a "you listen here, Missy" type response. Hell, she *liked* the way he played up being a curmudgeonly old man. It was part of his schtick. But he simply placed a weathered hand on her arm and squeezed.

"Sometimes you have to know when to walk away, kid."

You could only walk away when you had something to walk *to*. And Monroe didn't have anything else aside from her job. She didn't want to work anywhere else. She liked bouncing ideas around with Big Frank and having her weekly meetings with Jacob Sullivan. She even liked most of the rotating youngsters who came in and out.

"We can fix this," she said. "I just need to think about how we can get more people through the door and—"

"Roe." She knew he was serious when he called her that, because it's what he used to call her when she was a little girl and her grandpa took her and her sisters around to "Uncle Jacob's" place. He had no grandkids of his own. "Stop panicking."

"I'm not panicking," she said stubbornly. "But you're being rash."

"I've thought about this a lot." He released her arm. "I'm getting old and you should be off building something of your own, not working for me."

"I thought we were building something together." She hated herself for the pathetic little waver in her voice, for the fear that was so close to the surface right now.

Why did it feel like the last couple of years had taken her life and shaken it up like she was an ice cube rattling around the inside of a cocktail shaker? She didn't want things to change. Her life was comfortable, steady. Reliable. And she liked it that way.

"Give me a chance to turn this around." She swallowed against the lump in her throat. "Please."

Jacob's eyes searched hers and she got the distinct impression he was disappointed in her, which stung. But underneath the gruff exterior, he was pure kindness. Goodness. Monroe loved him like he was one of her own family and she knew he couldn't refuse her.

"I'm trying to do you a favor, kid." He shook his head.

"One month," she bargained. "Just give me a month to turn this place around and I swear to God, if it's not working then you won't hear another peep out of me."

"That's some bullshit if I ever heard it." He let out a raspy chuckle. "You won't be quiet until you're dead. It's what I like about you."

"You have my word." She caught his pinkie in hers and hooked him. She'd taught him how to pinkie swear when she was seven and he'd seen her doing it with her sisters— he'd always been fascinated by them. A pretty flock of seagulls, he used to call them.

"Dammit, Monroe. Fine. One month." He kept his finger wrapped tightly around hers. "But if after a month there's no change, then you'll let this place go out with dignity."

She sucked in a breath. The idea of losing the diner—of *failing* Jacob Sullivan—was like a punch to the gut. But what choice did she have? "I promise."

She gave him a fierce hug, hating how small he'd started to feel in her arms. No matter what it took, she would find a solution to this problem. The Sunshine Diner would *not* fail.

CHAPTER TWO

Ethan Hammersmith sat on the bed at his temporary accommodation—a rundown inn on the outskirts of a town called Forever Falls—while he sorted through his meager possessions. A traveler's backpack filled with a few changes of clothes, hiking boots, his passport, a document wallet, phone, and some toiletries.

If only people from his previous life could see him now. A year and a half ago, his family had nicknamed him "the suit" for his fancy corporate IT job and the penthouse apartment he lived in back in Melbourne, Australia. They'd stirred him up about his taste for top-shelf booze and for his desire to always have the latest tech gadget.

The biggest concern he'd had was chasing yet another promotion while planning a wedding. He'd worked long hours, always tethered to his laptop, a phone pressed permanently against his ear as he'd guided multimillion-dollar technology projects to success. He'd had a beautiful fiancée, a home with a view of the glittering city skyline, and the false sense of security that his life would proceed exactly as he had planned it.

Get married. Make partner at his firm. Have a few kids. Grow old and happy.

Simple, right?

But then one fateful day started a domino effect of changes that had taken every truth Ethan knew and ripped them all to shreds.

Now he was here, sitting on a faded quilt blanket and staring out into a green field in the middle of nowhere, small-town America. In the distance, the sound of cows mingled with birds chirping. It was sunny, and bright light streamed into the room, creating some pleasing warmth in the damp chill that the old building seemed to encourage.

Spread across the bed was all of Ethan's research. A notebook with a single name scrawled across the inside cover — Matthew Brewer — and the details of twenty-five men bearing that name whose deaths spanned the last five years. He'd printed out their obituaries and had visited the locations mentioned — two towns in Connecticut, one in Pennsylvania, another in Missouri, two in Nevada, another in New Mexico. Now he was in Massachusetts.

Ethan had spent the past year hunting for the man who'd given him life. Hunting for his real father.

But he was running out of options. After twelve months of traveling and researching and living day to day, there were five obituaries left. So far, he'd turned up nothing. It was difficult without much to go on besides a name, age, and a date range for the man's death, but Ethan wasn't going to stop until he found out where he came from. Until he closed the circle of lies he'd been fed since he was a baby.

A sharp knock at the door startled Ethan out of his thoughts, and he quickly scooped his papers back into the document folder, stashing it under the mattress of the bed as he'd done at each and every place he'd visited. He kept the obituary notice he'd found from Forever Falls and tucked it back into his wallet. Then he pushed up from the bed and crossed the small room in two and a half strides, opening the door.

"G'mornin'," he said.

"Good morning," Lottie May replied. The older woman ran the inn, and when he'd arrived two days ago, she'd agreed to trade room and board for his assistance, helping her with odd jobs.

She was all of five-foot-nothing, with tightly curled gray hair and sharp blue eyes. Ethan had quickly come to know her as a resolutely practical woman whose bark appeared worse than her bite. She lived exclusively in thick fisherman-style jumpers—sorry, *sweaters* as the Americans called them—and overalls.

"I need you to run me a few errands today," she said, motioning for Ethan to follow her.

He nodded and locked the door behind him. The hallway of the inn was in bad need of a facelift—the wallpaper was peeling in spots and had faded where the windows let in rectangular shafts of light. Floorboards creaked beneath their feet as they walked and the old staircase groaned as they descended. Unfortunately Ethan wasn't confident that Lottie's business was doing well enough for the investment the inn required, at least based on a few comments she'd made.

"I've got those two parcels there that need to go to the post office, and then I need you to go and see Harold at the hardware store. Here's a list." Lottie handed him a piece of paper, which had some random bits and bobs scrawled in hard-to-read handwriting. "Make sure he gives you the local discount, okay? I don't want him charging me extra on account of you being my proxy."

"Sure thing, Mrs. May."

"I told ya, it's Lottie. I've never been a Mrs. anything." Her raspy voice held a note of steel underneath it. "Now, you all good? I'm having some visitors over for lunch, so don't feel that you need to rush back."

Ethan made the decision *not* to ask what all that was about. Getting involved in other people's business wasn't part of his plan, and he wasn't about to knock back some free time. He'd looked up the address of the town's funeral home earlier that morning, and that would be his first port of call as soon as the errands were run and he got something to eat.

"No worries. I can amuse myself." He scooped up the parcels and headed toward the front door, pausing to pull on his coat.

As he exited through the front of the inn, he felt the heat of the older woman's gaze burning a hole in his back. She hadn't asked him any questions since he'd arrived, looking for work and a place to sleep. But something gave Ethan the impression that not much got past Lottie May, and while she might be keeping her mouth shut when it came to any suspicions or thoughts she had, that didn't mean she wasn't keeping an eye on him.

• • •

Ethan had never resented his name until the first Thor movie came out. Then the fact that he bore a striking resemblance to the lead actor and had the word "hammer" in his name became something of a joke. *That* he could laugh off. But when he packed his bags and headed to the U.S., it became more of an issue.

Because now people noticed his accent, too.

And they were looking at Ethan like he wasn't Ethan at all. Oh no, apparently it had gotten around the picturesque town of Forever Falls that Chris Hemsworth was there scouting a movie location. Now people had started approaching him for autographs, no matter how much he protested.

This was precisely how a man who was six feet three inches and built like a brick shithouse, as his father used to say, came to be hiding from a group of women who barely looked like they could lift a slab of beer between them.

But size, Ethan had come to realize, had *nothing* to do with fear.

He pressed his back against the side of the brick building, hoping that the group of women who'd been tailing him would pass right by the alley so he could get on with his day. Not to mention get some breakfast so his stomach would stop growling. Was that too much to ask? All he wanted was a little peace and quiet.

His plans to slink around Forever Falls, gathering information unnoticed, had been blown sky high the first day he'd set foot into the town. Despite the out-of-the-way accommodation and dressing to blend in, a single woman with an iPhone had ruined everything.

What the hell would Chris Hemsworth be doing *here* of all places? Sure, it was a cute town and he could see how in summer it would be very attractive to tourists. But currently it was at the tail end of winter, half the businesses were shut and waiting out the slow season, and the ground was covered in slushy gray remnants of snow. Oh, and it was colder than a polar bear's toenail.

Not exactly the destination for a box office star.

"I swear, I thought I saw him turn down here." One of the female voices sounded from the end of the alley.

"Maybe he went into the post office," another woman replied. "Damn. I was really hoping to get a closer look at him. I've been stalking his Instagram and he hasn't posted a story in over a week. Well, not one that he filmed himself anyway."

"See!" the first voice said. "I told you. It's definitely him."

Ethan rolled his eyes. For a moment he thought about approaching the women to clear things up, but what good would it do? How did the old saying go? The lady doth protest too much? Well, in this case it would be more like the doppelgänger doth protest too much.

At least if he failed in his mission here, then he had a fall back option: Chris Hemsworth impersonator. Luckily his mother had been born over on this side of the world, which had afforded him an American passport to travel on. Maybe he could move to New York, set up camp at Times Square, and grow his hair long. He'd probably make more than what he did now, traveling from town to town doing menial labor.

It was a good thing his former career had left him with a big fat nest egg, or none of this would have been feasible.

"Come on, I'm *starving*," one of the women complained. "Let's get bagels. I'm sure we'll find him later. I promised Micah I'd get him to autograph the Thor comic I got him for Christmas."

With deflated agreement, the women moved on and Ethan breathed a sigh of relief. Uncomfortable situation averted. Now all he had to do was make it two streets down to the diner so he could get breakfast.

Ethan walked to the edge of the alley and poked his head out to make sure the women were gone. Thankfully, it looked like they had disappeared into the bakery. Walking with intention, Ethan kept his head down and hurried along the town's main street toward the diner. It was fairly quiet, and he wove a path to avoid the clumps of half-melted snow.

The Sunshine Diner sat on the corner of Main Street and a smaller road that was lined with towering, leafless trees. The building itself was quaint, and like every other one around here, it looked as though it had leaped right off a painting. Strong and squat, it had red bricks and a colorful blue-and-yellow striped awning, with fairy lights glittering in the front window and a decorated chalkboard sign on the sidewalk, proclaiming a menu special of a spring fruits parfait with a side of cinnamon toast.

Ethan planted a hand on the black wood and glass door, pushing it open and breathing a sigh of relief at the comforting smells of bacon and coffee emanating from inside. The diner wasn't a fancy establishment, by any means. But they had a cozy booth right in the back corner that looked as though it would afford him a modicum of privacy.

If the eggs were good, that would be a bonus.

The diner was empty, bar one lone patron reading a newspaper, so Ethan headed over and took a seat.

A second later, a woman appeared at his table, notepad in hand. "Hi there, welcome to the Sunshine Diner."

She was striking. He couldn't exactly call her pretty—because such a word implied delicacy and there was nothing delicate about this woman. She had a lion's mane of ginger curls, penetrating dark brown eyes, fair skin and stark freckles that were like paint flicked across a blank canvas.

Hell, scratch *striking*. This woman was downright *arresting*.

"Hi," he replied, finding himself a little tongue-tied. It had been a long bloody time since a woman had stolen the words right out of his mouth.

"Would you like a menu or do you know what you're having?" She wore a bright yellow apron with Sunshine Diner embroidered across the chest, along with the cutesy logo of a cartoon sun and clouds.

"Eggs and toast would be good, sunny side up."

She smiled. "No hesitation, you must be hungry."

"Where I'm from we say 'I'm so hungry I could eat the crotch from a low-flying duck,'" he said with a wink.

The woman laughed, and it was a beautiful and unexpected raspy sound. "That's very creative. British?"

"Australian."

She nodded. "Want any coffee to go with your breakfast?"

"Yes, please." He'd kill for a decent Melbourne espresso right now, but the filtered stuff would have to do. That's what they served at most places in this part of the world. "I'll take some milk with it."

"Sure thing."

Ethan hadn't exactly wanted to prolong *any* conversation since he'd arrived on U.S. soil, but the intriguing redheaded woman had him wanting to know more. Her name badge had "Monroe" printed in neat letters. "Monroe, pretty name."

"I begged my mom to change it," she said with a rueful smile and a shake of her head. "But that would have ruined her theme."

Ethan raised an eyebrow. "Theme?"

"Yeah, I'm Monroe named after Marilyn. My older sister is Loren named after Sophia, and my younger sister is Taylor named after Elizabeth. It's a thing."

"Wow, she must have really liked those old movies."

"Couldn't get enough of them." A wistful smile crossed her lips. "I grew up watching things that were a minimum of forty years old. I couldn't tell you a damn thing about 90s culture, but if you want me to recite *The Birds* line by line I can totally do it."

"That's quite a talent."

"Most useless talent in the existence of talents." Monroe jotted his order down on her notepad. Then she paused, her pen hovering for a moment before she looked back down at him. "What's your name?"

"Ethan."

She scrunched up her nose. "You look like someone, but I can't place my finger on it."

Before Ethan could open his mouth to ask a probing question, a woman who looked to be in her late twenties approached the table, a little boy of about three by her side. He hadn't noticed them enter the diner, because he was facing away from the door. The woman had blond hair pulled into a bouncy ponytail and wore the kind of outfit that looked like athletic wear but was far too neat to have actually been used for working out.

"Excuse me," she said with a sheepish smile. "I'm so sorry to interrupt your breakfast, but my son is a *huge* fan."

She shoved the little boy forward, who looked up at him with huge unblinking blue eyes. The kid stuck his thumb into his mouth and continued to stare while Ethan scrubbed a hand over his face. This was getting ridiculous.

"I'm not—"

"Oh, we know. You were never here." The woman tapped the side of her nose to indicate she'd keep a secret. "But my boy, Mason, would absolutely love your autograph."

Mason continued to stare, and Ethan was pretty sure the kid was a cover for the woman to approach the table. Maybe he should learn how to sign Chris Hemsworth's name and get it over with.

Bad idea. That's only going to encourage more people to bother you.

Monroe was looking at him strangely, like something had clicked in her head.

"I'm sorry to disappoint you both," Ethan replied. "But I'm not who you think I am."

The woman didn't look discouraged in the slightest. There was a determined set to the way she made eye contact with him, like she wasn't used to hearing the word no. He'd bet money that she'd been raised by a "no is a jumping off point for negotiations" type.

"I give you my word," Ethan said. "I'm *not* a movie star. I'm just a regular guy who's passing through town."

Kinda. Okay, so maybe Ethan had a few white lies of his own, and that made him feel guilty as hell. But it was necessary at the moment, and these lies wouldn't hurt anybody.

"Look, I know Chris Hemsworth wouldn't actually come

here," the woman said, her voice low. "Trust me, even normal people don't want to stay in this town, so there's no way some Hollywood star would be here. But my son pointed at you on the street and said Thor. You wouldn't disappoint him, would you?"

The entitlement in her voice got under Ethan's skin. This was ridiculous—he didn't owe this woman anything. He opened his mouth to protest once more, but Monroe cut in first. "Peony, if you don't leave my customer alone, I'll have to ask you to go."

Peony looked toward Monroe with such derision that a lesser person might have flinched. But not Monroe. She stood with her shoulders squared and her deep, dark eyes unwavering.

"I don't have to listen to you," Peony replied with a heavy dose of snark. "I know you're only the manager. Mr. Sullivan still owns this place and my mom is still his doctor. So if you kick me out, I'll make sure your freckly ass gets fired."

"Try me." Monroe crossed her arms over her chest.

Peony's mouth popped open. "You're serious."

"As a heart attack."

Peony shook her head. "You're such a—"

"Mom?" The little boy looked up at his mother and she bent down to scoop him up, cradling him against her chest and shooting both Ethan and Monroe a nasty look before she turned on her heel and walked right out of the diner.

Monroe rolled her eyes. "She hasn't changed a bit since high school."

Okay, so Monroe went to high school here. He'd pegged

her for a local, but he was still pleased to have confirmation.

"I don't know what else I can tell these people." Ethan shook his head. "I'm not going to pretend to be someone I'm not."

Lord knew he'd been doing that *all* his life without even knowing it.

Ethan was about to thank Monroe, but she had already started walking across the floor of the diner, long red hair bouncing with each step. Against every sensible thought in his head, all of which told him there was no point getting to know *anybody* in this town unless it served his purpose, Ethan was officially intrigued by the fierce redhead.

Luckily for him, Monroe was a local. Which might mean she may *also* have information that he needed. Information that could end his year-long search for the truth of who he was. Information that might finally put his ghosts to rest.

But before he started asking questions, he needed to do a little quiet digging. He'd learned early on not to blaze into a town making his intentions immediately known, because folks tended to be cagey when that happened. But, much to his delight, it looked like he would be coming back to the Sunshine Diner.

CHAPTER THREE

Wednesday nights was Monroe's official night to visit her father. In reality, she dropped past at least every other day to check on him, but Wednesday was the day that was always marked in her calendar. She pulled her old Mazda up in front of her father's house — the house she grew up in — and killed the engine.

For a moment she simply sat there, exhaustion seeping into her bones. She was always the first one in and the last one out of the Sunshine Diner. Twelve-plus hours on her feet day after day took its toll.

At least today had featured some kind of highlight. A Thor look-a-like with a voice like warm honey and shoulders that could carry the world kind of highlight.

As much as Peony had ticked Monroe off, she *could* understand being drawn to a new guy. Hooking up in a small town was risky business. If it went south, *everybody* knew about it and most would pick sides. There were no secrets, not a shred of privacy. Monroe had been single for three years now and it was just the same old, same old. Nothing but a handful of Tims and Marks and Johns who cared about little more in life than fishing and their trucks.

No, thank you.

So yeah, she understood why a hunky out-of-towner would appeal.

"Why are you wasting mental energy on this?" she muttered to herself. "It's not like you're going to throw your hat into the ring."

And even if she did, a guy like that would have his pick. Who wanted a woman with a going-nowhere job, Sideshow Bob hair, and a cranky disposition? No, she needed to forget all about her day *and* about Ethan the Aussie hottie.

Burying her chin in her sweater as she stepped outside, a damp, icy breeze whipped past and ruffled her hair. Winter seemed determined to hang on as long as possible this year, and every time they had a few nice warm days in a row, a cold front would shock them back into their thick wool socks and down coats. Reaching into the back seat, she grabbed a small plastic crate which had been filled with food and grocery items, and then she hurried up the path to her father's front door. He opened it before she even had the chance to knock.

"Hey, Dad." She leaned in to give him a kiss on the cheek. His jaw was covered in gray whiskers. Some days he just didn't have the energy to stand at the sink and shave.

She could usually tell how rough his day had been by whether or not he'd shaved. But coming on too strong with her worry was never a good idea, because her father hated to be coddled.

"Monroe," he grunted, shuffling back to let her inside. He had a wooden cane in one hand, the top of it carved into the shape of a hunting dog, and his AFO—which stood for ankle foot orthoses, a type of brace that helped him walk more steadily—was propped against the wall by the front door.

Monroe quickly glanced away from the AFO. He was supposed to be wearing this new version around the house after he'd had a fall, but her stubborn father liked to wear his slippers and they didn't fit the brace. After the day she'd had, she didn't have it in her to broach the topic with him.

"I brought you goodies from the diner. Big Frank made some walnut and basil pesto, and I've got a bag of fresh pasta from the Italian place, as well as some olive bread and a hunk of that parmesan you like." Monroe hefted the box onto her father's dining room table. "Oh, and I went past the shops at lunch and I saw the new issue of *Woodworker's Journal*."

Her father's eyes lit up. "I've been waiting for this one."

She handed the magazine over and smiled as he excitedly flipped through it. Woodworking and furniture restoration had been a huge hobby of his before the accident, the one that caused a chain of events that would see him unwillingly retire early. These days the chronic pain had slowed him down, but her father could still be regularly found in his garage working on smaller projects, like building a new spice rack or refinishing a cupboard door. Working with his hands brought him an immense amount of joy and Monroe wanted to do whatever she could to support that.

"I saw they have an article about hand tooling with that guy you like." Monroe tapped the cover.

"You're a good daughter," he said, looking up with a smile. "Now be a dear and get me a cup of coffee, would you? I need to sit."

"Sure thing."

Monroe wandered into the kitchen and started the coffee. Then while that was brewing she unpacked the dishwasher and loaded the few dirty cups and plates from the sink. In the early days, her father had tried to refuse her help, but if there was one trait Monroe had acquired from him, it was stubbornness.

"Oh, there's some mail on the table for you," her dad called out from the living room. "How long have you been in your new place and you're *still* getting notices sent here?"

"Yeah, yeah." Monroe poured a cup of coffee for her dad and carried it out to him, landing an affectionate hand on his shoulder. "Be honest, you like seeing my name pop up in your mailbox."

He snorted. "More like I just wish all my daughters would actually move out when they say they're going to."

Monroe stifled a smile. Her father liked to grouse that his daughters always had one foot back in the family home—whether it was Monroe's mail turning up, or Taylor storing her bike in the garage because her new place didn't have enough space for a car *and* a motorcycle. Sometimes it was Loren hosting her weekly ladies' poker night at the kitchen table here, because with four daughters there was never enough peace to do it at her place.

All three of them knew he secretly loved how attached they were to their home, and to him. They might not have had the most money growing up, or the fanciest house, and they'd had their share of loss and heartache, but the Roberts family was never lacking for love.

"Make sure you check them," he said. "One of the envelopes looked very official."

Official? Frowning, Monroe went to grab the small stack of envelopes from the table. There were four in total—a bill for her cell phone that she *really* needed to get redirected to her apartment, some promotional crap that she didn't remember signing up for, a letter from her high school, no doubt some reunion invite that she would ignore, and…

Yeah, the last letter *did* look official. But it wasn't the Boston return address or fancy-looking serif font spelling out the name of an unknown law firm that had her worried. It was the fact that the letter was addressed to *Mrs.* Monroe Roberts.

And Monroe hadn't been a Mrs. for some time now.

She'd never changed her surname when she got married, something that Brendan had claimed to support at the time and had then thrown back in her face when things turned sour. Frankly, his family had never accepted her, and the idea of taking their name had made her feel ill.

Probably should have seen that *for the red flag it was.*

With a shaky hand, she tore at the back flap sealing the envelope shut, peeling the paper away in a jagged strip. Inside was a letter. Ice trickled through her veins, freezing her from the inside out as fear and reality slowly set in. The sheaf of paper trembled in her grip as she read, eyes growing wide and time slowing down so much that all she could concentrate on was the erratic thudding of her heart.

No. No, no, no.

Phrases like *we regret to inform you* and *incorrect paperwork* and *please contact us immediately* peppered the page. But it was a single line that stole the air from her lungs.

Unfortunately, this means that your divorce was not legally finalized and as of now, you are still married to Mr. Brendan James Ankerman.

Monroe stared at the letter in disbelief. Married? It'd

been three whole years since she caught her sonofabitch ex screwing around on her. Three whole years since the shock of finding out the other woman was her very own cousin, Amber. Three whole years since that one event tore a rift right through her family.

"Everything okay?" her father asked from the chair. "I saw it was a law firm and figured maybe you'd forgotten to pay that parking ticket from when you took me into the city for my specialist appointment."

"Uh yeah." Monroe's mind was spinning. How could this have happened? "I completely forgot about it. Not to worry, I'll make sure it gets paid."

She hated keeping things from her father, but there was no way she could tell him she was still legally married to her ex. When he found out that his son-in-law was having an affair, he'd wanted to punch the daylights out of him. Only Monroe's pleading had stopped him.

But it had been no use. Everything had fallen apart.

Her relationship with her aunt had deteriorated when it became clear she was taking Amber's side, even if *she* was the one who'd done the cheating. Amber's brothers had also stuck by their sister. The once close-knit Roberts family had come apart at the seams, and even though Monroe had been the victim in all of it she still hated that it happened.

She regretted...everything.

Not too long after it all went down, Brendan and Amber moved away. The divorce had been settled the following year, with minimal fuss. Monroe had just wanted it to be over as quickly as possible.

But this letter...

It was like ripping all those old wounds open all over again.

"I'm sorry, Dad. I can't stay." She stuffed the letter into her coat pocket and went over to say goodbye. He looked up at her with confusion clouding his dark brown eyes. "I just remembered...I think I left the back door unlocked at the diner."

"You're working too much," he admonished. "I know what that's like. You start to forget things because you're tired."

"I'm fine, I promise." She bent down and kissed her father's head. "Do you want me to cook up the pasta before I go?"

"No, no." He pushed up out of his chair. "I'm actually feeling pretty good today. Had a nice nap this afternoon, and I think the new pain meds are working."

"I'm so glad to hear that."

"Come here and give your father a hug."

Monroe let herself be wrapped up in his arms. For a moment, she was worried that tears might flood her eyes—because her whole world felt like it was flipped upside down—first the diner, now this. But she'd never let her father worry needlessly. He was one of the most important people in her world, and she'd swallow this whole thing down by herself if it would save him an ounce of pain. Her mistakes had already cost him his relationship with his sister, plus his nieces and nephews. Adding salt into that wound was totally unacceptable.

This was her problem to deal with and she would do it like she did most things these days—alone.

. . .

The diner was more than half full today. It hadn't been more than half full since…

She couldn't even remember.

A frown furrowed her brows as she slipped her apron over her head, watching the near-bustling main room over the top of the warming shelf.

Most of the patrons were groups of women. This wasn't odd in and of itself—they did a meager brunch trade on the weekend and there was a Pilates studio a few doors down, so they sometimes got a small influx after a class had finished. But today was a Tuesday. In late March. And the Pilates studio was closed for renovations.

It shouldn't be this busy for no reason.

Big Frank stood over the prep station, using tongs to carefully place muffins onto small plates. "Dare I say it, we're almost out of blueberry *and* chocolate chip."

Monroe shook her head. She couldn't remember the last time they hadn't needed to foist the leftover muffins onto her sisters or try to send them home with one of the servers. Monroe glanced at the grill and stovetop—both were empty.

"Is anyone ordering an actual meal?" she asked.

He shook his head. "I had one breakfast burger about an hour ago, and the usual scrambled eggs. But otherwise, nothing."

Huh. Half a diner full with no meal orders. She'd been so worried about getting butts in these seats after her chat with Jacob Sullivan that it didn't even occur to her a half-full diner could still make no money.

"You must be the only restaurant manager in the country who's frowning at the fact that they're filling *more* seats instead of less," Big Frank said with a chuckle.

"I'd be happy if we were filling seats with customers who ordered more than a low-profit snack. We need people filling these seats who are going to order an entrée and sides." She gestured to the dining room. "These people aren't those customers."

"Where do you think they're all coming from anyway?"

"I don't know." There were no events in town, not this time of year. "It's weird."

Monroe tapped a finger to her chin. Maybe if this was an indication of the type of clientele they were likely to draw, she could get creative with some muffin alternatives. Perhaps, a granola bowl and a rich yogurt from a local dairy farm might be a good inclusion? This could be a clever move, in her humble opinion, because it would help to increase the average price of those orders without increasing the time people sat at the tables.

Just as she was about to head into the office to look over their next order sheet, Monroe caught something interesting happening in the main room.

Ethan.

He was standing inside the door, but only just, and three teenagers were crowded around him, one boy and two girls. Almost every head in the diner was turned in his direction. Ethan had the distinct look of a piece of game in a hunter's crosshairs. With Jacob's bombshell about potentially selling the diner so fresh, Monroe felt her hackles rise. If she had any hope of lifting the sales for the Sunshine Diner, then they couldn't have people loitering and putting paying customers off. All Monroe cared about right now was making sure that this place didn't get sold. Jacob deserved a successful legacy, and it was her job to help make that happen.

Oh and sure, there was that whole "not divorced" thing to worry about, but Monroe had currently tossed that concern into a mental box marked "shit to deal with later."

She pushed through the door from the kitchen into the diner, walking with the kind of intent that made people skitter out of her way. Ethan caught her gaze across the room and for a second he looked relieved.

"What's going on here?" she asked.

One of the teenagers looked at her, scowling. She was about sixteen, dressed like she was twenty-five, and had the attitude of a two-year-old. "You can't tell me what to do. This is a free country!'"

"Asking a question isn't telling you what to do." She felt a surge of satisfaction when the kid's eyebrows jumped up. "And I was talking to Ethan."

"You mean Thor." The other girl giggled. "He looks just like him and sounds like him, too."

Ethan looked at her over the top of the teenagers' heads. It seemed like he might try to argue for a second, but instead he turned and headed out the door, his big frame squeezing through the tiny entry.

Do not pay attention to how broad his shoulders are.

"Darlene," Monroe called out to the waitress. "These three are looking for a table. Think you can squeeze them in down the back?"

The boy looked at the girls. "Uh, actually, we just came for—"

He made a loud *oof* noise when one of the girls elbowed him in the ribs. "We just came to check out the menu."

"It's on the website." Monroe held the door open for them and stared the kids down. If they wanted to eat, fine, but she was *not* going to put up with people loitering in her diner.

Not now that the stakes had been raised.

The teens trooped out and headed up the street, and she followed Ethan out onto the sidewalk. He looked even more delectable today. It was a little warmer out, and instead of a bulky coat he wore a fitted black motorcycle jacket that stretched across his broad chest and his jaw was coated in glorious golden stubble.

The second the door swung shut behind them, Monroe caught several people standing in the window, faces pressed to the glass. One person held up their iPhone and snapped a picture. On the street, a mother and daughter walked past, not even trying to hide the fact that they were gawking.

At least now she was clear on why her diner had suddenly filled up.

CHAPTER FOUR

So much for picking Monroe's brain and getting some breakfast in peace.

"You know, it's not normal for us to be so busy like this." Monroe's curly ginger hair was tied back into a voluminous ponytail. She wore a fitted top in a shade of olive green that suited her complexion and made her eyes appear rich and tinted with dark gold. "It's the strangest thing."

I've got some idea what it could be.

Ethan was still wearing his baseball cap to ward off the cold. He'd hoped the low brim might give a strong "leave me alone" vibe, but so far no luck.

The only person who seemed to have no clue about his celebrity doppelgänger status was Lottie May. He'd gotten up early that morning to help her haul firewood in from a big shed on the back of the property and had spent a few hours chopping up some more to keep the supply full. And she'd barely said a word to him the whole time.

Talk about bliss.

Ethan had always been a man with a laser-like focus on what he wanted—that focus used to be directed at things like corporate success. Now it was focused on finding out where his father died to see if he had any living relatives in America. That meant anything else was a distraction. Aside from helping Lottie, because the free accommodation served his needs, Ethan wasn't wasting time or energy on anything outside his goal.

"You don't have anything to say to that?" she asked, folding her arms over her chest.

"Nope."

"No speculation as to *why* people are hanging around you like flies on a cow pat?" Her lip quirked when he remained silent. "Nothing like, say, you bear a striking resemblance to one hunky action star and now all of Forever Falls is following your pied piper ass around."

Pied piper ass? To his surprise, the biggest, heartiest laugh Ethan had experienced in well over a year bubbled up from inside him. "You have a way with words, Ms. Monroe for Marilyn."

"Hmm." She cocked her head, studying him. "I can't think of a single reason why anyone would come here in slush season. Let alone someone from a country with decent weather year-round. So that begs the question, why *are* you here?"

"Contrary to popular belief, Australia isn't hot year-round. At least not the part where I live," Ethan replied. "Well, lived."

He would have to go back and pick up the pieces eventually. But right now there was no future. Only the present. And normally he would have gotten as *far* away from any kind of questions about himself as possible, but something in his gut told him Monroe might be the key to him getting the information he was searching for.

Ethan scrubbed a hand over his face, disappointment crawling through his system like poison. His visit to the funeral home yesterday had been less than helpful. The young kid—who was clearly the son of the owners—had been unsure what information he could and couldn't give out, which meant he'd been tight lipped. All he'd confirmed was what Ethan already knew from the obituary—that a Matthew Brewer, aged 57, had passed away three years ago and his funeral had been held there.

That was it.

Nothing about any relatives, or which cemetery he'd been buried in—there were two in town, and one just outside Forever Falls. And that was *if* he'd even been buried at all. Who knew? Maybe the guy had been reduced to ashes and was now decorating someone's fireplace mantel.

The past twelve months had been much of the same—asking questions and only winding up with *more* questions.

"And which part of Australia is that?" she asked, seeming genuinely curious. They probably didn't get too many international travelers around these parts.

"Melbourne. Although I'm originally from a little seaside town called Patterson's Bluff."

"Small-town boy, huh?" Monroe nodded. "I could see that."

"You saying I *don't* look like the Hollywood type?" he asked, raising an eyebrow and laughing.

"I'm saying that people in this town will latch onto anything if it provides some interest, and a mysterious stranger with an accent and a celebrity doppelgänger is about as interesting as things are going to get around here for a while. Do they really believe you're Thor? No." Monroe made a snorting noise. "But when the average man in his thirties here is either already married or an ex-boyfriend, you're going to draw attention."

Which was so *not* what Ethan wanted right now.

"At least now I know who's responsible for filling my diner," she said.

"You're welcome?" He had to phrase it as a question, because Monroe didn't sound pleased.

"I'll thank you when they're paying customers and not gawkers."

"I can't control what others do."

Lord knew that was the biggest lesson of the last year and a half. Because if Ethan had *any* control over other people whatsoever, then he sure as hell wouldn't be traipsing from town to town, chasing ghosts.

Monroe's lips twitched in amusement. "Can't help being good-looking, huh? What a hard life."

Okay now *that* was a prickle under his skin. Monroe didn't know anything about him, like he didn't know anything about her. She was mysterious, this woman, and for some bloody reason it made him want to peel back every one of her layers to find out what was underneath.

Bad move. You did not *come here to get involved with anyone, let alone a woman who looks like she's made of snark and shell.*

Maybe it said something about Ethan, but he tended to like women like that. Women with a firecracker energy about them. Women with strong personalities and spark and high walls, because watching all those things melt under his touch was the most satisfying thing ever.

Monroe was *definitely* his type. But that fell square into the bucket of distractions he really didn't need right now.

The latest obituary was folded up in his pocket. That's what he needed to focus on.

Matthew Brewer passed away on February 16th in his

home. He was a longtime resident of Forever Falls.

That was it. No names, no mention of a spouse or any kind of family. Not even a reference to anything he might have done in his lifetime. It was like looking for a ghost.

"You don't want to challenge me," he said, keeping his eyes locked on hers. Even though he'd only been in this woman's presence for ten minutes, there was something magnetic between them. Something that sparked and glowed.

He hadn't felt like that in a very long time.

"Maybe I do," she said with a teasing smile. "Maybe this is the only bit of fun I've had in a very long time."

Color him officially intrigued. "Sounds like there's a story there."

"A tale of woe, perhaps." She shook her head. "So are you coming in for a meal? I need all the paying customers I can get."

"I don't suppose you have a secret table out the back where I could eat my meal in peace?"

She cocked her head. "You know, I may just be able to help you with that."

• • •

Ethan followed Monroe's directions through the restaurant, ignoring all the looks tossed his way. She'd told him to go into the kitchen and find Big Frank. The first person he saw when he pushed through the swing door was a tall, built man with a bushy brown beard, warm eyes, and a sleeve of intricate tattoos up one bulky arm.

"You Big Frank?"

"Who's asking?" the man grunted. He looked like he could snap a human in half with his bare hands. Or a tree.

"Monroe sent me. I'm apparently causing a ruckus in your diner, but the eggs I had here yesterday were the best I've eaten in a long time. Not to mention, I'm hungry as hell."

Big Frank chuckled. "That's right, the movie star guy."

"Movie star *doppelgänger* slash unsuspecting victim of a town's worth of female attention."

Big Frank appraised him for a second, but then he must have decided that Ethan was all right. "Sit down, I'll make you some eggs," he said gruffly. "Can't let a man go hungry."

"Thanks, mate, I appreciate it."

Ethan was pretty sure this was peak small-town behavior—he could be anybody and they'd just let him into the back of the kitchen. In fact, it reminded him *a lot* of his hometown, which stirred some unwelcome nostalgia.

He watched Big Frank work the kitchen, moving with more grace than a ballerina—plating every single dish with care, even though it was mostly muffins and the occasional bit of French toast. After he slid the plates onto a shelf and tapped a bell, Big Frank cracked two eggs into a fry pan and got to work on Ethan's breakfast.

"Have you worked for Monroe long?" he asked.

Big Frank made a snorting sound. "I've been working here since that one was knee-high to a grasshopper. Started out as a dish pig when I dropped out of school and worked my way up."

"You've found your calling. I've eaten a lot of diner food in the last year, and this is top-notch."

The burly man seemed to puff his chest out a bit at the

compliment. "No sense doing a job if you can't take some pride in it, that's what my gramps always used to say. It's what I keep telling Monroe—she needs to find something to be excited about."

Frank shoved the mushrooms around a skillet with a spatula, scraping up the delicious little bits that stuck to the bottom.

"Being a diner manager isn't her life goal?" Ethan leaned back against the wall.

"She was supposed to have a cake shop, one of those fancy places." There was something sad about Big Frank's tone. It was obvious he'd known Monroe a long time and that he cared about her like she was his own kid. He'd peg Big Frank to be around fifty, and a tough-but-fair kinda guy. "You know she was on television for it. Won some big baking competition a few years back."

"Really?" Ethan's brow shot up.

Now *that* was a surprise. Not that he didn't assume Monroe had talent, but it was more that she seemed like the last person on earth to voluntarily go on a reality show. As much as he appreciated Monroe's spark, he wasn't sure that would translate well on television.

"Oh yeah, you should have seen her." Big Frank beamed with pride as he fetched the two slices of toast for Ethan's breakfast. Then he shoveled the mushrooms and home fries onto the side of the plate and slid the eggs over the top of the toast. "She was amazing. Every time she got herself into a jam she'd come up with the most creative way to come out of it. Her cakes were by far the best. Did Forever Falls proud."

"What was the name of the show?"

Big Frank passed the plate to Ethan and motioned for him to sit on a small wooden stool. Ethan balanced the plate on his lap and tucked into the food, his taste buds singing out in happiness as the first forkful passed through his lips.

"I honestly can't remember." He scratched the back of his neck. "Sugar something?"

"I'll have to ask her." Ethan chewed happily on his toast and eggs.

"I wouldn't," Big Frank warned. "She'd have my hide for even mentioning it."

"Why? Surely that's something to be proud of."

"I would agree with you there, but Monroe is…" Big Frank laughed and shrugged. "Well, she's a woman of her own mind. Smart as heck and a heart of solid gold, but she's more stubborn than a mule and she's got a tongue that could cut a person clean in half."

Ethan chuckled. "Yeah, I got that impression."

At that moment Monroe walked through the door, carrying a stack of dishes and coffee cups. Big Frank turned straight back to the grill, looking guiltier than a little kid who'd been caught stuffing his face with chocolate right before dinner. Ethan swallowed an amused smile—it was funny to see a guy who looked like he could intimidate the heck out of anyone clearly be worried about the wrath of a five-foot-nothing redhead.

Monroe looked from Big Frank to Ethan and then back again, as though suspicious of the sudden silence in the kitchen. But instead of saying anything, she simply left the dishes in the sink for the teenager working there and grabbed a fresh pot of coffee. Then she was gone.

"It was called *Sugar Coated*," the teenager said as he got to work pre-cleaning the dishes and loading them into the dishwasher. "The show that Monroe won."

Doing some homework on the oh-so-intriguing Monroe was exactly the kind of distraction he did *not* need right now. But something told him that wouldn't stop him from getting on Google later that night and seeing what interesting things he could find out.

• • •

To say Monroe's day had been frustrating was putting it mildly. The Sunshine Diner had been rammed from opening to closing and yet they'd barely made more money than usual. All those free coffee refills and people nibbling on a muffin for an hour had taken its toll on the day's profit. Who wanted to do triple the work for no more reward?

To make matters even worse, her ex had emailed. Turned out the reason the error with their divorce had been discovered was because Brendan was getting married…to Amber. Apparently it was "true love" and he hoped she "wouldn't stand in the way of what was meant to be."

Gag.

Talk about making her see red. That slime ball had not only reached out to demand that she contact the lawyers and do her part in correcting the mistake as quickly as possible, but there hadn't been an ounce of apology in his communication. Nothing which recognized the pain she'd been through, nothing which acknowledged the rift her family had suffered from his infidelity, nothing which showed he understood that her heart had been totally and irreparably shattered by his betrayal.

Because she'd loved him. Ever since she was a fifteen-year-old weirdo and he was the popular boy who'd unexpectedly welcomed her into his circle, she'd loved him.

Monroe jogged up the steps to her sister's house and jabbed the doorbell. The melodic chime echoed through the big house and a second later the door swung open. Loren looked as she always did—effortlessly glamorous in a colorful maxi dress with a big shawl wrapped around her shoulders, intricately beaded earrings shimmering against her long, blond hair.

"Hey, girl. Taylor is already here, the kids have been shipped off to Grandma's, and Rudy is out with the boys." Loren all but yanked Monroe into the house and enveloped her in a perfumed hug. "I'm *so* ready to open a bottle of wine."

"Sounds like heaven."

Monroe followed her sister into the house, ditching her boots by the door and hanging her coat in the hallway closet. They found their youngest sister, Taylor, sitting on one of the bar stools around the huge kitchen island. If Loren was the glamorous one and Monroe was the practical one, Taylor could be classified as the bold one. Her hair—which had been dyed a deep shade of crimson—was pinned up into a forties victory roll style. She wore black leather-look pants and a red top with a black cat embroidered at top right-hand side, the cropped sleeves of which showed off her tattoo sleeve perfectly.

"I always feel underdressed when I see you guys." Monroe walked over and planted a kiss on her sister's cheek. "I can't remember the last time I wore anything but jeans and a sweater."

"But it's such a cute sweater." Loren frowned. "Was it mine at some point?"

"Probably."

Loren's wardrobe was extensive, because she loved fashion and hated ever getting rid of things. Which led to both her sisters regularly "shopping" her closet.

"So," Taylor said, filling and then passing out the wineglasses. "It sounded like you had something on your mind. What prompted the family chat?"

Monroe plonked herself down onto one of the stools. God. How did she even *begin* this story? While she might be wanting to keep the divorce fiasco under wraps from her dad, she'd made an agreement long ago with both sisters that they would never keep secrets.

Besides, she wanted some advice and they were her go-to source of female wisdom. Given that their mother had passed away when they were all in school, they'd grown up learning to rely on one another. Loren made a great mother hen, and Monroe and Taylor had grown up fast to pull their weight in the family. They were as tight-knit as could be.

Monroe reached for her wine and took a long, steady gulp. When she placed the glass back down on the countertop, two sets of eyes were trained on her, twin worried expressions making her heart feel heavy as a bag of rocks. She reached into her purse and pulled out the letter from the lawyer and, without saying a word, she unfolded it and placed it on the center of the island.

Loren was the first to read it, clamping a hand over her

mouth, which caused Taylor to abandon her seat and peer over her big sister's shoulder.

Taylor shook her head. "Is this for real?"

"Yeah." Monroe swallowed against the lump in her throat. "Turns out I'm still legally married."

"Holy mac-and-cheese balls." Loren gaped at her. "Have you called the lawyer? I don't understand how this could happen."

"No, I haven't called yet. All I know, after some Googling, is that the lawyer Brendan originally used is no longer in business. I thought at the time he seemed a bit off, but I wasn't about to argue. I just wanted it over."

She still got nightmares about the day they'd all met in that big city office building. Monroe had barely eaten for a week before then and she'd almost fainted in the elevator. The whole time the meeting was going on, she hadn't even been able to look her ex in the eye, the betrayal still so painful that she wasn't sure she wouldn't either burst into tears or attempt to strangle him.

"What about your lawyer?" Taylor asked.

"I need to talk to him, too." Monroe scrubbed a hand over her face. "I was going to call him today, but then I got an email from Brendan and…"

Well, her mood had gone south faster than a stone plummeting off a cliff. Monroe then passed her phone around so they could all read the email. Yeah, maybe that wasn't the smartest thing to do, since neither of them had quite gotten over finding out their own cousin's involvement with the demise of Monroe's marriage.

"Fuck him," Taylor said, her nostrils flaring.

"Potty mouth! Thank goodness the girls aren't home,"

Loren admonished.

"Sorry, Lor, I know you hate cursing, but I stand by it." Her jaw ticked. "If he thinks you'll just leap to attention because he wants to marry that disloyal rat, then he can—"

Loren held up her hand to cut her mouthy sister off. "We get it. Brendan is the lowest, most gutter-dwelling form of human and that email is...something else."

"Just the *tone* of it." Taylor pulled a face. "The entitled, demanding tone that he has no right to use. And the threat that if you don't do your part he'll come back to Forever Falls and make sure it's done? Ugh!"

Brendan had always been a little entitled—he'd come from one of the wealthiest families in town, he'd always been good-looking and popular. But when he and Monroe had been together, he'd been more...grounded. Down to earth. It appeared that Amber and her unrelenting social climbing had brought out that spoiled rich kid side of him.

"If I have to see him again..." Monroe's stomach rocked at the thought of it.

She wanted to tuck herself into a ball and hide. If Brendan came back to Forever Falls then he would see that he'd won. Monroe was living alone in a tiny apartment that smelled like cabbage from the rolls made at the Polish bakery beneath it. She was chronically single, had given up on her dreams of opening a cake decorating business, and had little more in her life than the remaining family members who'd stuck by her.

All things considered, Brendan had broken the rules— broken their *vows*—and yet he'd walked away with everything he wanted. She couldn't let him see her like this.

"I don't know what to do," Monroe said. "I want to be

divorced, obviously. So I know I need to correct this, but the thought of having to go through it all again..."

It sounded like torture. Like taking a seam ripper and cutting through all the stitches holding her heart in one mangled piece. It had almost broken her the first time. Or maybe it was time to admit that "almost" was a lie she told herself so she could sleep at night.

There wasn't anything "almost" about it. She *was* broken.

"What's the rush on getting it done?" Loren asked, coming around to Monroe and wrapping an arm around her shoulders. Taylor joined her from the other side. "Just because he wants it done right now doesn't mean that you need to drop everything when he calls. You're not in a relationship with him anymore, therefore what he wants isn't your concern. If you need to take some time to think through it all, then do it."

"You're right," Monroe said with a heavy sigh. "I mean, it's not like I'll be getting married ever again, so there's no ticking time bomb for me."

"Exactly." Loren rubbed her hand in soothing circles on Monroe's back, and she felt some of the tension ease out.

"Thanks. I needed someone to tell me this wasn't as big a deal as I was making it out in my head."

"It's a pain in the ass, but ultimately a piece of paper is more trouble to him than it is to you right now." Taylor squeezed her. She opened her mouth like she was going to use another expletive but looked at her big sister and then thought better of it. "Screw him. Make him wait. It's about time he felt the consequences of his actions."

"What if he turns up here?" Monroe asked.

"He might, but so what? He can't hurt you anymore," Loren said. "You've already gone through the hard bit."

Monroe wasn't so sure about that. Because if she was being honest, the affair and the subsequent ill-fated divorce had changed her. It had changed her *family*. Three years ago, she'd been a vibrant woman with big dreams and confidence in her abilities. A woman who smiled more than she frowned. A woman who enjoyed dressing up for a night out, who lived for more than work and responsibility.

That was the hard part. Accepting that she'd changed and living with the fear that it would be permanent.

CHAPTER FIVE

Later that night, Ethan settled onto his bed at the inn with his laptop. It was barely six p.m. and already dark outside, a storm brewing in the heavy clouds and inky sky. He flicked the lamp at his bedside table on and set about Googling Monroe's baking show.

The show's graphics featured decadent cakes decorated with splashes of pale pink and yellow, sky blue and a lilac that reminded him of those candy-coated chocolate eggs his mum used to buy him and his brother at Easter.

Half brother, he corrected himself bitterly. If the man who'd raised him wasn't actually his father then that made Wayne his half brother instead of his full brother. It explained so much, since he and Wayne had always felt fundamentally different in some way, like they were on opposite sides of an invisible divide.

Now Ethan knew what it was.

Shaking off the memories, he went in search of a way to stream the *Sugar Coated* episodes. When he found them, Ethan skipped along until he found the section where the contestants were introduced and he almost choked on his own spit when Monroe popped up.

"Hi, I'm Monroe Roberts, I'm twenty-six and I'm from a small town called Forever Falls. I've wanted to be a baker ever since I was a little girl."

He scarcely recognized the woman on his laptop screen. Her bright ginger curls were tamed into long, sleek waves that fell in a lustrous sheet down her back, all the way to her waist. Her dark eyes were made up with an almost retro-style makeup with black eyeliner, and red gloss coated her lips. Her freckles were gone, presumably hidden with makeup. She was dressed in an emerald-green dress with fluttery sleeves and a V neckline, and dangly gold earrings hung from her ears.

"My specialty is layer cakes, the bigger the better." Her smile was pure sunshine and sass. "In fact, I love nothing more than creating a cake where all the special bits are on the inside. It's such a surprise, when you see this pretty but simple cake and then cut into it to find a crazy design like a special secret hiding there."

Ethan found himself grinning like a schoolboy. Monroe was charming, she knew how to work the camera, and she came across as friendly but confident. The other contestants seemed to like her, as did the three judges — one of whom Ethan knew because he was famous for his macarons back home in Australia.

He found himself binging his way through the episodes, fixated on this version of Monroe that seemed a whole world away from the woman who barked at people and hinted that she hadn't had any fun in a very long time. The more episodes he watched, the more curious he grew about why Monroe had walked away from her dreams of opening a bakery. What could have possibly caused her to give up on what was clearly an immense talent?

Ethan itched to find the answer.

But he wasn't supposed to be getting involved with *anyone* right now, let alone a woman who clearly had some baggage stashed away in a hidden closet. Hell, he'd left every single relationship he'd ever had behind when he'd boarded the flight bound for LAX. The man who'd lied about being his father, his half brother, his fiancée, his friends, colleagues…everyone.

Right now Ethan was alone in the world and that was exactly how it needed to be.

• • •

The following day Ethan helped Lottie move some furniture around the inn. There was an antique sideboard that was in bad need of repair, and Ethan had relocated it out to the shed. He wasn't much of an expert in restoration, but he'd agreed to take a look. At the very least he should be able to replace the hinges that had been busted, give the whole thing a sand back and a couple coats of stain to freshen it up.

Then he had the afternoon off, so Ethan headed back to the funeral home to see if he could glean any more information. He'd made the decision not to tell people he was trying to find his father, instead he had a story about looking for some letters his mother had exchanged with a man. Why? He was a deeply private person, by nature. And the questions that would be raised by him being open about his intentions weren't necessarily ones he wanted to answer. He was still working through his anger over the lies his mother had told him and yet he was still grieving her death.

It was complicated.

Therefore, he was being careful about where he started his search and the funeral home seemed like a discreet place.

Ethan pushed through the doors and walked into the funeral home's sedate waiting area. On first glance, one might easily mistake it for the reception area of a fancy doctor's clinic or even maybe a lawyer's office. There was an oak desk at the front, with a lamp and a vase of pink and white flowers. A glass coffee table sat in the middle of the room, flanked by two couches in a pale gray. Textured paintings of roses in soft, muted shades decorated the walls.

"Can I help you?" An older gentleman sat behind the desk, a pair of wire-rimmed glasses perched on his nose. He had silver hair and kind eyes that would no doubt make his clients feel comfortable.

"Yes, sir." Ethan approached. "I have somewhat of a strange request. I'm looking for a man who lived in this town and I believe he passed away a few years back. The obituary had the details for your business and I'm wondering if you might be able to provide me with some information."

The older man tilted his head, looking equal parts intrigued and wary. "That depends on what you want to know, son. We're not in the business of sharing our clients' private information."

That was the standard line he'd gotten at most places. Privacy and confidentiality, blah, blah, blah. But Ethan knew sometimes it was the smallest piece of data that could create a spider web of information. In his job, he'd often solved complex problems by starting with some small kernel and working his way out. This was no different.

He pulled the printed obituary out of his pocket and unfolded it, the lines heavily creased into the paper now. "I'm just trying to figure out if this man had any surviving family? My mother passed away recently, and I found some old letters with the name Matthew Brewer on them and I've been searching to see if he might have the letters she wrote to him."

Okay, so for someone who hated lying Ethan was certainly walking the tightrope of untruths at the moment. But, in his defense, his mother *did* have some old letters from the man who was his father. He'd found them pressed between the pages of a battered notebook. Sadly the envelopes had been thrown out, so there was no address or anything else that might aid him in finding his father.

"I'm sorry for your loss, son." The man picked up the obituary and Ethan caught the exact moment his expression changed—fleeting as it was—before dissolving back into neutrality. Interesting. "Yes, we buried Mr. Brewer. It was a…small funeral. He didn't really leave anyone behind."

Damn. Ethan nodded, but just as he was about to thank the man for his time, the older gentleman sighed.

"I wish I could say that all the dead are mourned equally, but Mr. Brewer led a very unhappy life. He was troubled, you see." The man slid the piece of paper back across the desk. "All I know is that both his parents have been dead a long time and he was estranged from any extended family. I can't really share much more than that, I'm afraid. If you want to find out more about him, maybe you could have a talk with Brian McPhee who runs the local ghost tour business. They were friends."

"That's very helpful, thank you so much."

"I hope you find what you're looking for." The man smiled kindly and Ethan bid him a good day before exiting the funeral home.

So, if *this* Matthew Brewer was his father, then he had no grandparents to meet. Didn't sound like there was a wife or kids in the picture, either. But at least Ethan had a name. He paused outside the funeral home and typed the name Brian McPhee into his phone. Then he added "Ghost Tours" next to it.

It was something. And right now, already so far into a currently fruitless journey, something was better than nothing.

· · ·

Ethan wasn't planning on stopping by the diner on the way back to the inn. A quick Google search had told him that the ghost tours office was only open Tuesday through Thursday and, of course, today was Friday. So he'd have to either send an email or wait until next Tuesday to speak to the man.

With that being his only lead, the plan had been to head back to the inn and get to work on the furniture restoration. But as Ethan walked past the diner on the way back to where he'd parked his rental, he noticed a piece of paper stuck to the front of the Sunshine Diner's front door.

No Chris Hemsworth impersonators allowed.

He snorted. Monroe was clearly yanking his chain.

Never one to turn away from curiosity, Ethan walked straight up to the door of the diner and pushed it open. The second Monroe met his eyes across the serving floor, she smirked.

Again, the Sunshine Diner was relatively full. The

clatter of coffee cups and the low din of chatter was kind of soothing.

"Didn't you see my sign?" she asked, coming forward. Today her red hair was scraped back into a braid, though several curls had escaped to frame her face. Her big eyes stared up at him, issuing a challenge, and she crossed her arms over her chest.

"I sure did. What have you got against impersonators anyway?" He grinned. The past year had been bleak, and sparring with Monroe might be the only bright spot in his day.

"Not impersonators in general, just those who look like Thor."

"Ah, got it. I'll be here tomorrow in my Elvis outfit, then."

She shook her head, her expression mock serious. "I doubt you could pull off that hair."

"You really want my pied piper ass to go somewhere else?"

She rolled her eyes. "You know what I want, paying customers. At this rate, the average time to consume a muffin is well over an hour while they're waiting for you to show up."

"You really think they're here for me?" He raised an eyebrow and swept his gaze across the room. A swift ripple of movement had everyone looking back at their plates so quickly, Ethan was worried someone might end up with whiplash.

Monroe stuck her hand into the pocket of her apron and pulled out a fist full of napkins. "These are phone numbers from people who've asked me to call them whenever you're in."

"They must be joking." Surely.

Although his gut told him otherwise. He'd already been asked out *four* times that morning, which was flattering but unwanted. The last thing Ethan wanted was a romantic entanglement.

"You're from a small town, so you know the boredom that sets in during the off-season." Monroe gestured with her right hand. "Not to mention the fact that dating when everyone knows your business is a *real* pain in the ass."

"Speaking from experience there?" He raised an eyebrow.

"Maybe."

Okay, so that was definitely a yes. Interesting.

"I don't know, I never found it too hard." That was the truth, but he conveniently left out the fact that he'd vacated his small town to go study in a big city before he'd even turned eighteen. But he wasn't about to go easy on Monroe, not when she might come between him and Big Frank's eggs.

"Of *course* you didn't," she said, shaking her head and laughing. "Do you find anything difficult?"

"Not usually." He couldn't help sprinkling a liberal amount of cockiness on his response and it had the desired effect—Monroe narrowed her eyes at him. "I'm practically perfect in every way."

She didn't seem to get the Mary Poppins reference.

"Your ego is majestic," she shot back.

"Fine, let me see what I can do."

He let out a whistle that was so sharp and so crisp it was sure to have every dog in the town running.

"You all should order some more food. The eggs are great!" He called out loud enough that everyone in the diner gaped at him, silence settling for a minute before the chatter started up again. "There you go, I've done my bit."

Monroe clamped a hand over her mouth to dampen her laughter. "That was exactly the kind of classy advertisement I needed, thanks."

"Sorry, this small-town boy isn't fancy enough for you?"

But before Monroe could get another barb in, Big Frank poked his head over the top of the warming shelf. "You two are bickering like an old married couple. Get a room already."

This time it was Monroe's turn to snort. "Please don't use the M word around me. You know how I feel about that."

Big Frank shook his head and went back to work. A ripple of awareness went through the diner, and Ethan overheard a woman saying to her friend, "Wait, are they *together*?"

Monroe must have heard it too, because she rolled her eyes. "Don't get any ideas, Ethan. You're not my type."

Although he couldn't help but notice how Monroe barely met his eye as she said it. Nor the fact that her voice was only loud enough for him to hear.

Ethan wasn't stupid. He *knew* he was attractive. He'd been waist-deep in attention for his looks since he was a cheeky blond-haired, blue-eyed surfer kid. Hell, he'd even done some catalogue modeling in his childhood and earlier teen years, which would never see the light of day if he had anything to do with it. It was a path he could have taken, but Ethan honestly found it boring as batshit. He much preferred to use his brain and spend his day solving problems.

"Too bad. You're *definitely* mine," he drawled, knowing full well that the tables closest to him could hear. Maybe it was silly but getting one back at Monroe for writing a 'keep out' sign was too much temptation for him to pass up.

Monroe almost choked. "Oh yeah, tell me another one."

"I'm serious."

Like during his modeling days, he found a focus on looks rather than anything else to be completely vapid. Not to say that Monroe wasn't attractive, she was...even if it wasn't in the most conventional sense. But he was attracted to so much more than appearance. She was a spitfire and a mystery and he would bet his last dollar that she was pure, combustible passion underneath it all. It was that hunt for the inner workings of a person that always got him excited.

You don't have time for that now. You're here for one reason and one reason only.

To find the truth.

"I don't know what game you're playing, Ethan," she said. "But you're skulking around town, visiting the funeral home and—"

"How do you know about that?" Had someone spotted him just now, or two days ago? Now that he thought about it, one of the women who'd asked him out had come up to him as he'd left the funeral home, which he'd thought was a bold move. Had that person been telling people his whereabouts?

Ugh, that's the last thing you need.

Now it was her turn to look amused. "Remember that

thing I said about small-town dating being a pain in the ass, well that goes for everything else, too. If you're looking for privacy, then you're in the wrong place."

Shit. Ethan scrubbed a hand over his face.

"I heard some of my 'customers' saying they saw you visiting and they were hoping you'd stop by here after." Monroe jerked her head toward a booth where women were sitting. They couldn't have been more than twenty-one or two. "Apparently this is your favorite place to eat."

They giggled when they caught him looking, and quickly turned away, only to peer back over a second later.

"I never asked for any of this attention," he said. "I wanted to come here, go about my business, and eat my eggs in peace. If there was something I could do to blend in, then I would absolutely do it."

. . .

Monroe knew she should be doing other things than verbally sparring with Ethan. Between the "surprise, you're still married" notice, the threat of her ex coming back to town, being run off her feet for minimal sales *and* her irritating, unwanted and unappreciated attraction to the mysterious Ethan, she was ready to call it a day.

Maybe she should just give up on small-town life and move to the woods to become one of those weird, off-grid people. She could hide away the rest of her life and live off nuts and foraged berries...or something.

Yeah, and then you'd eat the wrong thing and die alone in the middle of nowhere. Great idea, genius.

"Well, when you look the way you do..." Monroe

gestured to the arresting, masculine glory standing in front of her and made a huffing sound. "People will look. It's human nature."

"Is that your very roundabout way of saying you think I'm hot?" He grinned. "Thought I wasn't your type."

Oh dear, blush incoming. Unfortunately for Monroe, being a freckly redhead didn't make for a cute, pink-cheeked type of blush, either. Oh no. Transitioning into a full-on lobster face in three, two, one...

"It's not about my personal taste," she said, fully aware that she sounded about as legit as a shady man wearing a trench coat on a street corner. "It's biological. You're very... symmetrical."

"Thank you?" He raised an eyebrow.

"It's not a compliment, just a fact. And as much as I hate to say this about my fellow townsfolk, there's not a lot of husband material for those looking for it. Which means you"—she pointed at him—"are filling a need."

"It's hard not to make an inappropriate joke right now." The corner of his lip twitched. "But the last thing I came here for is romantic attention."

"While you're single, you'll be of interest."

Or even if you weren't single. Some people around here didn't consider that to be a barrier to entry.

Speaking of inappropriate jokes.

"I've got unfinished business here, so I won't be leaving for a while."

She should *want* his unfairly attractive ass somewhere else, so she could go back to having a half-empty diner of people actually willing to order a meal. That way she could at least work on getting the right kind of customers in. But

Monroe couldn't find it in herself to actually wish that he'd leave.

"I'm just telling it like it is," she said with a shrug. "You're a little too good at playing the mysterious traveler."

"You think I'm stoking people's attention on purpose?" He snorted. "I'm not."

"Well then let me give you some friendly advice," Monroe said, patting him on the arm and then immediately regretting it. Were those biceps made of pure stone? She'd bet he could swing a hammer with ease. *Stop it.* "Don't make it so easy for people to find you."

"I hate to break it to you, but this town isn't much bigger than a postage stamp. There aren't too many places to hide."

"Don't I know it," she said, hating herself for feeling so damn intrigued by him. "Why *are* you creeping around with an ulterior motive, anyway? You're not here as a tourist and as far as I've heard, nobody knows who you really are."

"First I'm making it too easy for people to find me and now I'm creeping around? Seems mighty contradictory to me."

Monroe could tell she'd struck a nerve. Ethan was definitely here with a purpose, and damn if she didn't want to know what it was.

You want to be distracted from your own shitty problems, that's all.

"Dodging the question?" she said with a nod. "Interesting."

"Why is it your business? I get the impression you'd be pissed if someone demanded to know what you were doing with your life and why you have such a visceral reaction to the M-word."

"I wouldn't be pissed, because everybody around here knows why I have such a visceral reaction to the M-word," she said flatly. "Let me catch you up: my ex was a cheating scumbag screwing around with my cousin. They left town together and now half my family doesn't talk to the other half."

Both his brows shot up in surprise. "People are assholes."

In spite of her bad mood, Monroe found herself laughing. "Ain't that the truth. I always preferred dogs to people, personally."

"Me too."

Something passed between them, a strange connection and a thread of understanding. She might not know what brought him here, but the man had come with more baggage than just the ones carrying his clothes. They were both a bit broken, both walled-off and untrusting of the world. It felt nice to find someone else like that—someone who wouldn't judge her for being wary. For being a little prickly.

God, the amount of times she'd had advice from the kindly old women around here that she should smile more and wear some lipstick if she wanted to hook a man…

What was the point? Hooking a man wasn't the hard part. It was sorting the good ones from the bad.

"So are you going to get rid of the keep-out sign?" he teased in that delicious accent of his. "I'm happy to sit in the kitchen again if it will make your life easier. You can hide me away like a dirty little secret."

The words sent a tremor of longing through her. It had been so *very* long since she'd indulged in a man, so very long since she'd used her body for pleasure instead of practicality and necessity. So very long since her heart had beaten for anything more than keeping her alive.

But looking up into the crystalline clear blue eyes of the man in front of her, Monroe felt her heart beat just a little harder than normal. Thump-*thump*.

"No need," she said, gesturing to the booth he liked that no one else wanted to sit in. "Take a seat. You want the usual?"

"Whatever you're serving is fine by me."

Monroe tried to ignore the innuendo in his voice, but the way he was looking at her made all the bad stuff of the last few days melt away. She had to remember, though, flirting with Ethan was like trying to stick a Band-Aid on a shotgun wound. It wouldn't fix a damn thing.

CHAPTER SIX

A sharp knock at his door drew Ethan's attention, and he paused the *Sugar Coated* episode playing on his screen. Monroe was in the middle of a "mystery pantry" challenge, which involved her having to make a cake with two traditionally savory ingredients.

"Coming." He got off his bed and went to the door. Lottie was waiting outside, arms folded across her chest. She looked pissed. "Everything okay?"

"I heard you were poking around the funeral home today," she said. "Word is getting around."

Dammit. Had that woman told *everybody* where he was? Ethan had spent his fair share of the past year in smaller towns—not to mention growing up in one back home—but the speed and fury with which gossip traveled in *this* town was mind boggling.

Ethan didn't say anything. He figured if Lottie had a question then that was on her to ask it. He hadn't done anything wrong.

She narrowed her sharp blue eyes at him. "Don't you have anything to say for yourself?"

"Did you ask me a question? Because I didn't hear one." He held his ground.

Ethan had spent the better part of his career dealing with egos—it was a natural part of consulting. It tended to attract ambitious, smart, Type-A folks who were used to being the most accomplished person in the room.

Wrangling a group of people like that took a few specials skills, namely the ability to stand your ground and the patience to let the other person show their hand before you showed yours.

Information was power, Ethan had learned. And that went double for personal information.

"I won't tolerate disrespect in my house," Lottie said, her voice hard as steel. "And I count the inn as my home."

"I'm not trying to be disrespectful," Ethan replied. "But as much as I appreciate that, I also don't tolerate people digging into my personal matters. So if you can see your way to respecting my boundaries, then I will do everything in my power to respect yours."

Lottie eyed him with reluctant acceptance. "You've got a way with words for a country boy."

"What makes you think I'm a country boy?" He'd barely told Lottie anything about himself, because she hadn't asked. When he'd turned up looking for a room and she'd offered a trade—a bed to sleep on in exchange for his hard-working hands—he'd readily agreed. But it wasn't like he'd brought a resume with him.

"You think a city boy knows how to chop wood the way you do?" She made a sound of disbelief. "Trust me, I lived in the city for a while and no suit-wearing, pasty-ass office dweller can do half the things you've done for me around here."

Ethan scrubbed a hand over his face, trying not to laugh because he had a genuine fear that Lottie May would clip his ears for doing so. "Right."

"You might have lived in the city, but you grew up some place small. You've worked with your hands."

Yeah, he'd done his share of work around his parents' property when he was a kid. But most of the scars on his hands had come from building computers and pulling apart other electronic devices to learn how they worked. He was a kid always with a screwdriver and a tube of thermal paste in his possession, and he'd made his money fixing up his mate's PCs so they could run better games without dishing out the excessive cash for new parts.

"That I have," Ethan confirmed.

"Then you know there are no such thing as secrets in a small town," she said. "Just the time between now and the point that somebody finds out what you're trying to hide."

"You think I'm hiding something?" He remained cool as a spring breeze.

"Follow me. You and I are going to have a talk."

Lottie started down the hallway to the stairs, without looking back to see if he would do what she'd demanded. Sighing, Ethan closed the bedroom door and locked it behind him, pocketing the key as he followed Lottie downstairs.

To his surprise, she bypassed the kitchen and went straight into her office, which was a small space behind the reception area in the foyer. Inside, there was little more than a desk, a filing cabinet, and two chairs jammed inside. Lottie reached down into a cupboard below the desk and pulled out a bottle of whiskey and two glasses.

"Sit," she said, pointing at one of the chairs.

Ethan lowered himself down and watched as Lottie poured two fingers of liquor into the glasses. She slid one across the desk to him and then held hers up in a brief salute before taking a long sip.

"Why are you trying to find Matthew Brewer?"

Okay, so they weren't beating around the bush. Duly noted. "Why do you want to know?"

"That boy never did a thing except cause people pain and I want to know why someone like yourself, who seems to have their head screwed on properly, is looking for someone like that."

Ethan's mind whirred. For a moment, he was tempted to tell Lottie the truth—but something held him back. She'd clearly known this Matthew Brewer, and had been hurt by him somehow. Family, maybe? The guy at the funeral home said both his parents were dead. Maybe she was an aunt, or a cousin.

"How did you know him?"

Lottie knocked back the rest of her whiskey. "That's not how this works, son. You don't get to ask all the questions."

"I think he had a relationship with my mother, and I'm looking for some letters that she sent to him." Ethan followed Lottie's lead and knocked his drink back. "She's dead and I've got nothing left of her. I was hoping to track the letters down and take them home with me."

Lottie refilled both their glasses, her eyes flicking back and forth as if she was trying to work something out. "If your mother *did* know Matthew, then I'm sorry for her."

"Why?"

"He was a bad egg, that boy. Always drinking, always causing trouble. Everybody around here knew him for mouthing off and picking fights." Lottie placed her glass down with a *thunk*. "You won't find anybody to say something good about him, and far as I know all his stuff is gone. His poor mother had to clear his house out after they found him dead and then she died a year later herself. Broken heart can kill a person, you know."

Questions danced on the tip of his tongue, all competing for attention.

"I don't even know if this is the right Matthew Brewer," Ethan admitted. "I've been all over this bloody country, hunting down dead men with that name."

"Seems a lot of effort for some old letters," Lottie said.

"My mother is worth it."

A lump lodged in the back of his throat—thinking about his mum now always brought up a storm of emotions. Grief, anger, aching loss, and love. Still underneath it all and after everything she'd done, there was love. He didn't know how to reconcile the kind and effervescent woman who'd raised him with the lies she'd told him since birth.

"Then I hope you're barking up the wrong tree," Lottie said.

"You knew him." It wasn't a question.

"His mother was a dear friend and I hated that little sonofabitch from the day he started breaking her heart." She stared at him across the table. "I don't want to see you wasting your time, Ethan. Those letters, if they ever existed, are long gone."

Something told him that Lottie wasn't telling the whole truth. But he wasn't going to push his luck tonight. When the ghost tours place was open, he could get a second opinion from the contact that the funeral home had provided him.

In the meantime, he needed to find out how he could go about getting information without every man and their dog watching his every move. For some reason, his mind drifted to his earlier conversation with Monroe.

She seemed to know how things worked around here. Maybe they could come to some kind of arrangement that would suit them both.

· · ·

Monroe was at her wits' end. The diner was *packed* again and nearly every table had been sitting there for a minimum of two hours, guzzling free coffee refills and barely ordering a damn thing. Didn't these people have jobs? If Jacob could see what was going on, he'd probably slap a "for sale" sign right over the door without giving her another minute to fix it.

She *had* to do something.

Surviving on barely any sleep, thanks to the mounting stress from both the diner and her divorce situation, she'd consumed more coffee than was healthy for one person and her nerves were critically frayed. Even Big Frank wouldn't come near her, which was saying something.

"Can I get you anything?" she asked as she stopped by a table with two women in their early twenties.

"I don't suppose if you know what time he's coming in?" one of them asked.

"Who?" Monroe asked.

"The Australian guy. It's Ethan, right? I wonder if he's related to the Hemsworths—maybe like a cousin or something? There's no way those similarities happen by accident." She looked at Monroe as if anticipating agreement. "It's genetics."

"He doesn't have a reservation," Monroe answered with

a sigh. Then she looked at the half-empty coffee cups and barely touched pastry which was all of two dollars toward the day's targets. This would not do at all. "And this is a diner, not a museum."

The young woman frowned. "What's that supposed to mean?"

Monroe stopped herself from saying what she really wanted to say—which was that people filling seats without buying anything were killing the business. Instead, she decided to take a more tactful approach. "People come here to eat and relax, not to have everyone staring at them."

"Oh. I didn't think of that."

"Besides, I'm pretty sure he's seeing someone." *That* was a total lie, but the women deflated and pulled out their wallets. Bingo! Maybe she'd just tell all the customers he was already spoken for and then they'd free up the tables so Monroe could concentrate on keeping the Sunshine Diner alive.

After the women cleared out, taking the pastry to-go, Monroe was wiping the table down when Ethan walked through the door and she felt something snap inside her.

"Out!" she demanded.

"Are you trying to kick me out again?" he asked, looking at her with his intense blue eyes.

"I'm not trying, I'm doing."

His jaw ticked and she got the impression he didn't like being on the back foot. "I don't care where we are, anyway. We don't have to be in the diner to have this conversation."

"You came here to talk to me?" She kept her face neutral, because she didn't want Ethan to know just how intrigued she was by him. Against her will, against her better judgment. Against the lessons she'd learned.

Most other guys would have taken off by now, rubbed the wrong way by her brash and forthright personality. But not him. Sure, Big Frank's eggs were good but…well, there were plenty of other places to eat.

Why did he keep coming back?

"You and I have a problem," he said.

"And that is…?"

"What did you call me?" He scrubbed a hand along his jaw. "The Pied Piper?"

"That sounds a whole lot like a *you* problem."

"Ah, but if I keep coming here then it's an *us* problem." He grinned and Monroe wanted to wipe the self-confident look off his face. "Which means there might be an *us* solution."

Monroe could barely remember the last time she'd been part of "us" anything. Clearly even in her marriage, she'd been alone.

"My solution is that I ban you from this diner." She folded her arms over her chest.

"On what grounds? I pay for my meals."

"I don't need grounds."

"That's not fair."

"Fair?" She balked. Then she grabbed him by the arm and hauled him out of the diner, fully aware that everyone was looking at them. When they were on the street and around the corner, out of earshot, she released him. "Do you think it's fair that this diner is failing and that people like Big Frank are going to be out of a job? Do you think it's fair that *I'm* going to fail my boss because I can't seem to fill the seats with actual paying customers? Do you think it's fair that people think that a small business should be able to offer McDonald's prices when we can barely scrape together wages for our staff?"

Okay, so maybe Monroe losing her shit at Ethan was a tad unfair. More than a tad, if she were being honest. But the pressure of it all was building up so hard and so fast that she wasn't sure how to deal with it.

"Hey," he said, holding up his hands. "Let's take this down a notch, okay?"

She sucked in a breath and brushed some flyaway hairs from her face. "Sorry. I know this isn't your fault, but everything is crumbling and…"

She felt a hot stinging sensation in her eyes and froze. No way, no how would she *ever* cry in front of a man again.

You're better than that. Tamp that shit down, now!

"I've got an idea," he said, tentatively reaching out with both hands and placing them on her arms, rubbing up and down in a way that was surprisingly soothing. "I think we can help each other."

"How could we possibly do that?" Monroe couldn't seem to help a damn thing at the moment, let alone assist some hot stranger.

"Hear me out."

She had no reason to say no. Either his idea would work or it wouldn't, so she might as well listen. She also couldn't say no to the curiosity winding through her system, lighting up parts of her that had been dormant for far too long. Parts of her that made her feel engaged again. That made her feel interested.

"Fine," she said with an air of skepticism.

"I won't be here forever. I'm looking for something and when I find what I'm looking for, I'll be out of your hair." He raked a hand through his blond hair, emotion playing in the crease in his forehead and the narrowing of his blue eyes. "Coming here, eating my eggs every morning…this is probably going to sound stupid, but it's the closest thing I've had to normal in over a year. It's the closest thing I've had to a routine."

Monroe cocked her head. "I can understand that."

"You said something yesterday that got me thinking. That while I'm single, I'll still be of interest."

"Yeah, I remember that."

"I want to go about my business without people breathing down my neck." He sighed. "It's important, this thing I'm looking for. *Really* important."

There was a vulnerability in Ethan's voice that made something catch in the back of Monroe's throat. For all her gruff and tough exterior, the ugly truth of it was that she was a total softie inside. She sniffled during Superbowl commercials and was known to give in to her nieces the second they set their puppy dog eyes on her. Easy target, that's what Loren called her. But it was being an easy target that had gotten her into the mess with her ex.

She'd been gullible. Weak. Stupid.

"You're in the wrong place for that," Monroe said. "Come slow season, people will throw pickles at a wall just to see which one slides the farthest."

Ethan looked at her like he wanted to say something, but he was hesitating for some reason. The push and pull was palpable in the air around him, and tension crackled like electricity.

"Spit it out," she said.

"I'm trying to find my father." He dragged his eyes away from hers for a moment, almost as if he hated saying the words out loud.

She blinked. "You think he lives here?" Dammit, she wasn't supposed to be interested.

"Lived," he corrected. "My father is dead."

"Oh." She frowned. "I'm sorry to hear that."

"I've been chasing dead men all over the country for the past twelve months and haven't found a damn thing yet. But I don't know..." He shook his head. "I've got a feeling this might be it."

"Why?"

"Because I think a man who knocks up a woman and then never has anything to do with his child is a bastard, and it seems like the man I'm chasing here fits the bill."

"I don't understand what any of this has to do with me."

"I need a cover, a way to walk around a little more unnoticed. Not to mention being attached to someone in this town might help me get access to more information." He let out what appeared to be a nervous laugh and for some odd reason, it made Ethan the Mystery Man seem even more gorgeous than usual. "I need to not be single."

Monroe opened her mouth and then closed it. Then she opened it again. "Wait, what?"

"I'm proposing a solution that might work for us both. You seemed to think if I was in a relationship then I might be able to go around unnoticed a bit more, and I'm not really looking for a relationship. You, on the other hand, look like you want to stab someone's eye out with a rusty fork at the mention of marriage."

"I'm not looking for any relationship, real *or* fake."

But wouldn't a fake relationship solve at least one of her problems? The threat of her ex coming back to town had been hanging over her head, the possibility of embarrassment at him seeing her pathetic life without him was like a noose around her neck. It was the fear that had grounded her into inertia with solving that problem. But if Brendan came back and saw that not only was she in a relationship with a man, but that she'd clearly gotten an *upgrade*…well, wouldn't that just be a wonderful way to stick it to the man who'd shattered her heart into a million irreparable pieces?

Wouldn't that be glorious revenge for him screwing her cousin behind her back?

"This is ridiculous." She shook her head, heart and mind arguing over the idea like they were playing tug of war.

"But if I'm no longer single, then people shouldn't be staking out your diner anymore right? I think they've given up thinking I'm actually Chris Hemsworth, but clearly they're not going to stop following me around and watching my every move unless I do something. I've tried to think of another way to fix this and I'm coming up empty." He took a step closer and Monroe felt the air still in her lungs. "I know you said I wasn't your type, but maybe you could fake being attracted to me."

If *only* he wasn't her type. Hell, Monroe would chance it and say that Ethan might be the "type" of every living being with a pulse and a preference for men. Universal hotness, at its finest.

"Look, I…" She couldn't find the right words. Because the right words would have been to tell the Aussie to get lost so she could go back to saving her diner.

But the lure of sticking it to Brendan was a strong one. When would she ever get the chance to do it again? This would be payback for all the tears she'd cried, all the moments of self-doubt and of not feeling worthy. It would be payback for her being stuck here, listening to the whispers behind her back and the pitying looks and the shame. Payback for the fact that he'd left all their dirty laundry flapping in the wind for the whole town to see.

And it would have the bonus of hopefully returning her diner to normal capacity so she could get back to working on a plan for how not to fail Jacob *and* mess up her carefully structured life.

"I can't believe I'm going to say this," Monroe said, shaking her head. "But yes, I'll fake it."

CHAPTER SEVEN

Ethan couldn't quite believe it. He'd anticipated the chance of Monroe saying yes to his outrageous plan was minimal, at best. But she had her reasons for agreeing, and it might not just be about clearing the non-paying crowds from her diner. Whatever it was, however, was none of his business.

And he wasn't about to look a gift horse in the mouth, no matter how surprising.

"I want to lay down some ground rules, though," Monroe said.

"Of course, I'd expect nothing less."

Pretending to be attracted to Monroe wouldn't exactly be a hardship, especially since there wouldn't be all that much pretending involved. Ethan might have spent the last year neglecting actual relationships in favor of hunting out a man he'd never get to meet, but he wasn't dead inside. He knew the way his pulse spiked whenever he saw her. He knew that his blood pounded a little harder in his veins when she set those intense brown eyes on him. He knew that given a few drinks, there was a risk he'd tell her all that to see if they'd end up in bed together.

Note to self: no drinking for as long as this takes.

"Good." Monroe nodded, pausing to wait as someone walked past them on the quiet side street. Then they were alone again. "First things first…I don't want you telling anybody this isn't real. Not a single soul. If we're doing it, then we're all in."

That *wasn't* what he'd expected her to ask for, but at least it was a request he could adhere to. What was one more secret on an already large pile?

"Done. What else have you got?"

"If I randomly ask you to kiss me out of nowhere, then you'll do it, no questions asked."

Interesting. They were doubling down on things Ethan had *not* expected. "I'm not afraid of a kiss."

"And third." She bit down on her bottom lip. "You'll need to meet my family."

"Uh…" Ethan wasn't above fooling some small-town strangers to get eyes off him, but fooling a person's real-life family was a whole other level of deceit.

"If I suddenly have a 'boyfriend' and I don't take you to meet them, that's going to be suspicious. You're hiding in plain sight, remember." She wrapped her arms around herself. "And it'll be good for them to see I've moved on."

"Even if you haven't?"

"I *have*," she said emphatically. "Mentally and emotionally, I've moved on. I just haven't been chasing down another mistake, but for some reason they think that's the final step in my 'healing.' So bringing you around will give me some reprieve there, too."

"And here I was thinking I'd need to put the hard sell on."

"You got lucky. This will benefit me as much as it benefits you." She stared up at him, and there was so much he wanted to know. So many questions he wanted to ask. "So, what are your conditions?"

"Only that you help cover my tracks so I can find out what I need to find out."

Worry flickered across her face, like a candle trembling

in the wind. "You're not going to do anything you wouldn't tell your mother about, right?"

"Bad example," he said, his throat tightening. "She's the reason I'm in this mess, so I imagine there would be plenty I wouldn't tell her if she was still alive."

Monroe nodded. "Well, maybe I'll add another condition to my list. Don't do anything illegal."

"It'll all be within the bounds of the law, I promise."

They stood for a moment, eyes locked, tension crackling between them like a log of wood popping and burning in a fireplace.

"Well, I have to get back to work," she said, suddenly seeming a little nervous. Or bashful, maybe.

They walked out of the side street and onto the main street, back to the front of the diner. Ethan's attention was caught on the big window. Multiple faces were plastered to the glass, a group of women who appeared to be having coffees openly watching the scene unfold outside.

"This might be your chance to show everyone you're all in," he said, a smirk tugging at his lips.

Monroe looked, ginger curls whipping over her shoulder. When she turned back to him, her cheeks were rosy as if she'd stood outside in the snow too long. "You're going to break some hearts, you know."

"Good," he said with a chuckle.

"You're a very curious man, Ethan…" She laughed. "I don't even know your last name."

"Hammersmith," he said with a sigh.

"No." She clamped a hand over her mouth. "Looks like Thor *and* has hammer in his last name. It's all very suspicious."

"Don't you start," he grumbled. "What are you going to tell people?"

"Not a goddamn thing," she said with an embarrassed shake of her head. Her cheeks were very red now—like twin scribbles of crayon on her freckle-covered skin. It was adorable the way she blushed to the extreme. "I prefer to let my actions do the talking."

Without warning, she pressed up on her toes and wrapped her arms around his neck, planting a kiss right on his lips. It was chaste in the scheme of things—all lips, no tongue—but it left Ethan feeling warm all over, and as she pulled away and scurried into the diner, he couldn't help a goofy grin spreading across his lips.

Well, that had gone *far* better than planned. He had no idea what to expect, and something told him Monroe was going to keep him guessing at every turn.

• • •

Monroe walked back into the Sunshine Diner, feeling the entire staff and every single patron looking at her. It would be all over town within seconds. For some reason, that made her want to puff her chest out a little.

Sure, the relationship was faker than the smell of those god-awful vanilla candles her sister liked to burn. And sure, Monroe had no intention of *actually* capitalizing on this thing with Ethan, apart from keeping a kiss in her back pocket should Brendan decide to show up. But for once, people were looking at her with awe instead of pity. And that was a nice change.

"What the *heck*?" Darlene, one of Monroe's longest

standing employees, followed her into the kitchen, her eyes wide and a delighted smile on her face. She had curly black hair peppered with silver and a smile that beamed against her brown skin. "Are you two dating?"

Big Frank looked up from the grill and raised a brow, clearly interested in Monroe's answer.

"He's only been in town a few days." Darlene blinked.

"I don't know if we're ready to put a label on it," Monroe replied, feeling her face shoot up a billion degrees. "We were going to keep it on the down low, but…well, you know."

"No I *don't* know, that's why I'm asking." She planted her hands on her ample hips and speared Monroe with a look. Darlene had five kids and twice as many grandkids and she did *not* suffer fools. "How do you go from writing a *keep-out* sign to kissing a man in the street?"

"It was barely a kiss."

That was the truth, if ever she'd told it. Her body had all but screamed *"WTF, girl?"* when she'd pulled away from him, desperate for more than something that might pass as a kiss for an eighth grader. Still, it didn't take much to get the gossip birds twittering. Hmm, she should probably text her sisters before they—

The chirrup of her phone told her it was too late. A message flashed up on screen from Loren that simply said: *Details. NOW.*

"This town is something else," Monroe muttered.

"I'm waiting." Darlene tapped her foot and even Big Frank was still watching.

"Hey, this isn't Dr. Phil hour. We're supposed to be working." Monroe grabbed one of the coffee pots that had finished brewing and stared both her employees down before heading back out into the dining area.

The questions kept coming, but Monroe had a knack for dodging questions when she wanted to. What was the first rule of deception? Don't be too detailed and stick to the truth as much as possible.

It's certainly what Brendan had done. The whole time he was screwing Amber, he'd been telling Monroe he was going to the yoga studio as part of his rehab for an old football injury. That's what made it so believable—because he *was* going to the yoga studio and he *did* have an injury that was playing up. That way if anyone saw him coming or going his story would check out. They didn't even need to text to arrange a "session" because he could book her through the studio's app.

Even better, Amber's town house was back-to-back with the studio. There was a small alley in between, with a gate into her backyard and another that led to the small courtyard behind the yoga studio. All they had to do was scurry across the alley, which barely ever had a car on it… until that time she happened to drive that way because a tree had come down and blocked her usual route to work.

"Monroe!" Someone called her name from the front of the diner. "Look!"

A delivery man with a huge bouquet of flowers waddled through the door, barely able to see past the green fronds and colorful flowers in yellow and orange and red. She walked over.

"Hey, Monroe. These are for you." He thrust the flowers into her hands and Monroe sneezed as a bit of greenery was all but shoved up her nose. "Enjoy."

She managed to wrap one arm around the large vase holding the flowers and plucked out the card wedged into the over-the-top display.

Monroe, dinner tonight at Deluca's. 8 p.m. Ethan.

He must have stopped at the florist on his way back to the inn, since the pretty shop was only two doors down. Flowers and then dinner at Forever Fall's only fine dining restaurant. He wanted to make a statement. He wanted *everyone* to know they were together.

A date? She hadn't been on one of those in years. She and her ex weren't the "date night" type, not after they got married anyway.

Maybe that's why the marriage failed.

"What the heck am I supposed to do with these?" she muttered to herself. She couldn't take them out the back, because it would be no good getting flower stuff near the food. And there wasn't a welcome desk or anything in the diner, because that wasn't their style.

Monroe walked back to the squished little booth that Ethan liked to sit at. It was free, for the moment. She plonked the flowers down and scrubbed a hand over her face, looking at the arrangement like it was an alien that had invaded her diner.

The last time she'd had fresh flowers in her house was the day after her wedding, because she'd kept her bridal bouquet and stuck it into a glass with water.

"It was all downhill after that," she said to herself.

Hard as it was, she knew it was a good thing. Monroe had gone through bad times and had the emotional scars to prove it, which meant the chances of her developing any feelings for her fake boyfriend were nil. Less than nil, even.

But that didn't stop her immediately thinking about what she was going to wear to dinner that night.

• • •

"You know how in those cheesy romantic comedy movies there's that montage of the girl getting ready for her hot date, and the pile of clothes keeps growing and growing?" Monroe planted her hands on her hips. "If I've been a bad person and I go to hell, *that's* what it's going to be. I'll have to die over and over under an avalanche of Forever 21."

Loren gasped, her eyes narrowing at Monroe, and she pressed a palm to her chest. "I do *not* shop at Forever 21."

"That's what you took from what I said?" She rolled her eyes.

"I can easily look past your melodrama, since, you know, I've been related to you for more than five minutes." Loren sniffed. "Classic Monroe."

"Whatever." She sighed and looked at herself in the full-length mirror of her sister's bedroom. "None of this looks good."

As soon as she knew that she would be eating at Deluca's, it was clear that nothing in Monroe's boring-ass wardrobe would do. So she contacted the rent-a-closet, aka Loren. Only her big sister seemed determined to put her in an outfit that made her look like Barbie's club rat BFF.

"What's wrong with a little black dress?"

Monroe raised an eyebrow and gestured to the dress Loren had forced her to try on. It was sparkly, had half a dozen spaghetti-thin crisscross straps at the back that would be likely to guillotine your head straight off if you put it on wrong, and had an unattractive gape at the front, which was where Monroe was pretty sure one's boobs were supposed to go.

You know, if she had any boobs with which to fill the dress.

"I'm not wearing this," Monroe said. "Maybe I'll just wear jeans and a nice top."

"You are *not* wearing jeans to Deluca's. In fact, I'm pretty sure they have a 'no denim' policy, anyway." Loren let out a long sigh. At that moment, Jesse, who was three and had been playing happily in the corner with her stuffed elephant and one of Loren's glitzy scarves, waddled over, something clutched in her chubby toddler fist.

"Red." She thrust the silky piece of clothing toward Monroe.

"Pretty sure redheads aren't supposed to wear red." Monroe crouched down and nuzzled her face against the little girl's chest, causing her to squeal and laugh. "But I think that would look *fabulous* on you, pretty girl. You're gorgeous just like your mama."

"Oh stop it, Roe." Loren riffled through her closet again, the clinking sound of metal hangers now burned into Monroe's brain. "You're beautiful in your own unique way."

"I don't need to be beautiful," she replied with a shrug. "If everyone were beautiful then the word wouldn't mean anything, would it?"

Monroe was happy being resilient and reliable, rather than beautiful. She knew she didn't tick society's boxes, what with her lack of curves and her wild hair and her overtly freckled skin. Oh, and her firetruck red blush. The Irish blood ran strong in her, and she'd inherited the stubbornness, too.

Loren walked over, her face stormy. She knew her big sister got annoyed when she said things like that. "Monroe Patricia Roberts, you will stop this ridiculousness right now. You *are* beautiful. I think it, Taylor thinks it, and Mr. Hemsworth certainly seems to think so."

"Don't call him that." Monroe laughed. "The poor guy's got a complex."

"All I'm saying is, you told me once after the divorce that Brendan cheating on you made you feel ugly and worthless, and what did I say?"

"That beauty is in the eye of the beholder and just because he didn't see it doesn't mean I'm ugly." Monroe repeated the words, even though she hated saying them. "I just…I'm not good at this girlie stuff, you know?"

She thought back to a time when she *was* good at it— before her marriage and in the early days, and while she was on *Sugar Coated*. Looking back at those photos was like looking at a stranger. It seemed like when she'd found out about the affair, all those bits of her evaporated into smoke. She'd forgotten how to be that vivacious, stylish, outgoing woman.

"We all have our strengths." Loren went back to picking through her closet until she found something else. "What about this? Maybe it won't make you feel so exposed."

The dress she held up was stunning and modest, yet elegant. It had a simple shallow V neckline and a hem that would float around her knees, with long, sheer sleeves and a tie that would help her fake a waist. The color was a muted sage green, with a subtle pattern of leaves printed onto the fabric only a shade or two darker.

"That's perfect." Monroe blinked. "Why didn't you show me this first?"

"I like playing dress-up." Loren grinned. "And I wanted to see you in that dress."

Monroe laughed and looked down at herself. "This is truly awful and I'm going to need your help getting out of it."

"Will you let me do your makeup?" Loren asked.

Monroe groaned. "*That's* what this is? A trap!"

"Hey, it's not often you come to me for help. A big sister has to take what she can get." Loren bent down to scoop up Jesse, who was trying to get into Loren's shoe stash. "So, what do you say? Makeup and hair?"

"Now you're adding things on," Monroe grumbled.

"We'll keep it subtle, I promise."

"Fine. But if you come near me with an eyelash curler I *will* defend myself. And if you send me out looking like a Bratz doll I will never forgive you."

"You have my word." Loren blew a raspberry on Jesse's cheek. "We're going to give Auntie Monroe a makeover, isn't that fun! Come on, baby girl, let's get everything set up."

Monroe watched her glamorous older sister walk away, a mixture of excitement and nerves rattling around in her brain. The old demons were there, sleeping. But only just— it wouldn't take much to wake them up fully and for Monroe to turn on her heel and hide out back home.

Going on dates wasn't her thing. Knowing that a whole town's worth of people would probably be scratching their heads and asking "why her?" made it even worse. The glow of satisfaction she'd experienced earlier had already faded a bit, because this was all for nothing. Lying to her sisters made her feel like crap, but right now she was in survival mode.

And maybe a little bit of revenge mode, where Brendan was concerned.

The lawyer's letter was still sitting on her kitchen bench and they'd called twice, leaving messages both times. Then her ex had texted again, saying that he wouldn't allow her to ruin his wedding.

Doesn't feel great, does it asshole?

Funny how he didn't seem to mind ruining their marriage, and now suddenly she was the bad guy. Let him sweat on it a little more.

It was time for Monroe to have the upper hand.

CHAPTER EIGHT

Ethan hadn't brought a suit with him to America, because who needed a suit to skulk around trying to find a dead man? It wasn't really a necessary clothing choice. But that left him struggling for his date with Monroe, since he'd picked the fanciest place in town and wanted to make a show of it.

A show big enough that hopefully people would leave him to his business.

Luckily, Ethan's bank account was healthy. His previous job had kept him flush and being the kind of guy who liked to analyze things, some light dabbling in the stock market had bolstered that further. He might be living frugally now, but that was only because he didn't want this wild goose chase to eat into his nest egg too much.

So it hadn't been too difficult to get himself something suitable to wear—a pair of dress pants, some proper shoes, a collared shirt.

He parked out front of the restaurant and took a moment to enjoy the view. Deluca's was an Italian restaurant situated in an old house on a hill. The windows were strung with fairy lights and a big old tree dominated the front of the property. Inside, a warm glow emanated, and he could see people sitting at tables by the windows, talking and laughing and touching wineglasses together. But it was the view beyond the restaurant that was truly spectacular.

Forever Falls was on the Atlantic coast, and the ocean view stretched out almost endlessly. It was dark, but the boardwalk below was lit with old-fashioned lamps, and he could see a few brave souls who'd gone for a stroll in spite of the cold. Heavy dark clouds gathered on the distant horizon and there was a sliver of purple light along the edge of the water. A storm was headed for them, and every so often he could see a ripple of lightning way out over the waves.

There was something magical about it. Something brutal and beautiful and raw, and if it wasn't for his hands starting to go numb, he could have stayed there for hours.

In some ways it reminded him of home — not of Melbourne, the cosmopolitan city obsessed with coffee and art where he'd spent the better part of the last fifteen years. But the small town he grew up in. It was on a bluff, with similar ragged and natural views. His childhood had been littered with days at the beach, digging his toes into the sand and trying to convince his mother to come into the water with him.

He'd loved her so much. Loved her with a force that always felt like it could break him in half. She'd understood him, his needs and his desire and she always knew exactly what to say to lift him up. He'd never had that connection with his father and brother because he had been quieter, more of a thinker. According to the old man he wasn't "blokey" enough because he wasn't into getting drunk at the pub or getting grease under his nails or putting up his fists. Thus, he'd always been left out of their little circle of two.

Now he knew why.

Shrugging off the memories, he turned and headed toward the restaurant's front door. Inside, there was a blast of warm air and it made his skin tingle for a second with the shock of temperature change. The hostess smiled warmly and guided him to the seat he'd requested—one right by the fire.

He was early, because it was important to never be late for a date. But he'd barely shrugged out of his coat when Monroe walked in.

Holy…

Ethan blinked. Was this the same woman who'd handwritten a "keep out" sign for her diner? The same woman who let her cactus prickles show without remorse? Surely not.

Monroe hovered in the doorway, her eyes scanning the room until they rested on him. It was like being hit with a bolt of lightning. She wore a green dress that had a timeless quality to it—flowing skirt, loose sleeves that tapered at the wrist, modest neckline that somehow looked sexier than if she'd worn something plunging. Her ginger curls were smoothed, though not completely tamed, and pinned above one ear so they fell neatly around her shoulders. She even had on a pair of high heels.

As she walked through the restaurant, heads turned and eyebrows raised. People knew Monroe, it seemed, and they were as shocked as he was.

"I left my coat at the front, I hope that's okay," she said to the hostess as she approached the table.

"Of course." The woman smiled and held her arm out to collect Ethan's coat. "I'll be back with some water in a moment."

Ethan pulled the chair out for Monroe and she sat, fiddling with the skirt portion of her dress so it didn't get rucked up underneath her. Something told him that either A, the dress wasn't hers or B, it had been a long time since she'd worn it.

Since the restaurant had been a house at one point, it had that cozy feeling of intimacy. There were tables scattered across the main area, and more in another room through an open archway. The fire crackled a few feet away, and there was a large bookshelf on one wall, styled with vintage leather books, interesting pieces of glassware, and other trinkets.

In the center of the table, a small candle flickered inside a glass and a single flower along with a sprig of rosemary sat in a small vase.

"You look *amazing*," he said, taking a seat on the other side of her.

Monroe made a little sound that told him the prickly woman he knew was *definitely* still there, even if she looked a little more polished on the outside. "If you're too good an actor then people will think you really *are* Chris Hemsworth."

Ethan shook his head. "Can't you take a bloody compliment?"

"Only if it's genuine." She smiled tightly.

There were no other tables within earshot, since the restaurant was nicely spaced out. So at least they could have an honest conversation, as long as it looked like a romantic dinner from the outside.

"What's not genuine about it? You're a beautiful woman in a beautiful dress, anyone can see that." Ethan shrugged.

He'd never been the kind of guy who was shy about giving a compliment where he felt it was due—and it was *always* genuine. Monroe looked at him like she was running a scanner over his face.

Warning, bullshit activator engaged.

Well, Ethan wasn't big on playing games. He said what he meant, and he meant what he said. For better or worse.

"All I'm saying is, you can drop the front if there's no one around to hear us." She paused as the hostess returned, bringing a bottle of sparkling water and two glasses. Monroe ordered a glass of white wine and Ethan opted for red. When the woman left, Monroe turned her attention back to Ethan. "So, you picked the fanciest spot in town."

"Naturally."

"Did you live the high life back in Australia?"

Hmm. She wanted to know more about him? Ethan had kept his cards pretty close to his chest, peddling the story about long lost love letters belonging to his mother and him being on a mission to get some closure over her death.

In a way, it was true. He *wanted* closure, though part of him suspected it would never come. If both his parents were dead, then what did he hope to find exactly? Maybe a relative, although if his father was the ghost he was hunting in Forever Falls, then it sounded like he might not get that, either.

"I had a well-paying job and a nice place..." He left out the part about the fiancée. "I used to eat out at places like this on the regular."

"What did you do for work?"

"I was an IT Program Manager."

She raised an eyebrow. "Sounds stuffy."

"I liked it. I got to solve problems and create solutions for our clients." He shrugged. "And it afforded me a lifestyle that suited my needs. Could have done without the office politics, though."

Monroe nodded. "As I always say, people are the most difficult part of any job."

Maybe he should be inclined to believe her—because a lot of signs had certainly pointed to her being a bit of a misanthrope. But Ethan wasn't the kind of guy to gloss over the surface of something—or some*one*—and he saw a big heart hiding under Monroe's protected exterior.

He'd also seen the flicker of empathy on her face when he'd confessed that he was looking for his father.

"So tell me, how'd the winner of an international baking competition come to be running a diner?"

Monroe's jaw twitched. "How do you know about that?"

Uhh crap. He didn't want to throw Big Frank under the bus, but how else could he have found out?

"Someone mentioned it in passing," he said, but Monroe's expression told him she was *not* buying it. "I Googled you."

Her mouth popped open. "Why?"

"Because I need to know this stuff if we're going to sell the whole fake relationship thing, right?" He shrugged. "I had a feeling you might be a little cagey, and if we want this thing to work then I need to know about you."

"The diner is run by a family friend and I've worked there for years. It used to be my after-school job." Monroe paused as the server came up to the table and delivered their wine. Ethan held his glass toward hers and she touched it to his, making a soft chime. "Eventually I worked my way up to helping with the bookkeeping and training new staff. Then when I decided I didn't want to go to college, my boss promoted me to manager while I was figuring out what I wanted to do with my life. That's it."

That's it? Yeah, not likely. Ethan found it interesting how Monroe had been so forthright about her divorce, like she used it as a shield. And yet her career seemed to be something she kept under wraps, *that* was the thing she protected with silence.

"And what about the baking competition?" he prodded.

Monroe sipped her wine and ran her tongue over her lips. Then she reached for a napkin and wiped all the glossy stuff off as if she couldn't stand the feel of it. "The baking competition was a fluke."

"Didn't look like it to me."

Her eyebrows shot up. "Just how far did your Googling go?"

All the way through the season of *Sugar Coated* that Monroe won. He'd binged the damn thing in less than two days, staying up late, mesmerized by her ready smile and cheeky eyes and her quick thinking. She was talented as hell—breezing through the challenges with creativity and adaptability and a boatload of heart.

She was a force to behold.

"I watched an episode or two," he said, sipping his wine and hoping that she didn't hear the lie of omission in his voice.

Monroe put her fingers to her temple and rubbed in circles. "Look, the baking competition was something fun. Call it a bucket list item."

"But you said you had dreams of opening your own bakery."

"It was all for the cameras," she said, shaking her head. "None of it was true."

. . .

Except it was.

Thinking back to that time was like thinking about another person. Monroe remembered the way her stomach tumbled and turned as they'd filmed the first round of auditions. She remembered the little handwritten affirmation she'd stuffed into the pocket of her dress—*I am smart, I am talented, I take risks.*

The words seemed strange to her now, almost like they were written in another language. Because Monroe wasn't the person who took risks anymore. She wasn't someone who used her talents and she certainly wasn't someone who considered herself smart anymore. Brendan had proven quite the opposite about her.

"Really?" Ethan looked doubtful.

He sat across the table from her with all his movie-star good looks. She was acutely aware of how the people around them looked at him, gravitating like flies to honey, though in a place like this, no one dared approach their table. His blond hair was a little long—like he hadn't bothered to have it cut in a while—and it curled around his ears. His blue eyes stood out against the inky black sweater hugging his muscled torso and the silver links of a bracelet peeked out from his wrist on one side.

"Really," Monroe lied. "Those reality shows are pretty

scripted. They often had us say things a few times, prompting us with particular wording so they could get the soundbite they wanted."

That was true, at least.

"I always wondered that," Ethan said with a nod. He reached for a bread roll that sat in a small basket between them and tore it open so he could swipe some butter on. Monroe did the same. "No ambitions for your baking talents, then?"

"It's more of a hobby. I make cakes for family and friends. "

"Tell me about the last cake you made." Ethan leaned back in his chair, cradling his wine, his blue eyes sharp and intelligent. Why did his question feel like a trap?

"Why would you want to know that?"

"Baking interests me. I tried it one time, but my muffins came out like rocks and I never tried again."

Monroe laughed. "You probably over-mixed the batter."

"Go on," he encouraged. "Humor me."

"The last cake I made was for my younger sister's engagement party. She's getting married next year, and she and her fiancé have a unique style. They're both tattoo artists. So I did a devil's cake in three tiers, with black fondant. Then I hand-painted some of their favorite tattoo designs on in an edible UV-activated food paint so that it glowed in the dark. She also loves piñata-style cakes, so I filled the cake with her favorite candy. It was cool actually, because all the candy was brightly colored and the cake was totally black when the lights were on, so when she cut into it all this rainbow spilled out."

Monroe grinned at the memory. Her sister had been

absolutely delighted.

"Sounds cool."

"It really was." Monroe sipped her wine. "We even did miniature cupcakes in the same devil's cake batter with a black frosting made using buttercream mixed with activated charcoal."

She bit down on her lip, aware that her voice had been getting higher and faster like it always did whenever she talked about her cakes. Baking was the only thing in the world that made her feel like she was good at something. Sometimes, when she was feeling low, she'd make an entire batch of cupcakes and spend an hour frosting them and fussing with all the little decorative details…only to then drop them off at one of her sisters' places because she couldn't stand the sight of them.

Really, it was more that she couldn't stand thinking about what they represented: lost opportunities. Discarded dreams. Failure.

"And what do I need to know about you?" she asked, turning the attention away from herself. "You're looking for your dad?"

Ethan sucked on the inside of his cheek for a moment, as if trying to figure out just how much he wanted to share. "Yeah. That's not the story I'm telling people, though."

"Okay, so what are you telling people?"

"That my mother died and I found letters from a man who lived in America. I'm trying to track him down so I can get the letters my mother wrote him, because I need some closure on her death." He raked a hand through his hair. "Truth is that when my mother was diagnosed with stage four breast cancer, I took a leave of absence from my job to help out at home. That's when she told me that the man I thought was my father wasn't actually my father."

Monroe gasped. "She lied to you all that time?"

"My whole life." He ground the words out, the muscles in his jaw ticking like she was trying to turn them to dust. "I lived with the man I called Dad and it turned out he wasn't related to me by blood. And my brother was only my half brother."

The words reached into Monroe's chest and wrenched something that she hadn't felt in a long time. "Did you find out why?"

"All she said was that being with my real father was a mistake and she didn't want me to know anything but love."

"But how is lying love?" It stirred up all the feelings of betrayal and hurt and shock that Monroe had felt when she stumbled on Brendan and Amber's affair. She knew what he was going through. Intimately.

"It isn't. It's selfishness." He shook his head. "All I know is that my real father is dead…supposedly."

"Do you believe that?"

He let out a humorless chuckle. "Well, I don't have much else to go on. So I have to believe it, otherwise I'd be widening my search by God knows how much. I have to think if she told me the truth in the end, there would be no point lying about that one detail."

"Makes sense."

"I want to be able to poke around and find out what I need to find out without people watching my every move, you know?" For a moment he looked truly pained and Monroe could see the toll this information had taken on him. "I left everything behind to come here and find out if

I have any family. I left my job, my house, my…"

He shook his head.

"I'll help you," Monroe said, the words shooting out of her before she even had time to think about the consequences. And there *were* consequences. She shouldn't be getting mixed up in other people's business when she had her own things to worry about.

Like her father's health. Like her not-quite-divorce. Like stopping her boss from selling the diner.

But something told her that a good deed wouldn't go astray, and despite the drama that Ethan had unwittingly caused, he seemed like a good person.

"I've lived here my whole life. I might know a thing or two to push you in the right direction." She nodded. "I can't promise anything, but you never know what piece of information might be critical."

"Thank you." Ethan's gaze captured hers across the table, the candle flickering in her periphery.

Something shifted in her stomach, like a piece of her shell had broken free and allowed her to feel the excited flutter she thought had died long ago. It was far too easy to be enraptured by a handsome, mysterious man. Far, *far* too easy.

But Monroe knew she could hold herself in check — after all, denying herself was what she did best.

CHAPTER NINE

Ethan and Monroe had agreed to meet the following day in the town square, so they could be seen together and so they could talk more about Ethan's father. Not long after their food had arrived last night, the restaurant had gotten quite full thanks to a large group that requested several tables to be pushed together. They'd sat close to Ethan and Monroe, and so they'd decided to keep their conversation light, in case anyone could overhear them.

The day was gray and chilly, and Ethan zipped his coat right up and tucked his chin inside the thick fabric. But he didn't mind the cold. In fact, there was something about being on the coast when it was frigid and damp that he liked. Maybe it was the juxtaposition to what people thought a beach *should* look like. Or maybe it was simply the rugged beauty of waves thrashing against the shore and the ripple of silver clouds across the sky.

It reminded him of his childhood—the quiet stretch of winter when all the tourists were gone and he could find himself alone on the beach. He used to go there to think, especially after an argument with his father.

He's not your father.

That was a complicated thought. Because Ivan Hammersmith was the man who'd provided for him all his childhood. He *had* raised Ethan. He'd taught him how to ride a bike and how to troubleshoot issues with his car and how to pour a beer properly. But he was also the man who'd mocked Ethan's need for time alone and who never showed an interest in any of his hobbies.

They were very different people. Too different, in some ways.

The worst thing about hearing the truth about his birth was not that he felt devastated—though he absolutely did—but that he felt like his life finally made sense.

"Ethan!" Monroe held her hand up in a wave as she jogged over to him. Her beautiful red hair was a splash of color against the otherwise muted surrounding. She wore a light gray knitted beanie, fitted jeans tucked into some sturdy boots, and a charcoal wool coat with a black and white checked scarf. "You're early."

He looked at his watch. "So are you."

"Punctuality is next to godliness," she quipped.

"I thought that was cleanliness?" He laughed.

"Probably." She shrugged. "Although I feel like one shouldn't need encouragement to keep up with their personal hygiene, right? That should be a given."

"Agreed."

The Forever Falls town square was a small square, with old-fashioned cobblestones on the ground and a huge, naked tree towering in the middle. There were a few buds that had started to sprout, hinting at the greenery soon to come. A monument sat next to it—well, maybe calling it a monument was a stretch. It was a small statue atop a podium that came up roughly to hip height on Ethan, and it depicted a plump seagull standing on one leg.

"What's with the bird statue?" Ethan asked, wandering over to it.

"Oh, that's Goldie." Monroe followed him, keeping her

hands shoved into her pockets. "The unofficial mascot of Forever Falls."

An inscription on the statue read: *Our beloved Goldie, who loved to eat and entertain. Thank you for putting a smile on all our faces. Love, the townsfolk of Forever Falls. RIP.*

"The story is that a local man thought he had found some rare golden bird. He came across this injured bird in a side street, and the feathers were a bright yellow-gold color. Being an avid birdwatcher, he thought he had discovered some new species and was convinced that he was going to have the discovery named after him."

Ethan raised an eyebrow. "I'm guessing that's not how it panned out?"

"Uh no." Monroe wrinkled her nose in amusement. "Turns out it was a regular old seagull who'd fallen into a vat of curry. A local restaurant was preparing for an open-air summer food festival and someone forgot to close the lid right before they transported it to the venue. Seagull fell in and they had to toss the whole thing."

"So the gold bird was just a curry-coated seagull?" Ethan snorted. "That's wild."

"Yep. The guy who found her took her to a vet and they got her all cleaned up, but the color didn't all come out. Turmeric, apparently. She got less colorful as her feathers turned over, but legend has it she never lost her golden sheen. Or at least, that's what people say." Monroe shrugged. "I was a kid when this all happened. But you'd often see Goldie around town. She was very friendly, and liked to follow the man who saved her, since he fed her. They used to have lunch together down on the boardwalk."

"Forever Falls, place with a funny name and a funnier mascot."

"That's right. Considering we don't actually *have* a waterfall or anything like it around here, it's a strange choice. But there are definitely worse places to live." The two of them set off in search of the fancy place that made good coffee. Not that Ethan would disparage the diner's coffee, but it certainly wasn't a reason to go there in and of itself.

"Have you ever thought about moving away?" Ethan asked as they headed into the Main Street Cafe, where there was already a short line forming despite it being earlier on a Sunday morning. A few people glanced in their direction, curiosity evident, but thankfully people left them alone.

"No." Monroe stared straight ahead. "This is my home."

"People leave their homes all the time," he said, rubbing his hands together to warm them up. They shuffled forward in the line.

"Not me," she replied stubbornly. "My family is here and that's what's most important to me in the world. I would never abandon them."

She seemed to realize the implications of her words and cringed, looking at him from the corner of her eye to see if he was watching her. He was.

"Sorry, I didn't mean that as a slight against your personal decisions. It seems your situation is a little different to mine."

He grunted. "You can say that again."

They ordered their coffees and headed back out into the crisp morning air. The sun had started peeking through the clouds and it already felt a few degrees warmer. Monroe pulled her beanie off and stuffed it into one pocket as they walked up the street. The quaint old shopfronts had a storybook look about them—narrow and colorful, like spines on a shelf. They had an old-fashioned barber and a gift store and a fancy paper shop with expensive-looking fountain pens in the window. Most of the shops were still closed, operating on off-season hours.

"So, what do you know about your dad?" Monroe asked. Their steps fell in time and despite everything in Ethan's life being so *not* the norm, he felt comfortable around her… like she genuinely wasn't judging him.

"Not a lot," he admitted. "As I said last night, I believe my mother when she says that he's dead. I imagine he would have been around her age—so sixty-something, maybe late fifties if he was a bit younger. Apparently he was from a small town, originally."

"Name?"

"Matthew Brewer." Ethan sipped his coffee. "Which is a name that's common as hell, it turns out."

He noticed the lack of reaction beside him—but not a lack of reaction indicating she didn't know the name. More a lack of reaction indicating she knew *exactly* who Matthew Brewer was and she didn't want to say a thing. He stopped, so he could look at her more closely.

"You know him." It wasn't a question.

Her tongue darted out to run across her bottom lip, like she was biding her time. But Monroe didn't have a stellar poker face by any means, and the wariness in her eyes was telling. "Uh, yeah. This is a small place, so lifers tend to know one another."

"What are you not saying?"

Her eyes dropped to the ground and she sucked in a breath. "I hope for your sake he's not your dad."

Hmm, so she seemed to have a similar impression of him that Lottie did. Interesting.

"Bad news?" he asked.

"Yeah." She nodded. "He got into fights a lot. Most Saturday nights he'd end up getting kicked out of one place or another. You know the kind of guy who is basically *always* on the radar of law enforcement? That kind of guy."

Stellar.

"Sounds like a model citizen," Ethan said drily.

"Like I said, I hope it's not who you're looking for."

"What about his family?"

"I don't know much about them. We steered clear of him, to be honest. Although his mom always seemed like a nice lady. She used to come into the diner sometimes with her friends—the lady that runs the inn, Lottie May, and another woman, Maura Michaels."

Maura Michaels. That was a new name.

"Who is Maura?"

"She worked at Harris Beech college, over in Kissing Creek. Some sort of admin position. But she passed away a couple of years back."

"Is everybody dead?" The words were out before he could even think about how callous it sounded.

Monroe shrugged. "That tends to happen in a town where more than half the people are retirement age and older."

Ethan sighed. "Sorry, it's just…every time I find something it feels like another dead end. No pun intended."

"Hey, no judgment here. I say blunt crap all the time." Monroe cradled her coffee between both hands and offered an understanding smile.

"Was his father ever around?" Ethan asked.

"I always knew Mrs. Brewer as living on her own." Monroe's gaze drifted into the distance like she was thinking about something. "You might want to try some of the guys he used to roll with."

"I got the name Brian McPhee from the funeral home."

Monroe nodded. "Yep, and you could also talk to the guy who runs the metal workshop just outside town. His name's Mike."

"Thank you." Another name on the list was a good thing—hey, maybe it would turn out that this fake relationship thing was even more useful than he might have thought.

"How long have you been looking?"

"Almost a year."

Monroe's eyes widened. They were heading away from the main strip now, and following the curve of the road down toward the boardwalk. "You've been going from town to town for a *year*? Wow."

"Fat lot of good it's done me," he replied.

"Your accent gets stronger when you're pissy, did you know that?"

He couldn't help but laugh. "Do I suddenly turn into Steve Irwin? Crikey!"

Monroe grinned. "You do have some funny words down under."

"This from the place that calls a remote control a clicker," he scoffed.

"Ooh, good one! But you got to lean into the accent. Pass me the *clickah*, this show's *gahd ahwful*." Monroe's cheeky smile could have lit up the entire country. "My dad grew up in Boston. People around here don't speak quite like that, but I swear my sisters and I picked up some of his linguistic habits."

"What about your mum? Sorry, *mom*."

"She's dead, too. See, more dead people."

Ethan cursed on his breath. "I'm so sorry. I must sound like a dick."

"Shush, no you don't. My mom passed peacefully and on her own terms." There was a glimmer of sadness in Monroe's voice—and in her eyes—but mostly there was a sense of fierce respect. "We miss her like crazy, obviously. My mom was a saint. But I remind myself that she chose to go out the way she wanted—at home, surrounded by family, no nurses fussing over her because she always hated that."

"My mother was the same." A wistful smile lifted his lips. "She always wanted to take care of everyone else, but hated anyone taking care of her."

Monroe bobbed her head. "Grief is a pain, but the first year is the hardest. I won't say it gets easier, but… I don't know. I guess at some point you make peace with it and try to remember all the good things you had, instead of the things you lost, ya know?"

"Cancer?"

"Yeah, the big C." Monroe shook her head sadly.

They followed the path onto the boardwalk, which was so long it seemed to curve around the entire town. Forever Falls was perched right on the edge of the ocean, with ragged cliffs on one side and a sweeping arc out to the other side. Planks of wood created a solid ground to walk on that ran alongside the beach. There were a few semi-permanent stalls that looked as though they served drinks and ice creams and food in the warmer months. But they were all boarded up.

There was a lighthouse in the distance, with strips of red and white almost like a chunky candy cane. A dog galloped along the beach and his two owners walked at a leisurely pace behind him. It was picturesque, for sure. Now that the sun had come out, it was pleasant to be outside. Not warm, by any stretch, but the latte was keeping his hands at a comfortable temperature.

"I can see why you wouldn't want to leave here," he said, staring out at the view. "It's really beautiful."

"Not everybody feels that way," she said bitterly. "Chalk that up to reason fifty-six why my marriage didn't work out."

"He wanted to move?" Ethan found himself curious about Monroe's marriage—and what her husband was like.

"Yeah, he wanted the city life. He said Forever Falls was the kind of place that would suck you dry if you stayed here too long." She made a derisive sound. "I think that's because he thought leaving made you more important to the people here. Like it was proof you were better somehow."

"So what were the other fifty-something reasons?"

She looked up at him, one brow arched. "You really want to know?"

"Well, if we want your family to think I'm good enough for you then maybe I should know what to avoid." Really, he was just curious.

"Oh well, let me count the ways. His family thought I was low brow, we could never agree on where to go on vacation together, he never wanted to put any effort in with my sisters and our sex life was…" She halted suddenly, like she was surprised at what had popped out of her mouth. "Nonexistent."

Now *that* he found hard to believe. Monroe was magnetic and passionate. Fiery. What straight man wouldn't find that attractive?

"Well, *our* sex life was nonexistent but he was still getting it on three times a week. Just not with me." She looked at him as if challenging him to say something, but what could he possibly say to that? "See, told you I was blunt."

"It's a good defense mechanism," he replied.

"Excuse me?" Monroe spluttered. "It's not a defense mechanism. It's just how I am."

Ethan chuckled and sipped his coffee. "Whatever helps you sleep at night."

. . .

Monroe felt like she was about to shoot fire out of her head, like the angry character in that kid's movie *Inside Out*. But not because she was angry at Ethan for saying it, more that she was angry at herself for being so transparent. She didn't like that he could read her so easily.

She didn't like when *anyone* could read her easily.

Her bluntness was absolutely a defense mechanism. Just throw it on the pile with its good friends sarcasm, snark, and self-deprecation. But while Ethan might think he was the one with the upper hand here, because he'd pulled this plan together, Monroe wasn't about to let him—or anyone else—think they could run rings around her.

"Just because we're pretending to have a thing going on doesn't mean you get to push my buttons." She drained the rest of her coffee and tossed the cup into a trash can.

He tried—and failed—to stifle an amused smile. "You're an easy target, Monroe. And a cliché, what with that fiery red hair of yours."

Her mouth popped open. "You did *not* call me a cliché."

"A lovable cliché?" He chuckled. "Come on, even you have to admit that's funny."

"Your sense of humor is warped."

"Nah, we Aussies just have an irreverent nature. That's what happens when you make a country out of a bunch of criminals." He shrugged good-naturedly. "Unless you want this to be our first public fight."

"God no." She blanched. "It's way too early for that. Although, maybe we should come up with a dramatic break up for when the time comes."

"Dramatic?" Ethan hooked his arm through hers, since there were quite a few people out walking along the boardwalk and across the sand, given the nice turn the morning had taken. "I was just going to go with the Post-it Note special."

"I take it back. You *do* sound like a dick."

He smiled and it went all the way up to his eyes, creating crinkles at the edges that somehow made him look even more handsome. Monroe had always liked people who smiled with their whole face, like they couldn't help the sunshine traveling all the way through them.

She was trying to think of another witty barb to throw at Ethan when she spotted a familiar face a few yards away. "Oh crap."

"What?"

"Big sister, twelve o' clock." Monroe cringed. "I was hoping to drag it out for a bit before you met them. Give us time to work on our chemistry."

"You don't think we have chemistry?" He looked affronted.

"I barely know you."

"You know more about me than any single person I've crossed paths with for the last year," he replied. "But fine, wound my ego if you must."

Monroe rolled her eyes. "I don't have the brain-space for your ego right now. And she's definitely spotted us."

"You going to call in one of those kisses now?" he asked, his voice low.

For some silly reason, it sent a ray of sparks showering over her. She'd been keeping the kiss in her back pocket for a very specific reason—a specific Brendan-related reason. But Loren was barreling toward them, powerwalking with her BFF Amy, like she always did in the morning. Rudy must be looking after the girls.

"No kiss, but look…enamored."

"Enamored?" Ethan raised a brow. "Despite the doppelgänger status, sadly I did not inherit any Hemsworth-level acting skills. In fact, I got kicked out of drama club in primary school."

"Argh. Just look at me like you want to take me to bed, then."

Ethan burst out laughing, which did *not* have the

intended effect she was hoping for. Great, the very thought of them doing the horizontal mambo made him laugh like he was watching some prime standup comedy.

"Gee, thanks for the ego boost." She folded her arms across her chest and then immediately dropped them—she didn't want Loren to think they were fighting.

"How about this?" Ethan stopped and tossed his coffee into a trash can. Then he pulled her into his side, wrapping one arm protectively around her shoulders and leaning down to whisper something in her ear. "Pretend I'm saying something dirty."

"Now it's my turn to laugh at you," she replied peevishly.

"Don't be like that. Just pretend I'm telling you all the things I plan to do when I get you back to my place tonight." He was so close she could smell him—no cologne, just earthy man. A touch of woodsmoke, like he'd helped to build a fire at the inn that morning. Something delicious under that. "Terribly wicked, unscrupulous things."

Holy moly. Monroe did *not* think that would have the intended effect at all, but sure enough the heat rose into her face, making her want to shrug out of her coat. Like she needed any help at all visualizing what it might be like to have Ethan toss her over one shoulder and haul her back to someplace where they could get horizontal.

Fact was, she'd thought about that already. A lot.

Too much for a woman who's all but sworn off men and intimacy of any kind.

Fact. But that didn't stop her body from giving her brain the middle finger and doing what it wanted—like making her warm and achy. Like making her want to press her thighs together to stop the subtle pulse between her legs.

Like making her imagine grabbing his hand and dragging him off to the bushes that separated the boardwalk from the path up to Main Street.

"Yeah, *just* like that," he said, his lips so close to her ear that she could feel the puffs of warm breath skating over her skin. "Get all nice and flushed so your big sister thinks I'm treating you right."

No wonder people were going ga-ga over Ethan. He was the kind of guy who was affable and funny and had a hidden sharpness that *really* appealed to her. On top of being good-looking there was a sexual magnetism to him that seemed as natural as breathing. And she was a poor old piece of metal who couldn't resist the pull.

"Monroe!" Loren waved and pulled her friend along toward them. She wore a big, beaming smile and Monroe knew she wasn't going to be able to worm her way out of his impromptu "meet the family" episode.

"You really *do* look like Thor." Amy shook her head. "I heard it, but I thought people were exaggerating."

"I'm sure if you put us side by side, it would be easy to pick out the real deal," Ethan said smoothly.

Loren raised her eyebrow, shooting Monroe a look that conveyed the kind of clear message only a big sister could. Of course, even while out on a power walk, Loren looked like a million bucks. Her long, blond hair was swept back into a bouncy ponytail and tight black and pink athletics-wear covered her fit body. How she looked so good after having four kids must have been some kind of witchcraft. In fact, Monroe was pretty sure Loren could still squeeze into her high school cheerleading uniform if she tried.

"Ethan, this is Amy. And this is my big sister, Loren. I

know you could probably tell because we're basically identical," she quipped.

"It's a pleasure." Ethan stuck out his hand to both women, one after the other, and suddenly the burning heat was gone, replaced by an easy Aussie charm that caused both Loren and Amy to giggle.

Actually freaking giggle. Like schoolgirls.

Ugh, one ticket to Vomit Town please. Express.

"Well, my little sister here did a *very* good job of keeping this a secret," Loren said, shaking her head. "Otherwise we would have invited you over for dinner a lot earlier than this."

Uh-oh.

"So, Tuesday night. We'll see you there. I know Taylor can't wait to meet you." Loren did her usual steamroller thing and Ethan blinked as though he wasn't quite sure what had just happened. Nobody ever saw it coming, because Loren was always sweet smiles and perky ponytails and she had that friendly, bubbly way about her that perfectly hid just how much of a Type-A control freak she really was.

It had amused Monroe to no end when they were in school, because she'd be able to bend students and teachers to her will without them having a clue. However, it wasn't as much fun when Loren aimed that power in Monroe's direction.

"Loren," she said under her breath. "There's no need to go all head cheerleader on this. Maybe Ethan has plans."

"It's fine," he said good-naturedly. "I'd love to be there."

"See?" Loren beamed. "Who can say no to a home-cooked meal anyway? Eight o' clock, no need to bring anything."

"I'm looking forward to it." Ethan kept his arm draped

around Monroe's shoulders. She was feeling overheated.

The reality of the situation was settling in—she was lying to her family. Getting their hopes up. Both her sisters had been at her to rejoin the dating scene for more than eighteen months, convinced that Monroe was "pining" for Brendan.

She wasn't.

If telekinesis was possible, she'd pop his head like a grape. There was no pining going on whatsoever. But was she in a hurry to get her heart bludgeoned to death with a metaphorical baseball bat all over again? No thank you.

"Okay, well we'd better be off before out heart rates get too low." Loren waved, then bent to whisper in Monroe's ear before she walked off, "He's *really* hot, you lucky thing."

Then the two women were gone and Monroe's cheeks were even more flammable than before.

"Your sister thinks I'm hot." Ethan nudged her with his elbow and Monroe wriggled out from under his arm.

"That makes one of us."

"I thought you said I was... How did you put it? Very symmetrical?" He smirked and, as if the universe was trying its best to poke her, it made him look even more attractive.

"Loren and I have very different taste. She likes beef-cakes." It was true, she'd married the high school football star for a reason.

"Beefcakes?" Ethan pressed a hand to his chest in mock offence. "I'm not some gym bro with no brains in my head."

"Could've fooled me." Monroe bit down on her lip to keep from laughing. As much as she hated to admit it, hanging out with Ethan was fun. He had a good sense of humor and people were looking at her like she was someone else. Someone…special. "I thought when you first walked into the diner, there's a guy who spends a lot of time at the gym."

Ethan snorted. "More like chopping firewood and playing handyman for the past twelve months."

Monroe appreciated people with complexity—people who didn't seem to fit your first impressions of them. Maybe it was because she saw herself that way, or maybe it was because sometimes she felt like when you lived in the same small place your whole life you got stuffed into a box with a label slapped on the front and nothing you did would remove it.

"What are you going to do when you find out your father's identity?" she asked.

"I honestly don't know," Ethan said with a sigh. He looked out over the Forever Falls beach, his eyes searching for something in the distance. In that moment, Monroe felt like she saw him, the real him… Not Ethan the Hemsworth impersonator. Not Ethan the hot Aussie stranger who'd wandered into town and caused a stir. Not even the man who flirted like it came to him as easily as breathing.

But the real Ethan Hammersmith, a man looking for his family. A man searching for something greater than himself. A man trying to figure out how to move forward.

And that was someone she could connect with.

CHAPTER TEN

Monroe and Ethan ended up going for a drive around the coast—he'd wanted to check out Mike's metal workshop and see if he was in, but the place was closed for the weekend. On the way back he offered to drive Monroe home. But the offer caught Monroe a little off guard.

"You don't have to do that," she said, looking out the window and staring at the coastline. The sun had really come through today, and it made the waves sparkle like someone had dropped a giant tub of glitter into the ocean. But like all days in late February, there were storm clouds on the horizon, and the closer they got back to Forever Falls, the darker it was getting.

"Despite my earlier comments, I'm *not* a dick. You were kind enough to show me around and give me a piece of information that might help me out," he said. "The least I can do is take you home."

Take me home...

She tried not to let her imagination run wild. "Seriously, it's fine. Just drop me at the square and I'll walk."

He shot her a look. "If this is about you not being comfortable with me knowing where you live, then that's totally fine."

"It's not that." She shook her head. "Maybe it should be, since I really don't know you. But we kinda jumped over a few hurdles where that's concerned. And something tells me you're good people, even if you like winding me up."

"I *do* enjoy winding you up," he admitted.

She narrowed her eyes at him. "Why?"

"It's part of Aussie culture. We're only polite to people we don't like." He winked at her and then put his eyes back on the road.

"Do you miss home?" she asked.

Ethan sighed. "I miss something that doesn't exist anymore. The life I had before my mother died and before I found out her secret…there's no point missing that, because it's never coming back."

"Ignorance is bliss, I guess."

It had certainly felt that way for Monroe — the time she had before she found out about the affair had been full of possibility. She had her whole family together, she had big dreams she was working toward, she had a relationship that she thought meant something. The diner had been running strong and she had the world at her feet.

"So, am I driving you home Little Miss Stubborn?" They were approaching town, the big sign saying WELCOME TO FOREVER FALLS growing larger off to the side of the road. It had been a long time since she'd seen that sign. A long time since she'd set foot out of her hometown.

"Fine," she conceded.

"Make it sound *more* like I'm holding a gun to your head." He laughed, reaching for his blinker so he could turn off the big coastal road.

"Actually, don't turn here," Monroe said. "Take the next exit."

"Sure thing."

Ethan drove them along a little way farther, taking a much smaller exit that led to a winding road through the back of Forever Falls. This part of the town was filled with small houses in various states of repair. Slowly melting snow drifts punctuated the streets, and large, bare trees lined both sides. The road swept left and then right, looking almost like a child had drawn the lines.

"Turn here." She pointed to another street. On the corner, a big yellow house sat like a candy shop confection amidst a sea of white clapboard and standard brown brick. "And then here."

"Why does this feel like you're leading me through a maze?" Ethan said as he slowed the rental down and then eased into a blind corner. "This isn't even a road."

The alleyway ran behind Main Street. On either side there were the backs of the shops, the section of restaurants and bakeries all with big green dumpsters behind them. As they moved into the retail section, the backs of the shops looked nicer. On the other side of the road were big fences, blocking off the backyards of the houses facing the opposite direction. The alley was barely big enough for Ethan's large rental SUV, and he cringed as they went through a particularly narrow gap.

"Then left here, immediately followed by a right." Monroe pointed. They were back on Main Street again and only a few blocks from her little apartment.

As Ethan pulled up at a stop light, he turned to her, a puzzled expression on his face. "Wouldn't it have been way easier to go down Main Street the whole way?"

This was why she didn't want him to take her home. Not because she had any concerns about him knowing her address or anything like that. But because Monroe had…a quirk.

Don't tell him about that. He's going to think you're ridiculous.

"Traffic backs up Main Street on the weekend," she said with a shrug. "It's quicker to take the back streets."

Ethan looked dubious, but in the end he shrugged. It was starting to rain now, and tiny drops splattered against the windshield. Monroe directed him to pull up in front of her apartment, which sat above the Polish bakery run by her landlord, Magdalena. The older woman was out front, ready to pull in her sign as she closed up shop for the day. She caught sight of Monroe in the car and waved, then she stopped and stared, not even trying to hide her curiosity.

"I think we're being watched," Ethan said.

"That's my landlord." Monroe laughed. Magdalena was fussing with the sign as if buying herself some time. "She's been trying to set me up with her nephew for years."

"Should I be jealous?" Ethan asked with an amused smile.

"He's thirty-three, balding, and he lives in his mother's basement. You have *nothing* to worry about."

"Maybe I should play the part so she doesn't get any ideas." Ethan had turned in his seat to face Monroe, a teasing smile on his lips. Oh how she wanted him to play the part. So, *so* badly.

"You're a little too good at this, you know. Am I your first fake girlfriend? Be honest now."

His smile was pure sunshine and warmth. Damn. There was something about Ethan that went *far* beyond his good looks. Because there were plenty of guys who were good-looking and thought that was enough to skate by on. Plenty who thought that gave them license to be a jerk.

But Ethan was something else. Yeah, at times he seemed like he could be a little broody and mysterious. But hanging out with him today had shown Monroe another side of him—playful, curious, heartfelt. As much as she tried to keep people out, hearing him talk about his search for his father had tugged at the soft, squishy bit she tried real hard to hide.

"Nope, you're my first. Fake relationship virgin right here." He grinned. "I don't know how this is supposed to work."

"Me neither," she admitted.

"What if I lean in and pretend I'm kissing you, then? Give your landlord something to gossip about."

"Works for me."

As Ethan leaned in, all the air left Monroe's lungs. Up close she could see the glorious details of him, the faint reddish sheen to some of the blond stubble on his jaw. The multiple shades of blue in his eyes. The tiny little mole on his right cheekbone.

And God did he smell good.

She let her eyes flutter shut as Ethan's cheek brushed hers. From any other angle it would look like they were kissing and, frankly, Monroe's body couldn't seem to tell the difference. It did all the things it usually would if she were actually being kissed.

When Ethan pulled away, she wanted to scramble out of the car and stick her head in a snow drift to cool down a bit. But that would make it obvious that she was all hot and bothered, and she *didn't* want him to know that.

"Think it worked?" he asked.

"I'm sure it did. It would have looked legit." She nodded.

"So, what's the next step in your plans?"

Yes, a change of conversation. Very good, brain.

"I need to go and see the guy who runs the Ghost Tours on Tuesday. Brian McPhee."

"Oh, right." Monroe knew Brian—he'd worked for her dad for a while, before he broke away to run his own business. "Want me to come with? He can be a little cagey around people he doesn't know."

"You'd do that?" His face lit up.

"Sure."

"Thank you, I really appreciate it."

"You know," Monroe said. "If I'm helping you with finding your father, then maybe this could be a quid pro quo thing."

"How so?"

"This stays between us, but…" She swallowed, finding herself feeling surprisingly emotional. "The diner is falling under hard times and my boss is thinking about selling."

"Really?" Ethan frowned. "That's no good."

"I convinced him to give me a month to see if I could turn it around." She let out a *whoosh* of breath. "Because what if the person who buys it decides to knock it down and put something else there? Year-round work isn't the easiest thing to find in a town like this. Most jobs are feast or famine with the flow of tourism, you know? People like Big Frank and Darlene have been working there forever."

And people like me.

"Whatever I can do to help, count me in. I can take a look at your business processes and bookkeeping systems if you like, see if we can tighten some screws to save money."

"Thanks." Monroe nodded. It wasn't exactly what she had in mind, but she appreciated his willingness to help. No wonder people flocked to Ethan—he was like a magnet. That's when Monroe had a snap of brilliance. She knew *exactly* how Ethan could help out the diner.

"Meet me tomorrow? You can have your eggs and then I'll walk you through my plan."

"Sure."

Monroe slid out of the passenger side seat and gave Ethan a wave. Maybe this fake relationship thing wasn't so ridiculous after all. In fact, if her plan worked the way she'd hoped, then this might have just been the best thing that could have happened to her.

• • •

Ethan shook his head vehemently. "No, absolutely not."

He was pretty sure that his darling fake girlfriend had lured him to the diner with the promise of a delicious breakfast, all under the guise of tricking him into her ridiculous plan. And that was saying a lot, since he took responsibility for the whole fake relationship thing.

"Oh come *on*, it'll be fun," Monroe cajoled. It even appeared as though she'd dressed extra pretty in an attempt to bend him to her will.

Her curly red hair was swept back into a low bun with several tendrils springing free around her face. She had a pair of silver hoops decorating her ears and a top under her uniform apron that was a pretty shade of green.

"I am not dressing up as Thor to hand out flyers," he said adamantly.

"Well, it's more about taking pictures than handing out flyers," she replied, smiling sweetly.

Oh no. She wasn't going to retract her prickles and be all sunshine and lightness just to get something out of him. He. Would. Not. Fall. For. It.

"It's the exact *opposite* of what I'm trying to do here, which is blend in. How is dressing up in costume and taking photos with people supposed to help me blend in?"

"You'll be hiding in plain sight," she argued. "Besides, you promised to help me."

"No," he repeated.

"Okay." Monroe nodded and sat back in her chair, biting on her bottom lip.

Ethan narrowed his eyes. "Why do I feel like you saying okay is just the calm before the storm?"

The corner of her lip twitched. "I don't know, why *do* you feel like that?"

"Hmm, maybe because I know a thing or two about fiery women. You never back down from a discussion quite so easily." He stabbed at a mushroom with his fork.

"Who says I'm fiery?" She wrinkled her nose.

"Me."

"Oh yes, that's right. You called me a redheaded cliché." She rolled her eyes. "I remember that."

"Well, you said I wasn't your type, so I guess we can call it even." He popped the mushroom into his mouth and chewed.

"I stand by it." She tried to sniff like she was quite happy insulting him, but he caught the sparkle in her eye. Monroe enjoyed the game, that much he could tell. "So you really won't even consider my idea? I thought it was smart."

"To bribe people to have a meal so they can get a photo with a guy dressed up as Thor?" He snorted. "And here I was thinking you wanted to make use of my business skills…not my abs."

"Awww. Are you worried I'm using you for your hot body?" She laughed and slid out of the booth seat across from him. "Maybe a hot Viking is my ultimate sexual fantasy."

"Yeah, yeah." He waved a hand and she disappeared off into the kitchen to get back to work, the sound of her laughter trailing behind her.

In spite of everything that had gone on this past year, Ethan felt lighter. Happier. Monroe, against all odds, had injected some levity back into his life when it was the last thing he'd expected. Hell, Ethan wasn't sure he'd smiled *once* since his mother died. Let alone laughed. Let alone felt a stir of something besides the driving need to accomplish his goal.

But the fact was, Monroe definitely stirred something. And for a few brief moments when he was around her, Ethan felt like the man he used to be.

CHAPTER ELEVEN

Dammit. Monroe really *had* thought dressing Ethan up as Thor to bring more paying customers into the diner was a smart one. A, because if he wasn't sitting mysteriously in his booth then there was no reason for people to linger unnecessarily. They could get what they wanted—a photo—and be on their way. And B, because Monroe had already tried all the "regular" ideas like trimming back shifts and reducing waste and adding some higher margin items to the menu.

If all the sensible things had already proven not enough, then maybe an outrageous idea would be the thing to move the needle.

Also, there was reason C…that Monroe *really* wanted to see Ethan dressed up as Thor.

In the kitchen, she found Big Frank at his usual spot by the stoves, flipping pancakes and managing a batch of bacon that was hissing and spitting in a pan. Darlene was swapping out the coffee pots and setting new ones to brew.

"Miss Monroe Roberts," she said. "I don't think I've seen you smiling quite so much since you came home with ten grand in your fist after winning that baking show."

Ten grand. All of which had immediately gone toward some renovations at her father's house to make it more accessible for him after his injury. What was left over had paid for the lawyers who helped her file her divorce.

The first part made her happy. But the second… Well,

what a waste of money that turned out to be.

"New relationships will do that," Big Frank said a little wistfully.

"You're such a romantic," Monroe teased. She thought it was adorable how the guy still clung to the soft and fuzzy notions of love and wasn't afraid to show it.

"Or sex," Darlene replied with a shrug.

Monroe's mouth popped open and Big Frank chortled at his station.

"What?" Darlene said, shooting them both a look. "I might be old, but I'm not dead. Lots of seniors have very active sex lives, you know. It's a healthy part of any marriage."

Monroe really did *not* want to think about Darlene and her husband getting it on. In large part, that was due to the fact that her husband had been Monroe's eighth grade science teacher and even now she could only call him Mr. Phillips.

"I can't believe you kept that secret right under our noses!" Darlene shook her head.

"Oh I saw something." Big Frank grinned. "Said you two were arguing like an old married couple."

"Well, let's not go crazy with the M-word." Monroe held up both hands. "It's nothing like that. He's only been in town a short while, so let's hold up on the serious relationship talk."

As if on cue, her phone started buzzing with a call from an unknown number. She had ten more minutes left on her break, just enough time to deal with whoever was calling her and then have a quick glance over the inventory sheet before she went back out onto the floor.

Monroe walked through the back part of the kitchen, past the supply cupboard slash office, and out the back door into the alley behind them. It was a nice day outside, so she figured some sunshine would do her good. She swiped her thumb across the screen of her phone.

"Hello?"

"Monroe."

Her breath caught in the back of her throat, almost painful in how fast it screeched to a halt. She would know that voice anywhere.

"Brendan," she replied coldly.

It hurt to hear him say her name. One, because he never used to call her by her full name. She'd always been "Robby" to him—a shortened form of her surname and what he'd called her ever since they were in high school. It was their secret joke. He'd whisper it as he held her at night, in the time when they used to touch one another without hesitation.

Those days were long gone.

"You haven't responded to the lawyers," he said. There was noise in the background, something that sounded like a coffee machine and the chatter of people. He was calling from work.

Smart…this is why you should screen your calls.

Only she couldn't. Monroe lived in fear that one day her dad might have a fall and a neighbor or medical practitioner might be calling her, since she was the first one on the next of kin list.

"I've been busy," she replied. "And you lost the right to expect *anything* of me the second you started screwing my cousin."

She could practically feel him wincing through the phone. "Isn't that old news now? I thought you would want to move on with your life."

"I *have* moved on. As far as I'm concerned, we're divorced and I've been living as such." Let him interpret that however he wanted—despite the fact that her life the past three years had been sad and lonely and gray. She would *never* admit it out loud. "So this matter of a bit of paperwork doesn't change anything for me. Hence why it's not a priority."

"I know what you're doing," he said. The noises in the background faded, as though he'd closed himself away in an office.

She could practically see him—wearing a dark suit and white shirt, hair styled in that way he prided himself on so it looked like he'd done nothing at all when in fact the process took half an hour and no less than four different types of hair product and styling tools. Brendan was handsome, there was no denying that. But he was also vain as hell.

"What? Working my butt off to take care of my father? Living my best life." She said the words sweetly, because she knew they would needle at him.

And yeah, maybe that made her a bitch. In her mind, Brendan deserved that and a whole lot worse.

"You're purposefully holding things up because I want to marry Amber," he snapped. "It's childish and, frankly, petty."

"Oh, childish like not being honest with your wife, and petty like purposefully choosing a lawyer from Boston to get back at me for not wanting to move there? That kind of childish and petty?"

The silence on the other end of the line was charged. Her ex could have quite the temper when he was backed into a corner. And right now, he was most definitely backed into a corner.

"You need to get over it," he said.

Get over it? Get *over* it? Did he really think that she could walk away from betrayal so easily?

"You ruined my family. My dad and his sister haven't spoken since you and Amber left town. I can't look my cousins in the eye in the grocery store. My Christmases are half of what they used to be."

"You can't always expect someone to take your side, Monroe," he said in that patronizing way of his that he knew got under her skin.

"I damn well can, especially when I'd done nothing but uphold the vows of our marriage."

"Ah yes, always the victim."

Oooh, now *that* made her blood boil! "I guess it's your turn to be the victim now, Brendan. I'm sure you can get the divorce corrected on your own, but I imagine that would be a much more complicated, lengthy process than if I cooperated."

"Why are you doing this? I can't believe you're being so difficult."

"And I can't believe you're expecting me to bend over backwards after everything you've done." She sucked in a breath. For some reason, giving her ex the metaphorical finger was surprisingly empowering.

She hadn't done this once through the failed-divorce proceedings. She'd been quiet and shaken, agreeing to everything so it would be over as quickly as possible. Emotions like grief and regret and sadness had overwhelmed her, blotting out her spark. Now, after enough time had passed, Monroe had regained that sense of her own backbone.

And she would *never* let a man walk all over her again.

"What did you say to me after I caught you with her? Oh, that's right. You said that I was too sweet and too nice and a little boring. You said I needed more bite in order to be 'interesting' to a partner long-term. So consider this me taking your advice, Brendan. I'm biting down, hard."

She hung up the phone and stuffed it into the pocket of her jeans. He wouldn't call back, not right away. She knew him better than that. The chances of him turning up in Forever Falls now was high, but maybe she wanted him to do that. Maybe she wanted him to see her with a big, hunky Australian man and realize that she had moved on and that she didn't miss him at all.

Feeling buoyed that she'd *finally* had a moment where she could get one back, Monroe headed into the Sunshine Diner. Her desire to get creative and save the place from sale was even stronger than ever.

• • •

The following day, Ethan went to see Brian McPhee at the ghost tours office. He arrived a few minutes earlier than the time he'd given Monroe to meet him, because he wanted to get a feel for the man before she showed up. He definitely appreciated her willingness to help him, but also wanted to get a bead on the man without any outside influences.

Ethan pushed open the door to the office and a small bell tinkled overhead. Inside was simple, to say the least. A single desk with an old-looking laptop perched on one corner, and behind it a mid-height shelf with neat rows of binders. There was a poster on one wall stating that this was a "National Best Ghost Tour finalist" eight years ago.

"Be there in a second!" a voice called from the back.

"No worries."

Ethan waited and a moment later, a man who looked to be in his late fifties appeared. He was tall and wiry, and his thin face had a slightly skeletal appearance about it. Ethan wondered if it added to the ghostly feeling of his tours. He looked like the kind of man who'd had a rough life. His dark goatee was heavily peppered with gray, and the hair on his head—which was the same salt and pepper mix— was drawn back into a ponytail.

The man set a cup down on his desk and the smell of instant coffee wafted into the air. "Can I help you?"

"You're Brian McPhee, right?"

He eyed Ethan warily. "That's right."

"Interesting business you've got here," Ethan said.

Brian settled into the seat behind the desk. There wasn't a lot of warmth to him, though he wasn't rude. He didn't smile readily, not even for a potential customer.

"Forever Falls has a long history of hauntings. We've got the Krick Mansion on the edge of town that's our biggest attraction, formerly owned by the Krick family but now stands empty." Brian took a sip of his coffee, his voice almost monotone like he was reading off a script. "There's also the graveyard hop where we explore three of our local historic grave sites. This time of year we only do tours on Saturday nights, though."

Ethan studied the man, wondering what he might be able to glean about his father from those he hung out with. He'd stared at a lot of faces over the past year, wondering this same thing.

The bell tinkled at the front of the shop and Monroe walked in. She was wearing her coat over jeans and boots, the same scarf she'd worn on the weekend a stark contrast to the ginger hair tumbling down around her shoulders.

"You're early," she said with a smile. She walked right up to Ethan and looped her arm through his. "Hi Brian, how's things?"

Ethan watched the cold reservation melt away from the older man's face and the corner of his eyes crinkle as he smiled in response. "Not bad at all, Ms. Roberts. Not bad at all."

There was a charming old-school politeness to him now and it was clear he held a lot of affection for Monroe.

"Brian is one of my regulars," Monroe explained to Ethan, as if sensing his surprise. "I think he's been coming to the diner ever since I was in high school and working there after school and on weekends."

"That's right." Brian nodded. "I stand by it still, best eggs on the East coast."

"Couldn't agree more," Ethan chimed in.

"So…" Brian looked at him, his barely concealed surprise creating a wrinkle in his forehead. "How can I help you? I'm guessing you're not looking to book a tour, then? I know your family has been through it all more than once."

"Not for a long time," Monroe replied. "But you're right, we came here for another kind of business."

Brian raised an eyebrow and cradled his mug between both hands. It looked like a promotional item, with the logo of another company stamped on the side, though it was difficult to make out, since half of the letters had rubbed off.

"Why don't you tell him, Ethan?" Monroe released his arm and nodded encouragingly.

"I, uh...I'm looking for some information on a man named Matthew Brewer."

It was almost like someone had poured concrete into Brian McPhee's veins. Ethan watched the man slowly harden, so much that he couldn't even tell if there was still breath flowing between his lips. He was damn sure at that point, that if Monroe wasn't at his side, Brian McPhee would have ordered him out of his office.

"Haven't heard that name in a while," he replied stiffly. He set the mug down on the desk. "And I'd be happy never to hear it again."

Interesting. Given the owner of the funeral home had made it sound like they were buddies, Ethan wasn't expecting him to say something like that.

"I think he may have had a romantic relationship with my mother," Ethan pressed. "She passed away a year ago and I found a series of letters from a man named Matthew Brewer. I've been trying to find the letters she wrote him, since they'll be all I have left of her."

The lie stuck in his throat a little more every time. It grated against Ethan's nature to deceive people, but in this instance, his need to find his father overrode that particular part of his moral center, especially since he was sure he wasn't hurting anyone.

"Mike's dead," Brian said flatly.

"I know. But I'm hoping someone might have ended up with his belongings or that someone may be able to confirm whether or not he had a relationship with a Marcie Jenkins."

For a moment after his mother died, Ethan thought about changing his name back to Ethan Jenkins. It was the name he'd been born with. But before he was one year old it had been changed to Hammersmith, when Marcie married the man who'd raised him.

"I don't have nothin' to do with Matthew Brewer or any of his associates anymore." Brian's expression remained hard. "I have no idea who ended up with his stuff."

"Do you know anything about a relationship he might have had?" Ethan pressed. "Please, man, I've been trying to find this out for almost a year. I just want to know if he knew my mother."

Brian's eyes flicked to Monroe and something in him seemed to soften a little. "This your boyfriend?"

Monroe cleared her throat. "Yessir."

"Look, I don't want to get dragged into any of Mike's shit, okay? I spent too many years doing exactly that and all it got me was a rap sheet and some jail time." He let out a breath. "But Mike used to talk about some woman who broke his heart. He left Forever Falls to go and chase some grand scheme up in the Cape. Apparently he met someone there and they were supposed to get married, but it turned sour. I don't know what her name was...but he was different after he came back."

Ethan felt a stir in his gut, like a flicker of intuition. "The Cape, as in Cape Cod?"

"Yeah." Brian nodded.

His mother had been to Cape Cod. He'd seen old photos of her when she was twenty-one, having her first legal drink in the U.S., because the drinking age was different there to Australia, and she'd complained about how in the first part of her holiday, right before her birthday, she'd have to make herself look older to be able to order a beer even though she'd been drinking legally in Australia since she was eighteen.

Ethan had been to Cape Cod a few months back, thinking that maybe someone there might know something. He'd gone to the bar where she'd worked for a summer, but the owners had turned over a dozen times and nobody recognized her name.

"What year would he have been in Cape Cod?" Ethan asked, already bracing himself for the answer.

"He would have been twenty-five or so, which woulda made it..." Brian scratched his head. "1988 or 1989, something like that."

His mother had spent the summer of 1989 at Cape Cod.

"And you have no idea who ended up with his stuff after he died?" Ethan asked.

"No idea and I don't want to know."

"Thanks, Brian," Monroe said. "Sorry to go digging around in stuff you want to forget. I promise we won't bring it up again."

The older man huffed. "You can make it up to me by booking a tour. Business is slow right now."

Monroe looked up at Ethan and raised both eyebrows

as if to say *how about it*?

"Sure," Ethan said. "Why not?"

Right now he would have agreed to just about anything, because he was feeling a spark of hope for the first time in months. This was a solid lead, a connection. And while he knew not to get his hopes up too much—he'd had leads before that didn't pan out—something told him that this one was worth investigating.

If that meant forking over some cash to thank the guy who'd pointed him in the right direction, then Ethan was more than happy to do it. Besides, he thought, looking down at Monroe's smiling face and her pretty brown eyes, being somewhere dark and intimate with her wouldn't exactly be a chore.

CHAPTER TWELVE

Monroe spent the rest of her Tuesday feeling like a bag of squirming kittens. She had all this twisty, turny energy that she couldn't seem to rid herself of, despite an unusually busy shift at the Sunshine Diner. They'd filled a reasonable amount of tables—some of the women Monroe had noticed first come in to gawk at Ethan had returned, and ordered more than muffins! Plus they'd had issues with an order from one of the local farms.

And yet…Monroe felt like she was a firecracker about to go off.

Helping Ethan out that morning had given her warm fuzzy feelings, because she could see the happiness it brought him. But then tonight was the "big introduction" and that was making her hellishly anxious.

Having Ethan meet her family was…gosh, she didn't even know.

On one hand, it felt awful and like she'd totally jumped into this situation without thinking through the ramifications…which she hadn't really. She *hated* lying to her family. Yet on the other hand, she knew it would ease some of their worries around Monroe's life.

Both her sisters had fussed around her like mother hens after the divorce, trying to shove her back out into the dating world, like throwing herself into another relationship was the only way to "get over" a bad breakup. Monroe was perfectly happy on her own, thank you very much.

Is that why you changed your outfit three times before you came over? Because you're happier alone and you don't actually care what your fake boyfriend thinks about how you look?

Monroe caught sight of herself in the big-mirrored doors on Loren's coat closet by the front door. She was wearing all black—jeans and a fine-knit sweater that hugged her body. Plus the ankle boots she'd discarded when she came into the house. Twin gold hoops hung in her ears and a delicate chain encircled the base of her neck, a single clear crystal hanging from it.

She felt...elegant. Which was something she hadn't experienced in a long time. And while she wouldn't tell Loren, it was nice to dress up. Not for Ethan, but for herself. It had felt nice to invest a little extra time in getting ready, beyond her usual throw everything on without looking in the mirror approach to things.

"Where's my favorite girl?" Her father ambled through the doorway, and Monroe rushed over to take his arm so he could leave the cane by the front door.

"I know you don't play favorites," she teased. "You just say that to make us feel special."

"You should feel special," he replied. "And don't you look lovely."

"Thanks, Dad." She pecked him on the cheek and saw he'd shaved. Or maybe he'd popped into the barber and had Mr. Donovic do it for him. "You're looking very handsome yourself."

"I tried to put a tie on but..." He let out a frustrated huff. "You know your mother always used to do that for me. I can't ever seem to figure the damn things out on my own."

For some reason, the image of her father trying to put a tie on made something stick in the back of her throat.

"You don't have to wear a tie, Dad. It's only dinner." She helped him navigate the hallway, stopping to pick up one of her niece's toys from the floor so her father didn't trip. "Not a black-tie gala."

"If you've deemed a man important enough to bring him home, then I want to make sure I look the part." He nodded. "It's a big deal."

"It's not a big deal."

"That's my Monroe, always the contrarian." He laughed. "You used to think I knew everything when you were a little girl. I had more trouble with Loren always asking questions, but you were agreeable."

"Well, being agreeable never got me anywhere, did it?" She walked her dad into the dining room. "Wouldn't you rather I have my own opinion on things?"

"Yes…so long as you agree with me." Her father gave a cheeky grin and Monroe couldn't help but laugh.

She squeezed his shoulders and then left him for a second to pull out his chair at the head of the table. Within seconds, Loren's little ones were all over their grandpa. Luckily for the family, Olly Roberts wasn't short on love to share around.

"Careful of Grandpa's leg, Kiara," Monroe admonished her niece gently as she climbed up into his lap like he was a jungle gym.

"Ki!" Loren called out as she came into the room, carrying a tray of cold cuts, vegetables and dip. Taylor followed behind. "What have I told you about being rough with people?"

"Sorry, Mom." Kiara, who was six, didn't quite know her own strength sometimes. She was a very active, energizer bunny of a girl and wore her hair in curly black bunches. It was *impossible* to stay mad at her and she knew it.

"Ah don't listen to your mom," Olly said to her. "That's what grandpas are for. Now tell me, what did you do in school today?"

Loren shook her head and rolled her eyes affectionately, placing the platter into the center of the table. Monroe and Taylor followed her back into the kitchen to help with the rest of the food and drink prep.

"It's fine for him to say that," Loren said once they were out of earshot. "But then when Tornado Kiara breaks something, I'm the one who has to teach her the lesson."

Monroe and Taylor exchanged looks. It was very much a tradition in their family that the men were all big softies and the women were the ones who kept things in order. Their mom had been the disciplinarian when she was alive, and their grandparents had fit that mold as well. Even Loren's husband, who was a college football star and as confident as they came, was very much the softie when it came to his kids, leaving Loren to enforce some order on their noisy, chaotic household.

"You look like you're taking a leaf out of my stylebook," Taylor said to Monroe. "I'm digging the all black. Makes your hair pop."

"Thanks." Monroe grinned. "Although, don't get any ideas about me coming into the shop. I'm going to keep my virgin skin away from your needles."

Taylor shook her head. "One day I'll convince you. You should see the piece I started work on yesterday for a new customer. She's sixty-four years old and she's always wanted to get a tattoo, but she was too afraid of what people would think. Then she was in a terrible car accident and ended up walking away with barely a scratch on her— but the car was *totaled*. She figured it was a sign to start living her life."

"What kind of design did she choose?" Monroe asked. As much as she wasn't a fan of the idea of getting a tattoo herself, she really enjoyed hearing the stories of all the people who walked into Taylor's shop to get themselves inked up.

"It's a floral piece that's going to hopefully turn into a full sleeve. We're incorporating her kids' names as well. She was a real trooper, didn't complain about the pain at all when we did the outline."

"How many kids has she had?" Loren asked, her voice slightly muffled as she had her head in the refrigerator.

"Seven."

"Seven?" Monroe's eyes went wide.

"That'll do it. Seven rounds of childbirth would mean she could take just about anything." Loren grabbed a bottle of champagne and another of a pinot grigio from the fridge and placed them on the kitchen island. "Who wants to play bartender?"

"I'll do it." Monroe grabbed the chilled bottles and headed out to the dining room to start getting everyone their drinks.

Loren's husband Rudy was sitting at the table now, chatting with Olly while he held baby Harlow in his arms. The little girl sucked eagerly on a bottle. She had a head of tight black curls and light brown skin, just like her dad.

Monroe went past and squeezed his shoulder in greeting and then raised a hand as Taylor's fiancé, Tim, walked in.

Tim and Rudy were about as opposite as could be. Rudy was always in slacks and a shirt, jaw clean shaven—he definitely had teacher vibes. Not to mention his years playing football had given him the physique of an athlete. Tim on the other hand was fully tattooed on both arms and hands, and was usually in a leather jacket. He had a gauge piercing in one ear and dyed his naturally fair hair boot-polish black.

But that was the awesome thing about the Roberts family—no matter what walk of life you came from, you were welcome at their table. And for the most part, everyone got along great. Amber issue notwithstanding.

"Good to see you, Monroe," Tim said, pulling her in for a brotherly hug. "We're excited to meet the new man."

"See, even Tim thinks it's a big deal," Olly said from his chair where Kiara was sitting on his strong leg while loudly reciting a song she'd learned in school.

For a minute, Monroe wondered if Ethan had any idea what he was getting himself into. In addition to the singing and the loud laughter coming from the kitchen, Harlow was grizzling because her bottle was over and the other two little girls were playing with dolls in the living room, where they could be easily watched from the table. Music started coming through the speakers carefully hidden away and Loren's off-key singing soon followed.

Their family was *loud*. Probably a reason why most of them were extroverts and they tended toward partners with that same preference—quiet people could feel a bit overwhelmed at a Roberts family gathering.

He'll hold his own. You have nothing to worry about.

She wasn't even sure why she cared. So long as their relationship seemed plausible and she could finally put her father and sisters' minds at ease over her mental and emotional state, that was all that mattered. Then when Ethan was ready to leave town, they'd "break up" and Monroe wouldn't be affected one little bit, thereby further proving that she really had moved on with her life.

At that moment, the doorbell sounded and Loren's giant yellow Labrador, Mimi, started barking like mad. There was a *whoosh* of golden fur and the clatter of toenails over floorboards as Mimi made a mad dash for the door.

"I'll get it." Monroe scurried out of the dining area and made a grab for Mimi's collar, hooking one finger into it so the big dog wouldn't immediately leap onto Ethan, as was her usual style of greeting.

When she pulled the door open, Ethan was standing there with a bottle of wine in his hands, looking like he was waiting for a GQ photographer to snap his picture. How did he look *so* good in jeans and a sweater? The soft fabric hugged his body and was the exact same shade of blue as his eyes. On the bottom he wore dark denim jeans and boots, and a coat was slung over his arm. As usual, his dark blond hair was rumpled and slightly curled around his ears.

"I would complement your outfit, but you gave me a hard time about that on our last date," he said with a sly smile. "But Goth Lite suits you."

She laughed and stepped back, holding a very excited Mimi in her grip. "Goth Lite, I like that."

"Who's this beautiful creature?" He crouched down and

gave Mimi a scratch.

"This is Mimi, and stop scratching her or she'll glue herself to your leg for the entire night." Monroe laughed. "Then it will take approximately six years to get all the dog fur off you."

"But you're such a gorgeous girl, aren't you?" he cooed at the dog, and Monroe couldn't help the goofy grin that spread across her face. So sue her, she was a sucker for a guy who loved animals. "Such a friendly, gorgeous girl."

Ethan stood and shut the door behind him, and Monroe was very aware of the curious eyes peering into the entryway from both the dining area and the archway leading into the kitchen. He must have sensed it, too, because he leaned in. The smell of his cologne hit Monroe as he brushed his lips against her cheek.

Surprised by how her knees felt so wobbly all of a sudden, Monroe accidentally released her hold on Mimi's collar. But because the dog was excited to be released— and because the polished boards were not her friend—she slipped and plowed into Ethan, sending him stumbling back against the wall and out of Monroe's grasp, which was probably for the best.

The last thing you need is to get hung up on how good he smells or how much you wanted that kiss to be a whole *lot steamier.*

"Oh my gosh, I am *so* sorry." Loren rushed over and grabbed Mimi, holding her out of trouble's way. "Let me put her outside. She's a little too affectionate for her own good."

"Where should I put this?" He held up the wine.

"I told you not to bring anything," Loren scolded in a

way that said he'd scored major props for not listening and bringing something anyway.

"And disappoint my mother's memory by being a bad guest? No can do." He smiled charmingly and Loren blushed. Monroe raised an eyebrow.

Her sister was so totally in love with her husband that nobody had seen her blush in a *long* time. Looked like Ethan's people skills were next-level.

"You can put it on the table." Loren herded Mimi out toward the back and Monroe took a few minutes to introduce Ethan around.

Everyone seemed eager to meet him and in true Roberts family style, he was given a chair, something to drink, and then had questions rapid-fired at him. He took it all in stride. In fact, he soon had Olly laughing at some joke about a failed attempt to do his own plumbing and was amusing Tim with a story about a friend's tattoo that had an unfortunate phallic aspect to it.

"Looks like you've found yourself a keeper," Taylor said as she sidled up to Monroe in the archway that connected the kitchen and dining area.

"A keeper for now," she replied. It was one thing to introduce a fake boyfriend to her family—which made her feel guilty enough—but she couldn't lead them to believe it was a long-term thing on top of that. "Honestly, it's not serious. But I'm having fun."

"I wouldn't expect it to be serious. It's not like he's been in town that long."

Monroe laughed. "Does everybody know the poor guy's movements down to the minute?"

"That's the quiet season for you." Taylor shrugged. "But

I'm happy you're putting yourself out there again. So long as you're actually letting him in."

"What's *that* supposed to mean?"

Despite her tough-girl looks and penchant for piercings and black leather, Taylor was the most emotional and introspective of the three sisters. She was the best ear to bend in tough times and could always offer some deep insight that would pass others by, Monroe included. The youngest Roberts sister had a gentle heart and the highest emotional intelligence of any of them.

"It means you've gotten very accustomed to pushing people away," Taylor said. "I've seen you do it with friends. I've seen you do it with guys. It's like you've spent the last three years closing your circle to the smallest number of people possible."

Taylor had a point. A few years ago, Monroe could always be counted on for drinks and trivia nights at the Forever Falls pub. She was the one who always put her hand up to help organize baby showers and bachelorette parties and surprise birthday dinners. She'd had a close but large circle of girlfriends who were now scattered up and down the East Coast, and she used to travel away for weekends to visit them.

After her divorce, Monroe couldn't remember the last time she'd even thought about picking up the phone to call people or organizing a weekend away.

"I've taken on a lot at the diner," she said. "Work has been busy and I don't have the time for lots of friendships."

"Especially not when those friendships require trust and you don't hand that out so freely anymore," Taylor said quietly.

Monroe watched Ethan talking animatedly with her father and her sisters' partners. Olly's smile was so wide and so genuine it filled Monroe with the most delicious warm and fuzzy feeling, and Rudy's loud, booming laugh almost rattled the paintings on the walls. It was like looking at a warped version of the past—where she had someone to love, where she had dreams and hopes and where she *did* let people in.

But this was fake. No more real than a stage play with props and costumes.

Ethan needed something from her and she needed something from him. Their arrangement didn't have room for things like trust and vulnerability and emotion, and Monroe certainly wasn't going to fool herself into thinking the scene in front of her was anything more than a means to an end.

"We should round up the girls and get them fed before dinner comes out," Monroe said, smiling like her sister's words had no impact at all.

...

An hour later, as they were finishing up their meal, Monroe was marveling at how well everything had gone. Ethan praised Loren's cooking and was doing well with all the questions. He was so good with people—charming, open, instantly likeable. She could learn a thing or two from that. Even in silence, his presence radiated, drawing her attention away from everyone and everything else.

Maybe it was the way his knee pressed lightly against hers under the table, or the way he'd taken her hand when they were selling the moment they'd decided to "date."

More like the fact that it's been years since you felt the touch of anything but your vibrator.

Celibacy was a bitch.

Ethan leaned over and slid an arm around her shoulders, pulling her close. God, he smelled good. Like a fresh fall breeze.

"If you keep looking at me like that, you're going to give people the wrong idea," he whispered. "Or maybe it's the right idea."

The rest of the table chatted amongst themselves. Monroe scanned the room to see if anyone was watching them, but Loren was getting ready to put the girls to bed and Taylor was busy teasing Tim in that flirty way that was adorable *and* pukey.

"I'm not looking at you like anything," she said under her breath.

"Yes, you are." He spoke right into her ear, sending a tingle of anticipation skittering down her spine. No doubt her sisters thought he was starting the foreplay early. "And you *should* be looking at me like you want to jump my bones."

"Maybe I'm a great actress?" She turned to him and lost herself in his incredible blue eyes. They were so perfectly clear they made her want to melt right into his touch.

"Liar."

She swallowed, ignoring how close his lips were. If she got any closer, she'd catch them with her own. "What makes you say that?"

His arm remained draped around her shoulder, his fingertips brushing an intricate pattern on her upper arm that made goose bumps ripple across her skin. "I'm good at reading people."

"Oh yeah?"

"I knew the first time you told me I wasn't your type, you were full of shit."

"You're so goddamn cocky." Monroe couldn't help but laugh.

"It's true. I mean, we have the blushing thing, which is as subtle as a ton of bricks," he said, and Monroe felt her cheeks heat up in response. Busted. "Nature's lie detector."

"You have no idea how often that got me in trouble growing up," Monroe said with a sigh.

"And secondly, I caught you staring when you thought I wasn't looking."

"You did *not*!"

"Did so. And since we've progressed from pretty pink rose to red fire truck in the cheek region, I'm going to call you the world's worst liar."

Monroe cleared her throat as she noticed that the conversation had died down at the table, and that everyone was watching them.

"I should clean up," she said to Ethan, pushing her chair back and extracting herself from his slow, deceptively sensual touch.

"I'll help."

"Please," Loren said. "Sit. You're a guest."

"I can't let my lovely girlfriend do it all by herself." He shot Loren a smooth smile.

Ethan helped her pick up all the bowls and plates, and then followed her into the kitchen. Monroe could hear her sisters already giggling and whispering about how

Ethan was so much better than her asshole of an ex. Low bar, for sure, but Ethan cleared it like a gazelle with springs on its feet.

"Well, look at you winning everyone over," she said, opening the dishwasher and rinsing off the plates before handing them to Ethan so he could slot them into the appropriate section. "Gold star, boyfriend."

"I didn't really do anything much," he replied with a shrug. "I guess that tells me all I need to know about your ex."

"And then some," Monroe muttered.

Ethan reached past Monroe to grab a plate, brushing her rib cage as he moved. "Why were you with someone like that?"

She bristled. "This arrangement doesn't include a free pass for you to judge me for my past romantic choices."

"No judgment, I'm just curious."

Monroe didn't shy away from telling people Brendan was a capital-J jerk. That was the easy bit. But talking about the man she *thought* he was for years before that... well, that was harder.

"I thought I loved him. I *did* love him," she said with a sigh. "When we were dating and in the early days of our marriage, things were great. He was sweet, attentive. I was attracted to his ambition and drive for a better life. I thought we were working toward the same thing."

"But then something happened?"

"Something *changed*." Monroe sighed. She continued rinsing the plates and handing them over to Ethan. "Brendan got this itch to move away from Forever Falls. He wanted to chase his dreams in the big city and I didn't want that. Sure, I had dreams. But I could never leave my family like that, especially not after Dad's accident."

"And he couldn't accept that."

"Well, I thought he did, at first. We had a few arguments about it and then he dropped it, so I figured he respected my view to at least wait, until…" She swallowed and shook her head. "God, I don't even want to think about anything happening to my dad. But I told him while Dad's alive I have to be here to help take care of him."

"And he took that as an excuse to cheat on you?"

"I guess so."

Monroe turned to the sink, suddenly hit with a wave of sadness. She didn't feel that often anymore—because she truly *had* moved on from Brendan. It was more sadness for the woman she used to be. Sadness that she'd allowed someone to hurt her so badly. Sadness that her family had suffered because of her mistakes.

Sadness that she'd lost a grip on who she was.

"It's not your fault." Ethan came up behind her and touched her shoulder, encouraging her to turn around.

"I know." Monroe tipped her face up to his, jaw set, determined that he wouldn't see her pain. That nobody would see her pain. Or her guilt. "It's on him."

"So why do you wear it like rocks on your back?"

"I don't." Her denial came too quick, too unsteady. He'd called her a terrible liar and he was right.

Ethan brushed her hair over her shoulder, toying with a rogue frizzy curl. He seemed to like her hair and was looking for any excuse to play with it. Funny, it had always been the bane of her existence. Carrot top, kids at school had called her. Fire crotch and matchstick and Raggedy Anne.

"You're beautiful," he said quietly. There was something about the way he said it, low enough that maybe it wasn't for show. For their act. Or maybe it was the way he looked at her—like he really saw who she was underneath it all. "Inside and out."

"Stop," she whispered, a strange combination of emotions knitting themselves together, creating a knot of feeling inside her. "You've already sold it."

"Have I?" His expression was hard to read now—guarded.

"Very well, I think." Her voice was husky. Want and need danced in her belly, twisting and twirling so that she had to press a palm against her stomach to quell the fluttery feeling.

Mistake. His eyes caught the movement—caught the intent—and when he dragged his gaze back up to her face, they burned. She grappled for some way to cut through the tension, but nothing came. "It's good for our…agreement."

"Right, our agreement." He smirked, as sure of himself as a guy who was used to charming women out of their skirts. Not that he'd told her much about his life, but she could only imagine that's how it was. "Do you remember what was included in our agreement?"

His gaze lingered on her lips. There was no point lying. She knew exactly what he meant. "That if I asked you to kiss me then you would do it no questions asked."

"Is this one of those moments?"

Her gazed flicked over his shoulder and she caught her sisters ducking back into the dining room, caught spying. "I don't want things to get messy."

Messy was the thing she avoided most in the world. It's

why she didn't date after her ex left. It's why she didn't want the Sunshine Diner to change hands. It's why she didn't want to deal with this whole screw-up of a divorce.

And having a fake relationship with a man you're impossibly attracted to isn't messy? Get real.

Ethan put his hands on her hips and pushed her against the kitchen counter, his hips flat against her belly as he wedged her in place. Then he inclined his head back toward the dining room. "They're spying on us, aren't they?"

"Absolutely."

"We should sell it."

His fingers toyed with the hem of her sweater, the stark black one she'd chosen because she knew it made the best of her red hair. Because she wanted to look good...to feel good. Her heart thudded in her chest and there was a tightness gathering in her belly, an instant ache between her legs, and a shakiness in her breath that she hadn't felt in a long damn time.

"It's not necessary," she protested, but her hands came up to his chest as if her body was the one at the control panel of her brain. His chest was hard and sculpted beneath her palms and she had to stop herself from rubbing against him.

Out of the corner of her eyes she saw a flash of movement. Loren.

"Okay, they're *still* watching us."

"Siblings," he said with a chuckle. "Always so nosy."

One hand came up to cup the angle of her jaw, and his thumb brushed the edge of her lip. He was waiting, holding himself in that delicious space of anticipation, looking for a green light. That was the arrangement; *she* was the one who had to demand the kiss. Not him. She hadn't known at the time that she was setting herself up for a trap. Taking away plausible deniability. Taking away the option to blame the kiss on him. Because they didn't *need* to kiss right now—her family had bought the act already, hook, line, and sinker.

But she *wanted* to kiss Ethan…and that was a problem.

"This is purely for maintaining our cover," she said, knowing that every word of it was a lie. A self-serving, self-protecting lie.

"Of course." His lips brushed the space next to the corner of her mouth, so close and yet the distance felt like pure, unadulterated torture. "Why else would we do it?"

"No reason at all."

"Are you going to hate it?" he asked, his lips so close to hers now that she felt the whisper of air between them as he spoke.

"Every second of it," she whispered. "You're repulsive."
Liar, liar, pants on fire.

He let out a rough, dark chuckle and the sound skittered along her spine, lighting up every part of her. He knew she was talking complete garbage, but thankfully he didn't call her out on it. Instead, he angled her head, tugging on her hair so that she was tilted up to him. As his lips brushed against hers, she sighed and curled her hands into his sweater, almost losing the ability to hold itself upright. Every nerve ending in her body sparkled like Fourth of July fireworks.

The first kiss was brief. Teasing. And she wasn't going to settle for wasting a lie on something that was over so soon.

She released his sweater, winding her arms around his neck and keeping his head in place so he knew this wasn't over. Not yet. She pressed her lips to his and the moment his tongue touched hers, her mind went blank. His fingers thrust into her hair, pulling her head back so he could take more, demand more. Taste more.

Unable to stop herself, Monroe pressed her hips against him, rocking back and forth until a wonderfully primal sound came from the back of his throat. He was hard against her and he wedged a muscular thigh between her legs, forcing an echoing sound from her lips.

"Maybe you *are* a good actress," he murmured against her lips, pulling away from the kiss with a dark fire in his eyes, "because you don't seem repulsed at all."

"I am." The crack in her voice betrayed just how much she wanted him. "I'm going to sneak off to the bathroom and throw up now."

"Sure you are."

A small gasp came rushing out of her as he slipped a hand under her sweater and palmed the bare skin at her belly. If they'd been alone her restraint would have shattered like a wineglass thrown at a wall.

But alas, they were not alone.

"We should finish the dishes," she said, forcing her voice to remain steady, to yank control back into her grip. "The kiss did what it was supposed to."

"I'll say so." When he smiled, it was like staring into the face of a wolf. "I'm going to need a clipboard or something to make it back to the dining room."

She did *not* need to think about that. Nor did she need to think about how she was going to be twisting and turning in her bed tonight without the object of her fantasies there to deal with her increasingly unbearable desires.

"That sounds like a you problem." She wriggled out of his grasp and began stacking the remaining dishes into the dishwasher.

Mercifully, Ethan only laughed in response. But Monroe knew that she hadn't exactly gotten out of this situation unscathed. It was already hard enough not to fantasize about Ethan Hammersmith, but now she had some reality with which to color those fantasies.

Don't think about his hammer, don't think about his hammer.

Luckily Loren chose that moment to enter the kitchen, since it must have been clear that the intimate moment was over. "How about some coffee?"

"Great idea," Monroe said. "I'll go and take everyone's orders."

And with that, she scurried out of the kitchen, quite sure that she resembled a tomato. Next time she and Ethan were alone, she'd make a note *not* to get baited into kissing him. Because she had no idea how much longer her willpower would last.

CHAPTER THIRTEEN

Ethan was convinced that he would make a terrible private investigator. Not because he didn't have a nose for sniffing out a lie, and certainly not for a lack of determination. Not to mention that he *loved* solving puzzles. Nothing gave him greater pleasure than finding the last missing piece of something that brought the glorious entirety into illumination.

But the two steps forward and one step back dance of investigation frustrated the hell out of him.

Every time he thought he had something solid in the search for his father, it felt like the past slipped through his fingers. He had been *sure* the Cape Cod connection would turn something up...but so far? Nada.

There was no record of his mother ever being there, even though he knew she had. And there was no record of a Matthew Brewer being there, either. Damn the 80s and their lack of internet. How did people find anybody before Facebook? And as much as he loathed the selfie-driven, filter-heavy behavior rampant on social media, it sure did make figuring out people's whereabouts a whole lot easier.

And really, grumbling over his lack of progress was better than thinking about the very thing his brain *wanted* to focus on—the kiss he shared with Monroe two nights ago.

That's not your brain wanting to think about the kiss, buddy.

True. But Ethan made it a rule that nothing below his

belt buckle got a say in any decisions. Especially now, when there were important issues in his life. Still, that didn't make it easier not to remember how she tasted like champagne and chocolate cake and smelled like a dewy spring garden. Nor did it make it easier for him to forget that her hair was like silk and her body was warm and soft and needy.

"Stop it," he muttered to himself as he locked up his room at the inn. The place was silent—which was strange for a morning.

Lottie was an early riser and she liked to get work going around seven a.m. Ethan usually woke to the sound of her banging around on whatever her latest project was, too impatient to wait for his help. But not today.

Today, the big, old building was eerily quiet.

He made his way along the hallway lined with guest rooms, the old carpet worn under his feet. He'd been working on sanding back the railings for the staircase and landing—preparing it for a fresh coat of paint. He'd suggested white, to liven things up, but Lottie wanted a more traditional British racing green. Trailing his fingers along the second set of balustrades that were now bare and smooth, he jogged downstairs.

There was a noise coming from the front of the inn. Reception area, perhaps? He followed the muffled sound out to the front desk. The door to the office was ajar, and through the sliver of space he could see Lottie sitting at her desk, crying. The soft sobs shook her shoulders as she looked at something in her hands, an old photograph perhaps.

There was something about seeing an old person crying

that was like a punch to Ethan's gut.

He wasn't sure why, but it always filled him with this overwhelming protective urge, even if he didn't know the person that well. That was something ingrained in him— that if he saw someone struggling, he should lend a hand. Or a shoulder to cry on. Or just an ear.

Knowing full well that Lottie was liable to snap the aforementioned ear clean off for intruding, Ethan walked up to her door and knocked. Her head snapped up and she brushed the tears away with the back of her hand.

"What?" she snapped. "Are you spying on me, boy?"

"No, I'm not. But I heard you crying and…"

"You thought you would stick your nose in my business?" She shoved something into the top drawer of her desk and then closed it.

"I wanted to make sure you're okay, that's all." He leaned against the door frame and nudged the door open a little farther. "I can't imagine you're crying without good reason."

Lottie leaned back in her chair and looked at him. Her eyes were red-rimmed and her cheeks had a pink sheen to them—but otherwise her demeanor still embodied the brittle, steel-spined attitude she'd had ever since he had set foot on her property. There was nothing soft about her.

"Grief is a strange beast," she said. "You think you've slayed it, and then out of nowhere it rears its ugly head to take you by surprise."

"So you're telling me I've got years of that feeling ahead of me?" His eyes lowered to the ground. It was difficult to grieve his mother when his feelings were so mixed up.

"I'm afraid so," Lottie replied with a nod. "No sense

lying about it, I don't think. Better to know what you're up against."

"I agree."

She stared at him for a moment, like she was trying to figure something out. There was something sharp and perceptive in her eyes, like she was slotting puzzle pieces together. "So, are you going to tell me why you're really here? Because I'm not sure I buy the story about the letters."

He wasn't surprised. Lottie seemed sharp as a tack. "Why not?"

"Usually that question would be followed by 'it's true' and yet you're looking to sidestep saying it."

"Ah, but if I protested too much then you'd pin my guilt on that." Ethan shrugged. "I know better than to try to change anyone's opinion of me."

Lord knows he'd spent way too much time and energy on that in his youth—trying to fit in with his dad and brother, trying to lose his computer nerd label in school, trying to shake the "entitled millennial" title when he'd first entered the workforce and started climbing the ranks.

"You're smooth," she said. "Too smooth."

"I'm not anything," he replied. "Just a man."

"A man with a mission."

"Sure."

"And you really think people will believe that you upended your entire life to look for some letters?" Lottie massaged the back of one hand with her thumb. "I'll only believe that if there's something specific you're looking for *in* the letters."

For a moment Ethan felt the weariness and exhaustion

of the past twelve months seep into his bones. Lying and searching and disappointment was hard work. In the early days of his travels, he had played things very close to his chest—because if he *did* find the town his father lived in, he wanted to be the one to decide if people knew Ethan was Matthew Brewer's son.

But now, after so many false leads and dashed hopes, Ethan felt himself—and his resolve to keep things private— slowing down.

"I'm trying to find out if Matthew Brewer had an affair with my mother," he said. "An affair which resulted in a son."

"You think he might be your father." The hardness drained from Lottie's face, leaving pure shock in its wake.

"What were your suspicions then, if not that?"

"I thought you were after money. Matthew owed a lot of people a lot of things." She stared at him, eyes roaming over him as if she were seeing things for the first time. "I figured you were here looking to sniff around his mother's estate, see if there was anything of value. Wouldn't be the first time someone had come poking around."

"He had a lot of enemies?"

"Enemies is a harsh word. More like he was indebted to a lot of people—some bad, some stupid. A few men have come around looking for him, not always knowing he was dead."

"Do you know anything about the time he spent in Cape Cod? My mother was there for a summer and I think that's where they met."

"I don't know anything about that." She shook her head. "He was always flitting off here and there. Not even his own mother could keep track of him."

"Do you know if he had a kid or a relationship with an Australian woman?"

Lottie was quiet for a moment. He could practically hear the cogs turning in her head and even though her face gave nothing away, Ethan had a strong tingling intuition in his gut. She was hiding something. Or thinking about hiding something.

How did he know? Maybe it was spending the past year analyzing every little detail he came across. Maybe it was because he'd become the kind of person who hid things and now he recognized it in others.

If only you'd developed that skill earlier.

"He had a few relationships here and there—almost married some poor lamb of a girl in his twenties. But she was from Arkansas. As for the kid thing..." Lottie shrugged. "I wouldn't have put it past him to knock a girl up and leave her to deal with it on her own."

That didn't really answer the question.

Yeah, Lottie was definitely being cagey. But why? If she wasn't related to Matthew in any way, why did she care to hide anything? Maybe he was just being paranoid.

His phone buzzed with a text from Monroe.

I have news! I'm on the early shift so I'll be home by 2 p.m. Come see me after that.

For some reason the text was like a balm to the wild, stirring feelings he was doing his best to swallow down. Seeing Monroe would lift his spirits and maybe she'd be able to shed some light on the Lottie situation. Was the older woman more connected to his potential father than she was letting on?

He texted Monroe back, confirming he'd head over that afternoon. When he looked up, Lottie was still studying him. She didn't trust easily—he understood that. These days Ethan didn't trust easily, either. He gave information away when it suited his needs, but trusting someone? Well, there was a small, dark part of him that wondered if he'd *ever* be able to trust again.

. . .

After a rather frustrating and fruitless day—where he'd tried to get in contact with the guy from the metal workshop, only to find out he was visiting family out of town for the week—Ethan headed to Monroe's place.

Part of him was curious to see the inside of her apartment. He had always thought you could tell a lot about a person by the things they included in their home and how they kept the space. What would Monroe's place reveal about his complex fake girlfriend?

Main Street was busy and he ended up parking almost a block away then walking along the street toward her apartment. He approached the Polish bakery and stopped at the small door he'd seen Monroe disappear into the day he'd dropped her off. Inside was a narrow staircase that led up to the top floor, which was stuffy and smelled like cabbage. At the top there was a tight landing with two doors.

Monroe had told him to come to the apartment marked 104b. He knocked and footsteps sounded inside. A few seconds later the front door was pulled open.

"I'm *so* glad you're here!" Monroe crackled with energy

and she all but yanked him into her apartment. She was wearing blue jeans and a silky top with a colorful apron over it.

Inside, he found a cozy place that was a contradiction of things—much like Monroe herself. Her living room and kitchen was one small area, and there was a bathroom at the back and a closed door which he assumed was her bedroom. In the kitchen, a hot pink stand mixer sat on the middle of the countertop along with bags of flour and other various baking ingredients and implements. All her utensils were pink and befitting of the woman he'd seen on *Sugar Coated*.

But then she had a poster on the wall in the living area that said: *only dead fish go with the flow.*

Ethan liked people who didn't fit squarely into one box, and Monroe was certainly that.

"What are you baking?" he asked, wandering over to her kitchen.

"I'm testing out a new recipe for some Thor-inspired cupcakes." A sly grin spread over her face. "Salted caramel and pecan, with a marshmallow and pretzel stick for the hammer. I don't know, but something tells me Thor would be a salted caramel kinda guy."

Ethan narrowed his eyes at her. "And why exactly are you making Thor cupcakes?"

He wasn't sure he wanted to know the answer to this. He should have known that Monroe wouldn't just drop the Thor thing because he'd said no.

"Well…" Monroe got her phone out of her pocket and pulled up an app. Instagram. "This is a post from *the* Chris Hemsworth, stating that he is currently in Byron Bay,

Australia, with his wife and family. Categorical proof that you are not, in fact, a Hollywood movie star."

"What does it have to do with the cupcakes?"

"You don't need to worry about blending in. So I figured, Thor cupcakes would go with a Thor costume, right?"

He rolled his eyes. "You're persistent."

"Like a zit on a teenager." Monroe smiled gleefully.

Ethan laughed and the sound came from somewhere deep and real inside him. Monroe was…something else. She was pushy and willful and irritatingly attractive.

"I promise, if you help me with this," she said, "I will do *everything* in my power to help you find out if your dad was the Matthew Brewer that lived here. You have my word."

And wasn't that all that mattered in the end? Finding out whether this was the town his father was from or not?

"Do I have any hope of saying no to you?" he asked, shaking his head.

"I don't think so." Her eyes sparkled. "It's probably best not to fight it."

"Can I taste some of your baking treats, at least? You know, as a consolation prize for being bullied into giving up all my dignity."

"Sure."

"The icing looks good."

"We call it frosting here, Mr. Australia. And it *is* good." She used a spatula to scoop some of the thick, glossy white substance into a triangle-shaped bag fitted with a silver nozzle. "Italian buttercream was always my favorite. She can be a tricky mistress, but the results are worth a little extra effort and care."

Monroe piped the frosting in steady, plump swirls on the top of two of the cupcakes. It was fascinating to watch her work, her wrist giving a light flick at the end of each swirl to create a perfect little peak. Then she dusted the tops with what looked to be tiny pieces of some kind of brittle or caramel. Or maybe it was a special salt. Then she stuck a pretzel stick into a small white marshmallow and placed it on top.

"It really does look like a hammer," he said as she handed it over. He turned the small cake around carefully to inspect it from all sides.

"If I was making them for an event, I would airbrush the marshmallow silver and gray so it looked more like a hammer. But for freebies, I think these will do fine." She peeled down the pink paper cup until the side of the cupcake was exposed. It looked soft and delicious. "See, a good cupcake is all about texture and ratios. You want the right balance of frosting and cake. The cake should be light and springy, not too dense. It has to be moist without being underdone. And the frosting needs to be silky smooth, with no graininess from the sugar as well as being the right amount of sweetness to balance the other flavors."

She bit into the side of the cupcake, not being delicate about it but getting a good amount of both frosting and cake.

"Hmmmm." The sound that came out of her mouth was the most sensual thing Ethan had ever heard and it shot through his system like a bullet. "That's delicious, if I do say so myself."

Ethan followed her lead and found himself making a similar noise. "That's *bloody* good. I could eat this every day."

Monroe glowed at the compliment. She'd ended up with a tiny dot of frosting on the tip of her nose, and Ethan didn't even think for a second before his hand reached out to capture it. She laughed and handed him a piece of paper towel to wipe his hand clean. As she did, their fingertips brushed and Ethan would swear something crackled in the air between them.

This woman surprised him.

"You're very talented," Ethan said. He took another bite of the cupcake and it was every bit as delicious as the first. "This is as good as any cake I've had from a professional bakery or cake shop."

She lifted one shoulder into a shrug. "Following a recipe isn't hard."

"But you're not following recipes, are you? You're creating them."

Her dark eyes lifted up to his and he saw something shift in their depths. "Don't you go saying I need to turn my hobby into a business, I get enough of that from my family and Big Frank."

"I don't think enjoyment needs to be capitalized." He polished off the last piece of the cake and enjoyed every single crumb of it. "But I have to question why a woman with so much talent would then go on a reality show if there was no ambition to take it further. If it's just a hobby, why compete?"

"At one time in my life I needed the external validation," she replied with a shrug.

Ethan wasn't buying it. It seemed like a canned answer since it was clear she'd been asked about this a lot. And really, nothing he had to say—words from a stranger, really—would change her mind.

"You really think a Thor costume and cupcakes are going to save the diner?"

"I don't know." She shook her head, and he caught the sadness rolling off her. "But I have to try. I figure you were able to fill the seats, right? Now we just need to get people to buy."

"I thought you hated the diner being overcrowded and busy?"

"Overcrowded with people spending five dollars and then sitting there for several hours. That's *not* how you make a successful business." She popped the rest of the cupcake into her mouth and balled up the paper liner, tossing it onto the kitchen counter. Ethan did the same. "I guess I was happy cruising for a while, making small changes and thinking that would be enough. Clearly it's not. And frankly…"

She wiped her hands down the front of her apron and his eyes tracked the movement. Then she reached for the ties behind her waist and released them so she could slip the apron over her head.

"Frankly," she repeated. "I don't want any more upheaval in my life."

"What do you mean?"

"I've lost my mom. I watched my dad go from an active, spritely man to struggling to deal with reduced mobility in his leg and foot. I lost my husband and the life I thought I'd signed up for. I lost…my future."

"If you're alive, you haven't lost your future, Monroe." He shook his head, rejecting the idea. "If you're still drawing breath, then you still have a chance to make your life what you want it to be."

"That's very poetic." She sighed. "And it's clear you're one of those people who's completely driven by your desire to achieve a goal."

"Why do you say that?" He wasn't going to deny it, because it was 100 percent true. But he was curious to hear her response.

"You put your whole life on hold to come to America in search of your father based on little more than a name and an approximate date of death. It's…" She shook her head. "Who *does* that?"

"Someone who thinks the truth is important."

He wished he could hear the thoughts swirling around in her head. But why did he feel so compelled to connect with her? To prove that she didn't have to worry about him hurting her like others had?

What she feels is none of your business. This is a fake relationship.

And yet…

He was thinking about agreeing to wear that stupid Thor suit to help her out. He was counting down the days until they were stuck in a creepy haunted house together because he thought it would be romantic. He was thinking about her more and more. Even more than what he was *supposed* to be thinking about.

"I was about to get married," he said, not exactly sure why he wanted her to know. "When my mum got sick, I was engaged. My fiancée had her dress all picked out and… we had so many plans. The house we were going to build, the family we were going to create, the dreams we were going to pursue together."

Monroe frowned, and for a second her eyes appeared glossy. But perhaps it was a trick of the light. "What changed?"

"Sarah was a great woman. She was smart and ambitious, climbing her way up the corporate ladder and being an inspiration for everyone." He'd loved her. *Really* loved her. "When Mum got sick, I decided to take a leave of absence from my work to move back home and support her. The company was great about it and Sarah was very supportive. She stayed in Melbourne and came down every weekend to see us. But…"

He still remembered the day he broke her heart.

"When Mum told me the truth about my father, something in me snapped. After the funeral was over I told Sarah I had to come here and find him. She thought I was joking at first." He shook his head. "And then she was angry because she wanted our wedding to go ahead and she felt like I was pulling the rug out from under her. Everything we'd planned, I wanted to put it all on hold for an indeterminate amount of time. We fought and she gave me an ultimatum: if I chose to leave, then that was it. No wedding, no relationship."

"And you still left?"

"I *had* to, Monroe." For some reason, he wanted her to understand. He wanted *someone* to understand. "I had to find him. I had to say goodbye to the relationship I never got to have, to what could have been. I had to close the circle."

"I'm sorry she didn't support you," Monroe said softly. "Family is everything to me, so I know why you did it. I had to sacrifice things for my family, too. But instead of leaving, like you did, I had to stay."

She came toward him, pressing a hand to his chest like she wanted to infuse him with her empathy. Like she wanted to connect. Ethan closed his hand over hers, feeling the warmth of her skin against his palm. He breathed in the scent of caramel and sugar lingering in the air, and he took in the glory of her—the halo of ginger frizz that framed her face, the dark, mesmerizing eyes, and every one of her freckles.

It had been a long time since he felt understood.

And now that feeling had come from the most unexpected and wonderful place. This might be a fake relationship, but the desire and desperation flooding through his body right now was anything but fake.

CHAPTER FOURTEEN

Monroe wasn't sure why she was feeling this way. Was it a sugar high? Some kind of hot guy magic? Or maybe she'd accidentally electrocuted herself and this was some kind of coma-dream?

"I guess we're not so different after all," he said. Ethan's blue eyes roamed her face and the pound of his pulse against her palm was surprisingly erotic. He was still holding her hand in place, and they were close.

So close.

"You're not as grumpy as me," she said with a laugh.

"I don't think you're as grumpy as you think you are. You care about your family more than anything, you take care of your colleagues, you work hard and…well, you've helped me and I'm just a stranger."

"You don't feel like a stranger," she said, without thinking about what it meant. Without thinking that it might shatter a barrier between them that she desperately needed.

But it was true. Ethan felt like someone she could have known her whole life—he was open, warm, self-effacing. He was exactly the kind of man she always dreamed of.

"You don't feel like a stranger, either." He slipped one hand along her jaw, driving his fingers into her hair.

The air snapped and popped around them and Monroe felt her eyes flutter shut in response, her body giving over to the need driving through her body. Giving over to him.

When Ethan's lips touched her own, tentative and gentle at first, and then harder and more searching, she melted into him. His strong arms wrapped around her body and pulled her close, cradling her.

She kissed him back, her lips and tongue finding a rhythm with him, and for a moment she let herself believe in it all—that this meant something, that she had this life, this future, with a man like him. She let herself drown in the fantasy of it.

Ethan backed her up and suddenly she was wedged between him and the wall of her apartment. She gasped as his body lined hers, hard everywhere. Solid and trustworthy and so, so decadent.

"We didn't talk about this," she said, her head rolling back and a soft moan falling from her lips as he kissed her neck. "What are the rules?"

"Ladies first?" His smile was wicked.

"I mean…" It was so very hard to speak when his hands were on her hips, solid and splayed with the tips of his fingers brushing the skin underneath her T-shirt. It was torture. "We only talked about a kiss."

"Do you want me to stop?"

His expression turned serious, but Monroe's mouth popped open before her poor brain even had the chance to have a say. "No."

The lust in Ethan's eyes was electrifying. He looked at her…

Like she was beautiful.

Like she was special.

Like she mattered.

And it had been a long time since anybody had looked

at her like that. It was addictive—a sugary lollipop of emotion that made her want more, more, *more*. But her heart screamed out for protection.

"This doesn't mean we're really dating," she said, sliding her hands up and down his chest, delighting in the way his muscles felt under her palms. "This is still a fake relationship because we both need something from each other. Sex doesn't change that."

He nodded and she couldn't tell if he was insulted by her need to draw a line in the sand. But she'd fallen victim to loving a man she shouldn't before—a man who was chronically unavailable. Who was willing to leave when she couldn't.

Which was exactly what Ethan had done to his ex.

And she understood his reasons—they were meaningful. Important. But he still left his fiancée behind and Monroe would never get left behind ever again.

"Is that it? Negotiations over?" He brushed his lips along her jaw, one hand skating up over her rib cage to palm her breast as he pressed her against the wall.

"Unless you want something?"

"Just you, naked. Under me."

"You have a way with words. I bet it works a treat on most women." She tipped her face up to his, needing to hang on to her defiance. Needing to hang on to her sharp edges and her walls and her prickly outer shell. Because the more time she spent with Ethan, the stronger the impulse was to shed those things...and she knew that was a bad idea.

She *needed* those things.

Without them, she would be exposed. The soft, squishy

parts of her that she tried so damn hard to hide would be ready for Ethan to take his aim.

His full lips tipped up into a devastating smirk. "It's going to work a treat on you, too, Monroe."

Heat trickled through her system, flooding her veins with delicious, sparkling warmth. When Ethan lowered his head to hers, his hand slid up the side of her neck and his thumb caught the underside of her chin to push her head back. He swept his tongue into her mouth, pressing his hard body against hers and wedging her against the wall. He kissed like he meant it. Like he wanted to consume her.

And she was pretty damn sure there would be a Monroe-shaped scorch mark on her living room wall when they were done.

Fake relationship or not, there was no denying the very *real* attraction. Monroe felt it course through her veins, pulsing in time with her heartbeat. She felt it in the tautness of Ethan's muscles, like he was an animal coiled and ready to pounce. She felt it...lower, too.

He thumbed her hardened nipple. "See, so quiet now."

"You always have a trick up your sleeve, don't you?"

He kissed down her neck, his fingers moving to the buttons running the length of the pretty top she'd found stuffed in the back of her closet, a relic from another time. He popped one open and then another, exposing her through the widening V of the fabric.

"No tricks," he murmured against her neck. "Because a trick implies you don't know what's coming and you, Monroe, know *exactly* what's coming."

"Do I now?" Her voice was husky, lust-fueled. She sounded so unlike herself that if she were only listening to audio, she wouldn't have recognized herself.

"I'm going to take you to bed." Another button slipped through its hole. Then another. "I'm going to keep you up all night. Then I'm going to buy you breakfast in the morning, like a good boyfriend does. And you're going to love every second of it."

"That a fact?" she whispered.

"Absolutely." When Ethan looked up at her, his blue eyes gleamed with intensity. His pupils were wide with arousal and it made her want to drown in him.

"Okay," she breathed. "Yes. One night."

"No regrets."

Could she determine that in advance? Monroe wasn't sure. But she nodded so he'd keep opening those silly, tiny buttons and keep kissing her.

Victory danced in his eyes, but Ethan didn't say anything else. Why bother? He had what he wanted. What *she* wanted, too. He lowered himself down her body, lips blazing a trail over her collarbone and down her chest. His fingers worked the remaining buttons and then he shoved the fabric aside and snapped the front closure of her bra open, exposing her to his mouth. A pleasant hum vibrated against her skin.

"Yes." The word hissed out of her, sizzling like water splashing a hot stove. She arched into him, her focus growing fuzzy around the edges.

"Tell me what you want," he said, his lips grazing her breasts.

God, no. It had been so long since she'd had sex that it had fallen off the edge of Monroe's attention. She hadn't missed it, hadn't craved it…not until Ethan had kissed her in Loren's kitchen. Not until this mysterious man had swept into her life and stirred up all kinds of things she had hoped she'd never feel again.

Her fingers threaded into his thick golden hair. The strands were soft against her palms, smooth and sturdy. Like him. She pushed his head lower—showing, rather than telling him what she wanted.

A rough chuckle vibrated against her chest and her instinct was to push him away, to shrink with embarrassment. But his lips were around her nipple and sucked, his tongue flicking against her in a way that drew a moan right from the back of her throat.

Her head fell back, knocking softly against the wall as her body turned molten beneath his touch. He scraped his teeth against her skin, gentle and yet the friction made fire race through her veins. How had she forgotten what this felt like? The need for more was a whisper in her bloodstream. Once he finished with one breast, he turned to the other, and she had to brace her hands behind her.

"You taste so good," he murmured, his face pressed against her skin. "I want to taste the rest of you."

"Yes." The word was out before she even had time to consider what he was asking. Or what she was giving away. "Bedroom. Now."

She grabbed his hand and pulled him toward her room. It was modest, like the rest of this place. Borderline barren. Just a double bed with a simple gray duvet and a nightstand with a lamp that she'd found for five dollars at the thrift store. No pictures, no decoration. Even the view was nothing special—since she looked right at the brick wall of another building.

Suddenly, she felt a little self-conscious even though she knew Ethan had been traveling across the country, with only a backpack to his name. But he came from more—the story about the life he'd left behind, the well-paying job in a big, fancy city, and the fiancée who matched him in drive and ambition.

That wasn't Monroe's life. That had *never* been her life.

But she pushed it all from her mind. Every doubt, every insecurity...none of it belonged here with them. Because for once in her damn life she deserved to feel special, to feel cherished. And a shitty bedroom wasn't going to take that from her.

Ethan finished removing her top and bra, pushing both off her shoulders and letting them fall to the ground. Then he hooked his fingers into the waistband of her jeans and tugged her forward, which was about the sexiest thing she'd ever experienced. There was a touch of arrogance in him, and she liked it. Because he *knew* he was attractive, he knew she wanted him and it was so nice not to have to pretend otherwise.

He popped the button on her jeans and pulled the zipper down slowly, making a soft grunt at the sight of what she had on underneath. Black lace, a touch of satin. She'd found some of her old lingerie when she'd gone digging for something nice to wear—finding a plastic bag with all manner of sexy things shoved into the back of her closet, behind a box of books and some old makeup that needed to be tossed.

"And you said you didn't know where this was going?" He pulled her jeans down, letting out a groan when he saw the little heart-shaped cutout in the fabric. "Bloody hell."

"Maybe I wore them for me," she teased.

"Did you?" he asked, helping her out of her jeans. He tossed them to the side, onto the pile containing her top and bra.

"No," she whispered. "I wore them for you."

His eyes were like twin blue flames and he eased her back to the bed, encouraging her to sit. Then he knelt in front of her and Monroe felt this surge of power go through her, like she finally understood that he didn't just have an effect on her. But that she also had an effect on him.

The way he looked at her...Lordy.

He kissed the inside of her knee and she couldn't help but smile at how tender and sweet it was, like a moment of truth in the haze of sexual attraction driving them forward. But that sweetness was soon consumed when he pulled her legs over his shoulders and opened her up. Monroe sucked in a breath.

"I love how you're freckled everywhere." He followed the brown dots with his fingertip, skating them higher up her inner thigh.

"I always hated them," she admitted. "The kids at school used to tease me."

"I think they're beautiful."

There were freckles and then there were *freckles*. Monroe had laughed once at a makeup tutorial Loren had shown her where girls drew them across their nose and cheeks in a delicate little spray, like a dusting of cinnamon. Monroe's freckles were clustered and stark and they were everywhere, summer or not. When she was on *Sugar Coated* the makeup artists had covered them up with dense foundation and powder, and for a time after Monroe had done the same.

But he looked at her like he enjoyed every part of her—all the bits she blamed on why her husband had stopped finding her attractive. Her small boobs, her unruly hair, her obnoxiously freckled skin. Ethan liked it all.

The higher his hands got, the tighter her body wound up. Her sex clenched as he brushed the very top of her inner thigh, anticipation turning her to molten liquid. This was it, her last chance to back out before it went from being an ill-advised fumble to something else.

He pressed his lips to her center through the thin satin and lace of her fancy underwear. A shudder rippled through her, and she curled her hands around the edge of the bed.

"You're excited," he said. His voice was low and rough and it made her pulse jump. "It's a bloody beautiful thing to see."

Her eyes closed, and she tried to push away the doubt and self-consciousness edging in. "That's because you make me excited."

He spread her legs with his palms, holding her wide open. "Tell me you want this. I want to hear you say it."

Her thighs were practically trembling under his touch and she couldn't remember the last time she'd felt like this.

"If you don't finish what you started, then I'm going to kick you out of this house so I can finish it myself," she said, her voice wavering. It wasn't like her to voice what she wanted so openly—because Monroe was used to hiding behind her snark and her prickles. Behind sarcasm and jokes. Behind her walls.

His wicked smile soothed any remaining fears about whether or not she could trust him with her body. This might not be a real relationship, but this *was* real attraction. It was real chemistry.

Don't let your heart get involved…

The light caught on the golden lengths of his hair as he kissed his way up her inner thigh. Warm breath brushed over her skin, excitement vibrating in the air around her. He lowered his head and brought his hands to her underwear, dragging it over her hips and down her thighs.

When he came back to her, his tongue brushed tentatively against the sensitive skin of her sex. She let her head roll back. Ethan must have taken it as a sign of encouragement, because the gentle, tentative first stroke was worlds away from the next. He feasted on her, using his tongue and his lips until it felt like all the blood in her body had rushed to that exact spot. She was weightless. Dizzy. Sublimely floating on a cloud of pleasure.

"Yes, Ethan." Her hips rocked against his mouth, one hand finding its way to his head so she could steady herself.

Her inner muscles clenched and she rocked against him, thighs trembling and her breathing coming harder and faster. Her mind narrowed to a pinpoint of euphoria and in that moment there was only one thing in the world—the feeling of his lips on her.

"I'm close," she gasped.

He growled against her, the vibrations skittering through her body and fracturing at the last second in a billion glittering shards. Monroe shouted Ethan's name, uncaring if her neighbors could hear them. All that mattered was the wave of release that was an avalanche on top of her. Burying her. Changing her forever.

Reminding her that this feeling was worth remembering.

• • •

Monroe's cries could very well have been the best sound
Ethan had ever heard. He'd certainly never had any
complaints in bed — because he wasn't one of those guys
who thought sex was all about his own orgasm — but this
was...something else.

That's because it's been a while. It's not her, it's sex.

Maybe. But something told him that was a load of self-
protecting bullshit.

He rested his cheek on the inside of her thigh, enjoying
the way she felt soft and smooth against him. There was no
tension in her muscles, not even a twitch. She'd given
herself over.

"All good up there?" he asked, knowing he sounded
more than a touch arrogant. But she seemed to enjoy the
game they had going — big, bad out-of-towner versus a
grumpy local. And he liked it, too.

"Not sure 'good' quite covers it." She propped herself up
on her forearms. Her big, brown eyes had a delicious
sleepy haze to them and her cheeks were flushed.

"You're stroking my ego." He kissed the inside of her
knee and rocked back on his heels, steadying himself with
a hand on either side of her on the bed. "I enjoyed that
very much."

"Me too." She watched him, like she was waiting to see
what his next move would be. A touch of wariness crept
back into her expression. Why, he had no idea.

The instance of distrust made his heart feel like it was
going to punch out of his chest. How did she manage to get

to him like that? His heart had no business here. But the relief he felt when she held her hand out and slipped her palm into his told him this wasn't a normal encounter. This wasn't normal sex.

It's just *sex. Casual, no strings or expectations required.*

He came down onto the bed, still fully clothed, and planted one hand on either side of her head. He pressed his face into her neck and kissed her skin, sucking in the scent of her perfume. It was lemon and something... Sweet with a load of bite. Like her.

Her hair was a mess, curls escaping all around her face from where she'd rocked her head against the bed. She was sex personified—gloriously messy and unrestrained.

"You're going to need to get undressed for the next part," she said, reaching out to smooth a palm up and under his sweater. He had a T-shirt on underneath and she tugged at it to get to his bare stomach. "You are ridiculously ripped. Honestly, it's almost a joke."

He let out a husky laugh. "Don't. I have a complex about my hideous muscles."

She rolled her eyes and laughed. "Mr. Aussie Hottie, driving all small-town women wild with a single glance. Yeah, you're a real Quasimodo."

"You saying I drive you wild?" he teased, nipping at her neck.

"I'd like to say no, but I guess my current position would indicate otherwise."

He pressed her against the bed, his lips parting hers for a searing kiss. She raked her nails down his chest and over his abs until she grabbed the hem of his T-shirt and sweater in one, and pulled them up and over his head.

Ethan helped the process along, tossing them onto the floor with her discarded clothes.

"Simply hideous," she said, eyes glittering and lips curved into a cheeky smirk.

"Hey, what happened to me driving you wild?" He grinned.

Ethan was so hard he was at serious risk of busting the zipper on his jeans. Monroe must have sensed it, because she reached down and cupped him through the denim, her palm rubbing up and down his length.

"I'll take *you* driving *me* wild as a consolation prize," he rasped out.

"Good choice. You know I like being in charge." She planted both hands on his chest and pushed him back. As she rose from the bed, she was a goddess who'd fallen down to earth. Aphrodite herself.

"I like you being in charge."

"Good." With a cheeky grin, she pointed at the bed. "Lay down. It's my turn."

He dropped down onto the bed and Monroe shoved him back into a laying position. This side of her was something else. Despite her hard edges, she'd never struck him as confident before. More defensive, protective, careful.

This moment was like watching a flower bloom into its full potential.

She dragged the zipper down and pulled both his jeans and his jocks over his legs. He levered his hips up to assist her, and her eyes never left him.

"I didn't think we would do this," she said as she dispensed of his clothing.

He grabbed the emergency condom from his wallet and

then lay on the bed—which was small enough that he took up most of the space—his cock hard and laying up against his stomach. Monroe let her eyes wash over him, as though she was cataloguing every detail.

"That's because I wasn't your type…supposedly." No sense in screwing with the dynamic now, he was going all in on the cockiness.

"No." Her tone was serious for a moment. "I never thought I'd be here with any man."

The words made him want to open his mouth and roar in pride that *he* was the one she'd chosen. He was the man who'd brought her to the brink, against all her expectations.

"Why me?"

It was a stupid thing, to go digging for information he didn't want or need. Their relationship was fake, his stay in Forever Falls was temporary, and she had more baggage than a Louis Vuitton store. All of it spelled out that anything more than a quick romp was bad news.

Yet he couldn't help being curious about her. He couldn't help wanting more of her.

"You're different than other people," she said. "At least, you're different with me."

He had absolutely no clue what that meant.

But she shook herself, as if giving herself the reminder of why she was here. Then she crawled onto the bed and over him, her knees digging into the soft covers on either side of his hips. She leaned forward, her breasts brushing his chest. Reaching for him, she wrapped her fingers around his cock in a way that drew a deep moan from the back of Ethan's throat. Then she plucked the foil packet from his hand and dealt with their protection.

"You might have to go slow, okay?" She sucked in a breath, a little flash of uncertainty flickering in her eyes. "It's been a while."

Ethan smoothed his hands up her thighs. "All you gotta do is say stop if you need to, okay? I'm here to make you feel good."

She nodded.

He slid his hands to the inside of her thighs and delved between her legs. The sharp sound of her gasp sent endorphins rocketing through him. She was so hot. So wet. Her forearms came up to brace against the bed, bringing her face close to his. Her hair fell in a curly sheet around them and it was like being under a blanket fort with her.

He pressed one finger inside and then two. The gentle rocking of her hips matched the timing of his strokes, and he felt her quiver.

"That's good." Monroe's lips grazed his cheek as he warmed her up. "So good."

He watched the pleasure roll over her face like a storm. In here, it seemed that she was a lot easier to read. There was an openness he hadn't seen in her before, a willingness to let him get a peek behind the curtain.

"You're sexy as hell, you know that?" He growled as he felt her clench around his fingers and she hummed in response.

His hands were all over her—cupping her breasts, grabbing her hips, parting the slick folds of her sex. She panted, and her head dropped down so that her forehead rested against his. He could see her eyes in detail at this closeness, all the shades of brown from the almost black ring around her irises, to the coffee and chocolate shades in the center.

Working Monroe up into a frenzied state was incredible, but his cock was begging for release. So when she dropped her hand down between them and filled her palm with him, Ethan groaned.

"Monroe." He thrust slowly into her palm. "I need to be inside you."

"I'm ready."

Sliding his hand over her backside, he guided her down on him. When he pushed inside, easing them into position and giving her a moment to adjust, he had to shutter his eyes for a brief moment. She was tight and so hot he had to stop himself from finishing with one thrust.

Monroe crushed her mouth against his, greedily seeking his tongue. Nipping at his lips. Encouraging him. Teasing him. He sank his fingers into her backside and thrust up into her, burying himself over and over.

"Ethan," she moaned, rocking back and forth to meet his pace. "I think I'm going to…oh yes."

She clenched around him as she came, her moans turning to cries as she tipped over the edge again. He wanted to hold on—to let her have her moment before he sought his own release—but the sight of her face flushed with pleasure and the sound of his name on her lips was too much. He buried his face against her hair as he came, wrapping his arms around her so tight it was like he never wanted to let go.

Her lips peppered his skin and when she sighed, a satisfied hum vibrating against his chest, Ethan knew that neither one of them was faking it.

CHAPTER FIFTEEN

Sometime later, Monroe stirred. An unfamiliar scene greeted her.

Her bedsheets were rumpled, the duvet piled into a messy heap at the foot of the bed. Outside her window, the sky was indigo velvet. Inside, the room was almost dark, with only the glow of a streetlamp below to keep them from being plunged into shadows. It had been light out when they'd stumbled into her bedroom and then…

She looked up at Ethan. He had one muscular arm flung across her pillow and she was nestled into the space next to him, her cheek against his chest and one of her legs draped over his while he curled an arm around her shoulders. It had felt so perfectly normal. Familiar, even though it shouldn't.

Real.

It's not real.

She swung her feet over the side of the bed and pressed them into the cool floorboards, steadying herself. He was breathing soundly and there was something almost angelic about him—with his rumpled blond hair and warm gold stubble and the slight smile hovering on his lips. It was almost like he was an angel who'd tumbled out of the sky and landed in her bed.

Shaking her head at herself for being so corny, she got out of the bed and pulled the duvet up and over him, making sure he was warm. Ethan didn't even stir.

Monroe slipped a bathrobe on, shivering a little at how cool the apartment felt as she pulled the belt tight. Stuffing her feet into some slippers, she headed into the living area and softly closed the door to the bedroom behind her. Out here, she *was* greeted by a familiar, albeit long-forgotten, sight.

Her kitchen was creative chaos, with flour dusted across the countertop and just less than a dozen cupcakes still sitting in the tray. The surface was littered with tools and ingredients and for a second Monroe wondered if she'd figured out a way to turn back time.

Only back then, she'd lived in a small but beautiful home, with a pretty garden full of edible blooms that she loved to use in her baking. A place that had personal pictures on the walls and a kitchen full of things she loved to use.

These days she often grabbed something from the diner to eat at home. Or perhaps a quick meal from one of the local takeout places. Often, she didn't even bother with that, opting for a piece of toast and some peanut butter instead.

But now, looking at this kitchen that reflected who she used to be, Monroe wasn't sure how to feel.

She knew more than anyone how dangerous it was to dream. Disappointment was the misalignment between desire and reality, and she'd been misaligned for a very long time. But the way Ethan made her feel…

She couldn't help grinning like a fool.

Her hands itched to work, to create. She went into the kitchen and cleaned up the mess from her cupcakes, popping the little cakes without frosting into an airtight container. Then she put the frosting in another container and popped it into the fridge. In seconds, her cupboard doors were open and she was pulling more things out—a cake tin, another bowl for her stand mixer, cocoa power, and more butter.

The possibilities were endless.

Monroe dusted off old tools, even digging some out of a box she'd kept stored under her tiny dining table ever since she'd moved in. The oven beeped as she set it to preheat and then she lost herself in the process of creation, feeling hope kindling in her chest.

Feeling like…maybe she could be this person again.

· · ·

Ethan spent all day Friday and Saturday thinking about seeing Monroe. The night they'd slept together, he'd awoken to find her pottering around her kitchen, the smell of chocolate cake wafting in the air. He'd stood by the bedroom door and watched, enraptured, as the woman he'd seen on *Sugar Coated* came to life before his eyes.

She was vibrant. Luminous.

He'd been so enamored, in fact, that they'd taken a shower together, kissing long and slow and touching one another until they were dizzy with desire. Then they'd ordered pizza from the only place still open, and had eaten it while watching a movie on her couch.

But he hadn't spent the night.

Something told him that Monroe's transformation was a warning sign that he shouldn't get too close—she needed a man who was going to be there for her long-term. A man who had plans to set down roots and to give her everything she deserved. But Ethan wasn't that man. If it turned out that the troublemaking Matthew Brewer of Forever Falls wasn't his father...then he'd be moving on, leaving her and the town behind so he could chase the next ghost on his list.

For some reason, the thought settled uncomfortably in his gut. The idea of walking away from Monroe didn't feel good. Which was *precisely* why he couldn't get too involved with her. Sex was one thing—and he enjoyed the hell out of it—but sleeping over and allowing either one of them to think this was real was only setting them up for near-future disappointment.

Even if it turned out that this Matthew Brewer *was* his father, then why would he stay? There was no family, from the information he'd gleaned, and it sounded like everyone hated the man. Ethan would simply close the loop on his life and figure out what came next.

But as he pulled up to the front of Monroe's apartment, there was no denying the excited feeling in his stomach. The anticipation swirling like butterflies that made him fidget in his seat until she suddenly appeared at the little door next to the bakery, an emerald-green coat wrapped around her slim frame, and offsetting her hair to perfection.

She raised one mitten-covered hand in a wave before she opened the passenger side door and slid into the seat next to him. The scent of vanilla hit his nose and Ethan almost hummed at how good she smelled.

"You've been baking again," he said, starting the engine.

She yanked one mitten off and then the other, stuffing them both into a pocket of her coat. Her cheeks were pink from the damp, chilly air; the temperature had dropped suddenly that afternoon. "I have, actually. But don't worry, I showered."

"Ah, so that delicious smell isn't cupcake icing then."

"Frosting." She grinned. "And no, I uh...put some perfume on."

Perfume. He'd never smelled anything like this on her before, not in any of the times they'd been together—like on their fake dates or the dinner at her sister's house.

Don't get excited that she wore it for you. She probably just felt like smelling nice. No. Big. Deal.

Only it did feel like something special and maybe that was because he'd thought about her when he'd gotten dressed that night. He'd worn his leather jacket, even though it was probably cold enough for the puffy coat, because he wanted to dress up.

Monroe leaned over and inhaled. "You smell pretty good, too."

"Soap and shampoo, the rest is all me." He turned his head and they were so close that he could easily kiss her. He wanted to. Actually, what he really wanted was to say screw the haunted house and take her right back upstairs and to bed.

Get a grip man. You're not a horny teenager.

Clearing his throat, he pulled back and was surprised to see a flash of disappointment in Monroe's eyes. Or was that wishful thinking?

"I looked up where we have to go," he said, deciding to leave bad ideas alone. "Tour starts at one of the historic graveyards and then we go to the mansion after that."

"Great." She nodded and settled back into her seat,

yanking the seat belt across her body.

Ethan pulled slowly out into Main Street in the direction heading out of town. He'd already programmed the address into his phone and the robotic voice directed him to keep along Main Street for several blocks.

"Don't listen to that," Monroe said, pointing. "Take Carlisle Street."

Ethan frowned. "This is the most direct route. I looked it up."

"Who's lived in this town their whole life, huh? Carlisle is quicker."

She was doing that weird thing again—wanting to take back streets and going some strange way out of town.

"What's the rush? We have plenty of time." Ethan went through the intersection of Main and Carlisle, ignoring her directions. He felt Monroe tense up beside him, almost as if she was shrinking against the door.

"Good to know even people in fake relationships argue about directions," she grumbled.

He slowed down behind a small train of cars at a red light. Being Saturday night, there were a few people out and a restaurant had warm lights glowing in the windows and the outlines of people sitting down to a meal. Out of the corner of his eye, he watched Monroe. There was something going on with her. Something weird.

Her eyes locked on a place as they sat at the lights. A yoga studio?

"What's going on?" he asked. Yep, she was definitely looking at the yoga studio. It had a big sign in the front saying "for lease" and was otherwise dark inside.

"That was my cousin's yoga studio," she said, tearing her

eyes away. "The cousin who was having an affair with my husband."

The barely suppressed anger in her voice hit him like a fist to the solar plexus. *That's* why she avoided this part of Main Street, so she didn't have to drive past the scene of the crime.

"Shit." He glanced over at her. "I'm sorry, Monroe. I had no idea that was why you didn't want to drive down here."

"It's a stupid thing, I know." She shook her head. "That I'll take any other street and drive out of my way not to go past it, but every time I look at that place…"

The lights changed and the traffic started moving again. Soon the yoga studio was behind them.

"You shouldn't let them have that kind of power over you," he said. "This is *your* town, not theirs. You were the victim of their bad behavior, you were the one who gave everything to your marriage and got nothing in return."

"You say that with a lot of confidence for someone who wasn't around at the time it happened." Her expression softened and she seemed to relax again now that the studio wasn't in sight.

"I may not know you well, but I know enough to see what a good person you are," he replied. And he meant every word of it. "I saw how you were with your dad at dinner, how much you care about your family. The fact that you spent most of your prize money fixing up his house to give him a better quality of life, it all points to how big your heart is."

"It's not the fact that my marriage ended that upsets me so much." She shook her head. "It's what it did to my family."

"Her side of the family didn't believe you?"

"It was more that Amber made them believe I was standing in the way of true love." She snorted. "If that was the case, then why didn't Brendan leave me first? Why go behind my back? Because they were cowardly, both of them."

"But the family didn't agree?"

"Nope. My dad was *furious,* and he got into a massive argument with his sister about it. I'd always been close with my aunt and my cousins, but after that…" She blinked and something shimmered in her eyes. He had to fight every instinct in his body not to pull the car right over to the side of the road and haul her into his arms. "My dad said they betrayed the values we held as a family by supporting Amber and the affair. He basically told my aunt that she'd raised a horrible a person with no moral compass and my aunt returned the barb by saying he'd raised a daughter who didn't know how to hold onto a man."

Ethan whipped his head toward Monroe. "That is complete bullshit."

"You're defending my honor," she said with a laugh. "How romantic."

"I…" He didn't even know *what* to say.

"I know my aunt was angry and defending her daughter because my dad took the first swing, but it hurt. A lot." Monroe swallowed.

"Did your dad tell you what she said?"

"No, I was staying with him after I'd moved out of Brendan's and I picked up the phone to call someone…I heard the whole thing myself."

"Ouch."

"Things were never the same after that. I couldn't look any of them in the eye knowing they thought it was my fault, even if they were only trying to save face. But I miss what we used to have as a family—these huge Christmas lunches with everyone under one roof, all the noise and laughter and…" Her voice wavered. "The affair didn't just ruin my marriage, it ruined my family."

He shook his head. "That's a bloody awful thing to happen."

"Relationships are never only about the two people in it. When you're with someone a long time it bleeds into your family and your friendship groups. Untangling that is messy."

"Unless you walk away and leave the other person to deal with it all."

It might have sounded like he was talking about her ex, but really he was reflecting on himself. "That's what I did to Sarah. I left and she was the one who had to deal with the aftermath."

"She gave you an ultimatum, Ethan. It's different." Monroe pressed a hand to his arm. "You'd experienced a massive loss and a huge shock. It's no wonder you wanted to break away from it all and figure things out. If you love someone, you should support them through those difficult times, not try to guilt them into putting someone else's needs before their own."

"That's what I always thought. I would have gone with her, if roles were reversed." He knew *that* down in his heart. He would have done anything for her.

"Of course you would have." Monroe said the words like

they were a fact carved in stone.

"You seem pretty confident for someone who wasn't there when it happened," he teased, echoing her words from earlier.

She laughed. "Touché."

"Thank you, though. Some days I don't even think I understand why I have this driving need to find out who my dad was. I know it won't make a difference—he's gone. I won't ever get the opportunity to know him."

"Sometimes the important things don't make logical sense," she replied with a shrug. "But we know it on a gut level when something is right."

Being with Monroe is right.

The thought flashed up, unbidden. Unwanted. But it resonated like the gong of church bells through his body, stretching on and on. For the first time in so long, it felt like he could just…be.

He wasn't trying to impress the directors at his work, he wasn't trying to fit in with his half brother and Ivan, the man he'd called Dad. He wasn't trying to keep Sarah happy by being everything she needed and planning a wedding that was far more extravagant than he truly wanted. He wasn't trying to reach a level of success that would prove to the man who raised him that all the things he'd teased him for were worth something.

"You okay?" she asked, and he laughed. Monroe was the one who'd been forced to face a bad memory because he didn't want to let her give him driving instructions and now she was being sweet and caring toward *him?*

"I don't know how it would be possible to *not* be okay around you," he said.

She turned away to look out the window, but he caught a quick flash of a smile on her lips and growing rosiness in her cheeks.

• • •

Outside, the sun was setting. A thick band of orange and gold lay across the horizon, and the purple-blue of night was close behind. They'd reached the outskirts of Forever Falls, meeting Brian and the rest of the people attending the tour at the gates of one of the oldest cemeteries in Massachusetts. They'd walked around the grave sites, listening to stories about a few mysterious deaths and local urban legends.

Monroe had to admit, Brian was quite the storyteller. You'd never get that impression of him meeting him on the street, but it seemed like when the sun began to set and he got out into the night air, his skills came to life.

Now they had a few minutes to wander around before it got fully dark and before they headed to the haunted mansion for the night's main event. The group was small— two older couples who were visiting, and a gentleman who was writing a book and doing the tour as part of his research.

Ethan chatted away with one of the couples, who'd apparently been to the west coast of Australia several years back, and they wanted to pick his brain about a potential trip back there to visit Melbourne and Sydney. Monroe was looking at one grave in particular, being careful where she stepped so as not to disturb anything, when Brian approached her.

"Can I have a word?" he asked, his hands shoved into the pockets of his coat.

"Sure."

He turned his back on the group for a second and Monroe frowned. She knew Brian well enough, but couldn't think of a reason that he'd want to talk to her privately.

"It's about your boyfriend," he started. "And the stuff about the letters."

Monroe nodded, curiosity piqued. "Okay."

Brian let out a sigh. "Look, I probably shouldn't be telling you any of this, but if the letters are likely to exist anywhere then they'll be with Lottie May."

"Really?" Monroe raised an eyebrow. Everybody knew Lottie May—she was a Forever Falls lifer from way back, independent to the core and known to have a bark worse than her bite. She came into the diner sometimes, and there were a lot of stories that had swirled around about her over the years…

She'd been single for as long as anyone could remember, no kids. No family. Things that were unusual for a woman of her generation. Not to mention the fact that she'd run the inn on her own for years, well past when most people would be looking to retire. Monroe was sure her dad said that there'd been suitors over the years and possibly a secret relationship of some kind, but the woman was locked up tighter than Fort Knox.

No easy feat in a town like Forever Falls.

"Why Lottie?" Monroe asked.

"When Mrs. Brewer died, the executor of the will was some guy from out of state. A distant cousin or something, and he didn't really want anything to do with it. They hired a company to pack all the things up and get rid of it. The executor guy came and picked through to see if there was anything of value, but there wasn't of course." Brian shook his head.

Monroe echoed the movement. "Then what?"

"Everything else was supposed to go to the dump. I knew that because I was doing some removal work at the time. On the day we were loading everything into the truck, Ms. Lottie turned up in tears."

"Tears?"

"Yeah, I never seen nothing like it. That old lady is hard as nails and I never seen her cry before." He raked a hand over his hair. "But she begged me to keep some of the stuff. Nothing fancy, you know, just some photo albums and that kind of thing. Sentimental stuff."

"And you let her?"

He glanced around as though wanting to make sure no one was overhearing. "I decided to use that moment to take a smoke break and I told Ms. Lottie as such. When I came back she was gone, and so were two boxes."

"Why would she want Mrs. Brewer's things?"

"I don't know. They were friends, I guess." He shrugged. "I remembered it after you and your man came past my office. But she made me promise that I'd never seen her that day, not to mention I'd get in trouble for letting someone go through the stuff, even though none of it was worth even a penny. So, do with that information what you will, but you didn't hear it from me."

"Thanks, Brian, I appreciate it."

"I trust you, Monroe. Your family has always been nice, even to the likes of me."

Monroe's father had given Brian a job when he couldn't find work anywhere in town, because of his checkered past—a past that was deeply entwined with the troublesome Matthew Brewer. But Olly thought Brian was a good guy, if a bit naive, and that he'd been swept up in the wrong crowd.

It was that job that had helped him get back on his feet and be able to start his ghost tours business.

"I promise I won't breathe a word of it to anyone besides Ethan. Finding his mom's letters is really important to him, so I'm glad you told me."

Brian nodded and then headed back toward the group, catching the eye of the male writer and engaging him in conversation. They were due to leave in five minutes and head to the haunted mansion.

Monroe's mind was swirling and a little flame of hope flickered in her chest. If Ethan found out that his father had been from Forever Falls, then maybe he'd have reason to stay. And for some reason, that made her feel far, *far* happier than it should.

CHAPTER SIXTEEN

Ethan parked his rental at the Krick mansion, along with the other tour participants. The building was a behemoth, two stories with a generous-looking attic up top. The windows had shutters that were all painted a uniform navy blue, which contrasted against the pale gray weatherboards. Or maybe they were green? It was hard to tell in the dim light.

"Are you ready to be scared?" she asked with a grin as they got out of the car. Her cheeks were flushed from the cold and she looked as happy as a kid about to enter a candy store.

He glanced up at the big old house. "I guess this is a bad time to tell you I don't love scary things?"

"Really?" Monroe rubbed her hands together as they walked over to where Brian was standing, waiting for the tour participants to assemble. "Not into horror movies?"

"Nope." He shook his head and wrinkled his nose. "Why would I want to watch something where the whole purpose was to freak me out? I watch movies to relax."

"But it's romantic, having an excuse to grab someone's hand in the dark and snuggle up close."

He raised an eyebrow. "Is that why you brought me here?"

"I could have done that a lot cheaper by finding some crappy B-grade horror movie on Netflix," she pointed out, but Ethan pulled her into his side anyway, his arm draping around her shoulders.

It felt familiar and comforting to have her lean into him. Was that because they were out in public and it was part of the show? Or because she wanted to?

Monroe's hair spilled down over his coat and her gloved hand rested at his chest. It stirred something inside him, like an awakening of a part he'd buried this past year. The old Ethan who had a twenty-year plan for the future, who had goals and aspirations, and who knew where he was going. A man who knew that he wanted a loving partner at his side and a family to come.

But his sense of family had been deeply shaken.

"Welcome to the Krick mansion," Brian said, motioning for the group to come closer to him. "This is one of the most haunted mansions not only in the state, but in the whole country. Built in 1875 by Theodore Thomas Krick for his family, this house is more than seven-thousand square feet in size and reportedly took a team of 100 men almost two years to build it. You'll find an incredible amount of workmanship inside, including hand-carved moldings, hand-turned wood balustrades on the big staircase, and other fine work that we don't see in modern buildings."

"That doesn't sound too scary." Ethan lowered his head and whispered into Monroe's ear. "Maybe I won't need to hold your hand after all."

"I don't get scared," she said, looking up at him with a cocky smile.

"Oh no, I meant for me. You're my protector, okay?"

She laughed, nudging him with her elbow because she knew he was just teasing. "Big bad Thor's afraid of a few little ghosts? I don't believe it."

"But you're not here to appreciate the architecture of a bygone era, right?" Brian flicked on a torch and started to hand them out to the group. Now Ethan knew why they'd signed a waiver at the tour office—looked like they were going into the house in the dark, at least to start the night off.

Ethan had to hand it to him, Brian was quite the show-man.

"Follow me, folks, and watch your step. I don't want anyone getting hurt, but this is an experiential tour so I want you to have the full effect. We won't have the lights on for a while." He started up toward the stairs.

Monroe held their torch and she flicked it on, sticking it under her chin as if she was about to tell a ghost story. "Oooh spooky."

"Don't antagonize the otherworldly spirits," Ethan said drily. "Those people are always the first to die in horror movies."

"Pfft." Monroe waved her hand. "I know all the horror movie rules. One, always check behind you. Two, don't run up the stairs when you can go out the front door. Three, never say 'I'll be right back,' and four, definitely, absolutely do *not* go down into the basement."

"I feel much safer now, thank you," he quipped.

"You're really missing out. The horror genre has a lot to offer." They trailed behind at the end of the group and followed Brian into the house. "*The Shining, Texas Chainsaw Massacre, The Exorcist,*" she said. "Or if you like something more modern, *Get Out* was phenomenal. Hell, I'd even put *Scream* up there because it was so fresh at the time."

"Pass." Ethan shook his head. "I prefer my movies with more explosions and less stabbings."

They paused in the foyer of the old house, torchlights bouncing all around. There was definitely something eerie about the house.

"Let's get to the heart of why this house has the reputation it does," Brian said to the group. "Upon its completion in 1875, the Krick family moved in. There were seven of them in total—Theodore, his wife Emily, their three daughters Patricia, Grace, and Lillian. Plus Emily's mother, Rose, and their maid, Anna. Within five years, only one of them was left alive."

Someone in the group gasped and Ethan felt goose bumps ripple across his skin. There was a coldness to the house, as though he could gauge the emptiness and loss by the temperature.

Okay now you're being ridiculous.

"Grace was the first to die in the house. Within days of them moving in, she contracted a bacterial illness and passed away. A year later, the youngest girl Lillian drowned in the bathtub upstairs. But no one was ever able to figure out why, because she was very capable of bathing herself and there was nothing to indicate she'd slipped and hit her head, or anything like that."

Brian paused for a moment, letting the creaking of the old house and wind outside amp up the tension.

"Theodore's grief caused him to struggle in keeping control of his life and his business started to suffer. He turned to alcohol and was often found wandering the grounds, drunk. Two years later his wife fell down the stairs and died, and many speculated that Theodore pushed her in a drunken rage."

Brian continued on with the story, slowly walking the group through the house. Monroe and Ethan lingered behind, their torch off. Monroe reached for Ethan's hand. "Scared yet?"

"It sounds like a whole lot of bad luck to me, not the interference of supernatural forces," he replied. "But I *do* think this place is creepy."

Outside the wind whipped a tree branch across the glass and they both startled, giggling nervously. Monroe squeezed Ethan's hand. It was hard to be scared with her touching him—because whatever part of his brain was responsible for fear was being steadily overridden by the part responsible for…well, other parts of him.

She released him as they had to pass through a narrow doorway, and Ethan let his hands drift to her hips as he followed her. Ahead of them, torchlight bounced around a dining room, glancing off some eerie carvings of crows on a wooden piece of furniture.

Monroe slowed and Ethan pressed up behind her, feeling the curve of her backside brush the front of his crotch. It was probably horribly inappropriate that he was getting hard thinking about Monroe and the breathy sounds she made when she came while Brian was talking about the grisly murder of the Krick family's maid. But Ethan could only seem to concentrate on the heat coming from Monroe's body and how he could touch her stealthily in the dark. They paused in the dining room and he wrapped both arms around her from behind, holding her hard against him. She didn't try to break free. In fact, she rocked back against him as if encouraging him.

He leaned forward, bringing his lips down behind her ear. "Are you doing that on purpose, Monroe?"

"Doing what?" she said quietly, her innocence belied by the cheeky look she threw over one shoulder.

"How does this fit into your rules for surviving a horror movie?"

"Not great," she admitted. "The ones who have sex usually end up dead pretty early on."

"Shame."

The group moved on up ahead, but Monroe stayed stock-still. As the sound of Brian's talking grew softer as they moved into the next room, the torchlight fading, Ethan's senses were heightened. The sound of Monroe's breath grew louder and he could swear he felt her pulse jumping as he trailed his hand down the side of her neck, sweeping her hair to one side.

"This is very naughty," she whispered as he pressed his lips to her neck. "Someone might catch us."

Her skin was warm and the enticing scent of her perfume wound through his bloodstream. "You mean the ghosts might catch us."

She kept her head tilted to one side so he could keep kissing her. Ethan found the hem of her sweater between the lapels of her open coat, and slipped one hand up underneath. Warm flesh greeted his eager fingers and he searched higher, finding the curve of her breast and the lacy texture of her bra.

When he pinched her already hard nipple, she gasped and pressed back against him, rubbing her backside where Ethan was already rock hard.

"This is so wrong," he muttered. But that made it even

more exciting.

He spun Monroe around and pressed her to the wall, something rattling above her head. "You're so bad," she whispered. "I love it."

He crushed his mouth down to hers, kissing her hard and deep, his hand still palming her breast. He wanted nothing more than to strip her down and spend the whole night exploring her body, learning all the things he missed last time and savoring every single second with her.

How could he want her so much? So soon?

Her hips rocked against his, encouraging a soft yet guttural sound from his lips and the way she gripped onto him was everything. There was something about the darkness, the people in the next room, the fact that this relationship was only supposed to be for show...all of it made the kiss hotter than anything Ethan had experienced before. Or maybe it was none of those things.

Maybe it was one factor and one factor only: *Monroe*.

This woman was under his skin. She was in his head and knocking on his heart and dancing in his mind.

"You're so sexy," he murmured against her lips, planting one palm on the wall next to her head. "And this isn't supposed to mean a bloody thing, but I can't keep my hands off you."

"I don't want you to keep your hands off me, Ethan." Her lips found his again and she coaxed him open, her tongue sliding against his. "Don't stop."

He reached down for the back of her leg, finding her knee and hooking his palm behind it so he could drag it up and over his hip. Her coat bunched and he pressed against her, applying pressure where he knew she wanted it. He was right, because one brush of the sensitive spot between her legs and she was mewling.

"Monroe? Ethan?"

Ethan jumped back at the sound of their names being called from within the house. Oops. Looked like the tour leader had realized he'd lost two of his group.

"Come on," Ethan said, taking Monroe's hand. "We'd better catch up before Brian worries."

"Such a Boy Scout," Monroe teased.

"For now." He lowered his lips to her ear. "But when this tour is over, we're going back to your place, okay? You told me not to stop and I don't plan to."

"Good." She stared him right in the eye, meeting his intensity with her own. That was the part of her that he found so attractive—that fighting spirit, that willfulness.

Tonight, he was going to watch her come undone all over again.

• • •

Monroe was on pins and needles the whole way home after the ghost tour. She had information to give to Ethan, but part of her was worried that if she brought it up now then he'd go right back to the inn. And the selfish part of her didn't want to risk that happening.

She wanted Ethan in her apartment. In her bed. In her arms.

You shouldn't feel like this.

She tried to tell herself it was just sex, but the fact was she'd never found casual hookups appealing. Because a hot guy was one thing, but Monroe needed more than abs and a great smile. She needed to be attracted to what was underneath all of that.

And when it came to Ethan…he ticked all the boxes. Big heart, sense of humor, family values. The way he'd been with her father and sisters the night of the dinner at Loren's house, well that alone would have been enough to have Monroe falling head over heels.

What if he doesn't want to stay?

He had baggage. They both did.

This wasn't like falling in love the first time and not knowing the pain that could come. They'd both loved before, both lost before.

Ethan pulled the car up in front of her apartment building and killed the engine. "You're quiet," he said.

"So are you."

The lights of oncoming vehicles played across his handsome features, making his eyes glow blue and his jaw seem even sharper and more devastating.

"I'm wondering what it means if we go up together," he said.

"How so?"

"For something that's supposed to be fake, I'm having a hard time drawing a line in my head."

Her breath caught in her throat. He was so open, so willing to let her in. That made him unlike any other man Monroe had ever known—it made him unlike *her*. But maybe she could learn a thing or two from him about speaking her truth. About putting herself out in the world even if the outcome was uncertain.

"Me too," she admitted. "I don't have all the answers. But I know I very much want you to come upstairs and I wouldn't be mad if I woke up tomorrow morning and found you sleeping next to me."

The car interior was dead silent for a heartbeat. Then two. Three.

"I wouldn't be mad about that, either," he said.

It was raining outside and the windshield was streaked with water, blurring the traffic lights and car lights. It looked like a Monet painting, soft-focused and beautiful.

"So we're doing it then?" she said, her breath stuttering. "Putting fake on hold for a night?"

He reached for her hand and brought her fingers to his lips. The warm breath felt good on her skin and the pressure of his kiss even better. "Let's do it."

They got out of the car and ran through the rain, reaching the door beside the bakery in a few seconds. But it was enough for the unrelenting drops to saturate her hair, and they stumbled into the stairwell, running up the steps as fast as they could. Ethan's hands were already on her as she fumbled with her keys. The door opened and they tumbled through. Ethan pushed it shut behind him and shrugged out of his coat, hanging it on the hook by the door, and she did the same. The water dropped onto the floor, making soft *plink, plink, plink* sounds.

Then, without hesitation, he crushed his lips down to hers, making her stumble back against the couch. The tightly-coiled restraint they'd held in the car ride home snapped—it happened instantaneously and irreparably. His hands were in her hair, his lips coaxing hers open, and she met him with passion. He tasted of mint and rain, smelled as heavy and powerful as a thunderstorm.

She couldn't get enough of him. Every moment he

wasn't with her, she wanted him to be. Every moment they were together, she dreaded it ending. Whenever her phone pinged, her heart hoped it was him.

"God, you taste good." His hand came up under her sweater to palm her breast.

Her head dropped back as he kissed along her neck, stubble scratching and teeth gently scraping. She fisted her hands in his hair, trying to keep her balance. But there was no point. Resistance was futile.

Ethan Hammersmith had totally and irrevocably knocked her world off its axis.

It shouldn't be this way. They were supposed to be faking it. And technically Monroe was still married…

Shit. She still hadn't told him about that. Why? She had no idea. Part of her rationalized that it didn't matter. It wasn't like she'd seen her ex—her ex who was engaged to someone else—and this thing with Ethan wasn't real.

It isn't real. It isn't real. It isn't real.

Maybe if she thought it enough times then she would believe it.

But the way he was kissing her now—like it was the key to their shared survival—tempted her to believe otherwise. She would tell him. About the divorce, about Lottie. Everything.

Tomorrow.

"Ethan," she sighed as he pushed his other hand underneath her sweater and felt around the back, growling in frustration.

"Hmm-mmm." His mouth was otherwise occupied with sucking at the skin on her neck.

"Front closure," she gasped.

He fumbled with the bra, finally getting it open, his breath hissing with satisfaction. Now he could touch her more fully. His hands were at her breasts, thumbs brushing her peaked nipples. Everything ached. Everything *yearned*.

No matter how satiated she felt after one encounter, her hunger for him returned with force.

"Yes," she moaned.

But Ethan wasn't content to stop there. He planted his hands on her hips and hoisted her up onto the back of the couch, roughly nudging her legs apart with his thighs so he could get closer. She wrapped her arms around his neck and hauled his mouth down to hers. Through her jeans, she could feel the hardness of him. He pressed between her legs, smoothing his hands around to her butt so he could rock against her. But it wasn't enough.

"Undress me," she whispered. "I need to feel you."

• • •

Goddammit. What the hell was he doing right now? His head was in a tailspin. He wanted Monroe with a hunger that he'd never thought was possible. It shocked him. The strength of his feelings were…

Unpredictable. Unstoppable.

He yanked her sweater up over her head and shoved the open bra from her shoulders. She arched for him, letting him have it all. He toyed with Monroe's hair, pushing it back over her shoulders because he loved nothing more than watching those curls spring free and loose down her back. He couldn't stop himself from wanting to be here more than anywhere else on the face of the earth.

With her. For her.

Monroe reached for the hem of his sweater, yanking the fabric up and trapping his arms above his head. "Ugh, those awful muscles again."

A wicked grin curved on his lips, almost blotting out the worries flying around in his head. "You can turn the lights out, if you want."

"Never." Her dark eyes almost glowed in the soft, orange light of the standing lamp in the corner of the room. Outside, rain splattered the window in a steady beat. "I don't want to miss a second of this."

"Me neither."

Did she feel it, too? That connection. That spark. That thing that told him this could be everything.

If he wasn't careful, he'd dig a hole he'd never escape from.

"I'm glad you're here," she whispered.

Seeing Monroe be vulnerable with him…God, it was everything. Because she didn't give out her truth easily or freely or often, as far as he had seen. But as he'd gotten to know her, peeling back her layers one by one, he'd seen the side of her that she'd shamed and hidden away. The side of her that had been hurt so badly in the past.

Guilt stabbed him in the gut. A storm cloud of doubt loomed over them—his indeterminate but inevitable departure. His newly formed trust issues.

Ethan had no idea what he was going to do about any of it. But right now, none of that seemed important. At least, not as important as showing Monroe what she meant to him. He wanted to drown in her. He wanted to love her so hard that the only option was for her to fall asleep with her body curled up next to his. He wanted to hold her and promise her that everything would be okay.

But you don't know that. Everything may very well not *be okay.*

He stroked a hand up and down her back, tracing her spine with his fingertips as they kissed. Slow this time. Gentle and exploratory. Monroe slipped down and grabbed Ethan's hand, leading him around to the other side of the couch.

They were both topless and in their jeans, and Monroe shimmied hers over her hips, letting them slide to the floor. He followed suit, both of them stripping down until there was nothing between them. Ethan pulled Monroe into his arms and lowered them to the couch, so he was sitting and she was straddling his lap.

Her arms draped over his shoulders and the back of the couch, and she looked at him with that sexy, coy smile he'd come to love seeing on her.

"What?" he asked.

"Nothing." She rocked her hips back and forth, teasing him. Not that he needed it; he was already harder than granite.

"Doesn't look like nothing." He nuzzled the side of her neck, enjoying the way she always sighed when he hit her favorite spot.

Monroe reached for a blanket that was hanging over one arm of the couch and wrapped it around her like a cape. It was a little chilly in the apartment and he pulled the blanket around him, too, trapping them together inside.

"I was just thinking…" She looked down, her telltale flush creeping over her cheeks. "This has been good."

218 FOREVER STARTS NOW

"Good?" He raised an eyebrow. "The way you were screaming my name last time I'd say it was more than good."

"I don't mean the sex." She could barely look at him. "I mean, working on things together. Having a partner in crime."

You shouldn't be doing this.

He was getting in too deep. *She* was getting in too deep. None of this was supposed to be about helping one another improve their lives. And it certainly wasn't supposed to be about feeling proud of it. But he would be lying through his front teeth if he denied that it felt like sunshine and the good parts of life he thought he'd lost. In fact, being with Monroe felt a whole lot like putting himself back together. Like being the Ethan he was before his life had fallen apart.

"You're about to say something sweet," she said with a smile.

Shit. It terrified him to think she could read him so easily. That even if he tried to hide things from her—like the softer parts of him—she could sniff them out with ease.

"I'd rather taste something sweet." He shook the unsettling thoughts from his head and reached down between them to find her wet and ready. He toyed with her sex, drawing a sharp gasp from her. "You're a goddess, Monroe."

"I'm just a woman." Her eyes fluttered shut and she rocked against his hand. "Just your average, run-of-the-mill person."

"No, you're not." He said the words so harshly that her eyes snapped open and her mouth dropped open in surprise. "You're a wonderful, full-of-potential person."

For a moment they just sat there, staring one another down. Dammit, he knew Monroe's confidence issues were none of his business but he wanted her to see in herself what she saw in him. He wanted her to *believe* she was capable of everything she'd set out to achieve before the demise of her marriage and the family fallout that had broken her heart.

"You are so much more than what you give yourself credit for," he said, shaking his head.

Monroe looked away, but he drew her face back to his, forcing her to meet his gaze. He looked at her long and hard, wanting more than anything for her to see that he was sincere. That he...

That you what? Care? That you feel something for her?

They were dangerous thoughts. Pointless thoughts. Because he was inching closer to the truth and once he did, there'd be nothing else for him here. No more ghosts to chase, no family to find. Nothing. At some point he had to go back to Australia and pick up the pieces of his shattered life.

She rolled her hips up, encouraging him to press at the spot between her legs, seeking out her entrance. "I want you, Ethan."

The words were like a sledgehammer to his restraint. How did she slay him like that? How did she take everything he thought he knew and snap it clean in two?

She grabbed a condom from her bedroom and brought it back, still wearing the blanket. It was huge and swept the ground around her, making her look like Little Red Riding Hood. Ethan sheathed himself and pulled her back onto his lap.

"You're magnificent," he told her, cradling her face with both his hands. "And you should never think otherwise."

She kissed him long and hard, and he grasped her hips, pulling her down and making her sink onto him. When it felt right, he pushed up, burying himself inside her, rewarded with her sharp gasp so close to his ear that he felt it right down to his toes. It was perfect.

He rocked back and forth, thrusting up deep each time. He lost himself in her body—in the springing curls on her head and the soft, demanding lips and her silky, freckled skin. He lost himself in her dark gaze and her wandering hands and the needy little whimpers she made as he held her tight.

"Yes, Ethan," she moaned as her thighs clenched around his hips. He smothered her words with a kiss, driving one hand into her hair and keeping his other arm wrapped around her waist, holding them as close as possible. "I..."

His heart stuttered, not knowing whether he wanted to hear what she was going to say next or not. Not knowing whether he was strong enough to withstand it, given the ticking countdown that would soon lead him away.

"I like you a lot," she whispered, looking him right in the eye as she touched his cheek.

"I like you a lot, too, Monroe."

It turned out that Ethan hadn't lost himself at all.

Because he was exactly where he wanted to be.

CHAPTER SEVENTEEN

Monroe stirred sometime later—was a minute or an hour? Who knew? Heck, it could have been a week for how sleepy and relaxed she felt. Ethan was beneath her on the couch, naked and warm. She laid her head on his chest and his big arms held her in place, the blanket covering them both.

She could hear his heart beating. The steady thump lulled her into a state of bliss and contentment, and he gently stroked her back.

A thought struck her out of nowhere—this was the happiest she'd been in a very long time. Not just since she'd separated from Brendan, but for quite a while before that, too. On her long, lonely nights she'd reflected on the past. Her marriage had been over well before she found out about the affair. She just hadn't admitted it to herself.

"What are you thinking?" he asked. "I can hear your brain cogs turning from here."

She smiled. "Nothin'. You turned me to mush."

"Good. That's how it should be."

Monroe watched the shadows shifting on the floor beneath the window overlooking Main Street. The rain was pouring even harder now and it caused the light to shift and distort. Ethan looked utterly delicious. His blue eyes were hooded and his hair was sticking out in all directions, a reminder that they'd been a little rough and ready with one another in the best way possible.

"I found out something that might help your search," she said.

That hazy, dreamy look on his face vanished like a magician's trick, replaced by coiled anticipation. "Tell me."

"Brian pulled me aside while we were in the first part of the tour, but he made me swear that we would keep it on the down low." She searched his face. Could she trust him not to rat Brian out? "I need you to promise that you won't break my word with him."

"How can I promise that before I even know what you're going to tell me?"

"Because I have to keep living here, Ethan. This is going to be my home for as long into the future as I can see." She sucked in a breath. "And I don't break promises."

They stared one another down for a long moment, bodies still entwined, hearts still scarred. But eventually Ethan nodded. "Okay, I won't tell anyone."

"Brian thinks that if there's any evidence left of the letters they'll be with Lottie May."

"Lottie?" Ethan blinked. "Really?"

She told him the story about the removal of Matthew's mother's personal effects after her passing, and how Lottie turned up begging Brian not to trash the sentimental items.

"She *did* indicate that they were friends." Ethan rubbed a hand over his face, like he was trying to wake himself up. "She cornered me after I'd visited the funeral home, wanting to know why I was poking around in things. She said she hoped Matthew Brewer, at least this one, wasn't my father, and that she blamed him for his mother's death."

"But he died before his mother." Monroe shook her head.

"I think she meant more that his mother died of a broken heart."

"Oh." Monroe let some memories roll around in her head. "Brian said she was crying and I don't think anyone has ever seen Lottie cry. Not even that one time that she slipped and broke her arm in three places."

A strange expression crossed over Ethan's face. "I've seen her cry."

"When?"

"She was looking over something in her office and I went to see if she was okay. She snapped at me, like I thought she would, but…" His eyes flicked back and forth like he was running a memory on loop in his head. "She was reading a letter, I think. She shoved it in her office drawer when she saw me standing there."

"I guess no matter how tough someone seems on the outside, we all have our own personal heartaches."

"Like you," he said softly, his fingers toying with a curly strand of her hair. "You have a tough shell, but on the inside you're like a big old bundle of fairy floss."

"I am not!" Then she laughed. "What's fairy floss?"

"How can you protest without even knowing what I'm saying?" he chided.

"I get the context from your tone."

"Fairy Floss is that sticky pink stuff they serve at carnivals and amusement parks. I think you call it something else?" He screwed his nose up while he was thinking. "Cotton Candy."

"You call it Fairy Floss in Australia? That's adorable." She laughed, but then she narrowed her eyes. "And I am not Fairy Floss or Cotton Candy or any other sweet, soft thing on the inside. Just because I let you in my pants doesn't mean you get to psychoanalyze me."

She was only defensive because of how true his comment hit. Monroe *was* soft and squishy on the inside. Back in the day, pre-betrayal, she'd been way more soft and squishy on the outside, too. Hence, her getting hurt so badly.

"I call it like I see it," he said, continuing to play with her hair. "It's not a bad thing, complexity is sexy."

"Said no man ever," she scoffed.

"*I* think it's sexy. When you meet a person, you want lots of layers to peel back and interesting things to discover. How boring would it be if you met someone and then that was it—no discovery, no learning, nothing to figure out."

"You just like puzzles." She laughed. "I'm pretty sure most guys want their women to be straightforward. What you see is what you get."

"Not me," he said resolutely. "Besides, nobody is truly one-dimensional and anyone trying to appear that way is hiding something or acting the way they *think* they should act."

"And this concludes our psychoanalysis hour with Dr. Ethan Hammersmith."

He cringed, but then shook his head as if trying to shake something off.

"What?" she asked.

"My last name. I can't stand the sound of it now." He offered her a weak smile and Monroe's heart almost burst right on the spot, flooding her with empathy for this incredible man and all he'd been through. All the lies he'd been told and the secrets he'd had kept from him.

Like you're any better. He doesn't even know your divorce failed and that technically you're still married.

She opened her mouth to tell him, but no words would come out. What if he branded her the same as his mother, just another woman who'd lied to him? And it was a lie, if even only by omission. At the beginning it didn't seem to matter, because all this was meant to be fake. They owed one another nothing, had no promises beyond their arrangement.

But now…

You care about him.

She did. Deep down she knew that Ethan was special to her, that what they had *wasn't* just some arrangement with benefits. That he was the kind of man who had the potential to open up and heal her battered heart, and that she could do the same for him.

But if she told him the truth now, would she even have the chance to explain herself? He'd gotten what he wanted: information. He knew that if his father grew up here, Lottie would likely be the one to have answers.

He didn't need Monroe anymore.

"Hey?" Ethan caught her chin and tipped her face up. "You okay? You went deathly quiet for a minute there."

"Just tired," she said weakly. "You wore me out."

"You sure?" There it was, an opening.

She could tell him everything now and hope that he wouldn't walk out on her. She could hope that this fragile bond would survive her truth and that maybe there was a tiny hope Ethan might stay.

It's a hope on a hope on a hope.

Deep down she knew the odds were stacked against

them, but the thought of having him leave her now, after the night they'd shared, after the passion that had burned brightly between them, after the realization that he meant something to her...she wasn't sure her heart could take the pain of it.

How could a heart like hers withstand another blow?

"I'm sure," she said, the lie tasting bitter on her tongue.

Part of her knew this would come back to bite her, but she promised herself that she *would* tell him...just as soon as she found the right moment.

• • •

Ethan could *not* believe he was in this predicament. Moreover, he could not believe that he'd let himself feel good about helping Monroe, especially when it came at the expense of his own dignity.

But here he was, dressed as Thor and crouching down to take pictures with two little boys whose smiles were pure sunshine. Monroe was standing next to him, a tray of Thor-inspired cupcakes in her hand. They'd changed the plan a little from her initial idea, getting some vouchers printed to hand out with the cupcakes offering people a discount if they came back and spent a certain amount, rather than rewarding them with a cupcake after having a meal.

Ethan might have been a tech guy, but working in consulting had taught him a thing or two about fostering customer relationships and the importance of a goodwill gesture. He and Monroe had put a business plan together for the Sunshine Diner, working on it over the three nights since the ghost tour. That was their routine now—during the day she worked at the diner and he continued helping Lottie at the inn and continued searching for a connection between his mother and father in Cape Cod. At night he and Monroe planned and had dinner and made love until they both collapsed in a tired heap in her bed.

He loved every second of it.

Well…except this.

"Don't you look like a real superhero!" a woman said, eyeing him with a smile curving on her bright red lips. "Do you take pictures with adults as well as kids?"

"Sure." He smiled good-naturedly, shooting Monroe a look out of the corner of his eye, but she was too busy trying not to laugh to offer him any sympathy.

They'd bought his costume from a shop one town over—black and gold chest plate, a red cape, wrist cuffs and, of course, a hammer. The costume was cheap and Ethan was pretty sure that it was made of 100 percent polyester, but according to Monroe it was tight in all the right places… whatever that meant.

The woman came to stand next to Ethan, handing her phone to a friend. She slid right up next to him, slipping one arm around his waist and leaning in so that her breasts squished against him.

"Say cheese," the friend called out as she took a few photos.

"You really do look like him," the woman said, shaking her head.

"Oh really? That's the first time I've heard it," he quipped. "Make sure you grab a cupcake and come back to the Sunshine Diner with your voucher."

"Oh I *will*." The woman giggled and went back to her friend, collecting her goodies from Monroe on the way.

Darlene poked her head out from the front door of the diner, a big smile on her face. "I have to tell you two, we have reservations for the next few weeks. Nobody ever makes a reservation!"

And *that* made it all worth it. Seeing the beaming smile on Monroe's face and the lightness in Darlene's voice, knowing that he was doing something to help a business that made an impact in their lives…yeah, wearing a cheesy costume was totally worth it.

When there was a lull in activity, Monroe came over with a near-empty tray of cupcakes. Three little cakes were left. "Nobody wants this one because it has a wonky marshmallow."

"I'll take it." Ethan swiped the cupcake off the tray and used the pretzel stick to pry the marshmallow hammer off. He stuck it into his mouth and chewed.

As they were standing around, Taylor approached them with a wave. She wore black jeans with a frayed slash across one knee, motorcycle boots, and a bright red leather jacket over what looked like a Metallica concert T-shirt. Her tattoos peeked out where the jacket sleeve ended on her right wrist.

"I heard there were cupcakes going around," she said, reaching for the tray. "Or are these for customers only?"

"Nah, you can have one. We're pretty much done anyway," Monroe said. "All the vouchers have been handed out and I think I have tortured poor Ethan well enough, making him take photos with people and wear that costume out in the chill for two hours."

"It's hot." Taylor winked and took a bite out of her cupcake. "Damn, Monroe, this is amazing."

"It's just a cupcake."

"No, it's not *just* anything." Taylor looked over to Ethan. "Can you try and talk some sense into this woman? She shouldn't be working here putting money in someone else's pocket when this is what she can create."

"Maybe I don't want to work for myself," Monroe said, frowning. "I get that you've always had issues with answering to people, but—"

"You haven't?" Taylor snorted. "Please. Independence and a stubborn streak run in every Roberts woman in our family. It's part of our DNA."

"You're as bad as Loren," Monroe grumbled.

On the surface people might think them very different—especially with Taylor's leather and tattoos, versus Monroe's curls and freckles. But under all that surface stuff, he could see how similar all three sisters were. How fiercely they loved one another, to the point that they didn't mind ruffling a few feathers to speak up for something they believed in.

"Running a business is a whole lot of work," Monroe said, looking to Ethan for support.

"I think Taylor has a point." He shoved the last bit of his cupcake into his mouth and savored the perfect blend of salty and sweet. "You're exceptionally talented and while I know you take your job here very seriously, I think you could do more."

She gaped at him. "You're supposed to take my side."

"I take the side of truth." He shrugged in a sorry-not-sorry fashion.

"I knew I liked you," Taylor said with a grin.

"You can have him." Monroe rolled her eyes. "One boyfriend, going free."

"I already got my dream man, no offense." Taylor patted Ethan on the arm. "All right, I'd better get back to the shop. I promised Tim I'd bring him back a coffee."

Ethan waved as Taylor made her way off down the street.

"I stand by it," Ethan said to Monroe. "I admire your tenacity and desire to breathe new life into the diner, but your talent is wasted here."

Monroe opened her mouth like she was about to shoot a comeback at him, but something stopped her. Instead, she sighed.

"I've thought about it a lot over the years," she admitted. "Dreamed about it, even."

"Then why not pursue it?"

She looked at the lone cupcake sitting on her tray. It was a small morsel of perfection—the shape, size, color… everything looked professional. They'd spent all morning listening to people gushing over how good her baking tasted and he saw the pleasure Monroe took in hearing it. She *loved* to bake. Anyone could see that.

"Hey, if baking is purely about the joy of creation, then don't let anyone tell you that you have to make it a business," he said. "But something in my gut tells me that it's not a lack of desire holding you back. Am I wrong?"

"No," she admitted, barely meeting his eye.

"Then what is?"

"I guess… I don't trust that good things will last." Her dark brown gaze dragged back up to him. "What if I fail?"

"What if you don't?" he replied. "What if instead you create something amazing?"

"Were you born with enough confidence for an army, or did you acquire that somewhere along the way?"

Ethan dropped his fake hammer down and slipped an arm around Monroe's waist, drawing her closer. "I simply believe that I'm living my life for a reason. That reason has changed a bit in recent times, of course, but it's not confidence so much as an understanding that I'm doing what I'm meant to be doing. Do I have any idea if I'm going to succeed? No, because nobody knows the future. But does that deter me from trying? No, and it shouldn't deter you, either. What's the point of living if you don't try anything new?"

Monroe let out a long breath and her eyes sparkled when they looked up at him. He saw her now, every part of her. The sad bits and the vulnerable bits and the hurt bits and that tiny, flickering flame of hope that hadn't yet been extinguished.

"You deserve to try everything," he said softly. "Every single thing you want."

She pressed up onto her toes, the tray clattering to the ground as she wound her arms around his neck and pressed her body to his, kissing him long and deep. Her lips coaxed his open and her tongue slid into his mouth and her hands drove into his hair.

This wasn't a kiss of lust. It was raw and open and terrifying. It was a kiss that promised a future, the kind of future that Ethan had once dreamed about, a future that still hovered in the back of his mind like a ghost.

A future that he could see with Monroe.

She pulled back, one hand cupping his jaw, and she looked him deep in the eyes. There was something about the way she looked at him that said maybe she saw all the bits of him, too.

She opened her mouth to say something, but before she could, a voice called out, "Monroe!"

And at that moment, based on the way she stiffened in his arms, Ethan had the feeling that something was about to go horribly wrong.

CHAPTER EIGHTEEN

Oh no…not now.

Monroe's breath stuttered in the back of her throat. It was a good thing Loren wasn't standing next to her, because Monroe let out every curse she knew under her breath. The irony was not lost on her that the very thing she'd requested at the beginning of their arrangement—a kiss without questions that she could use like an ace in her back pocket should her ex show up—was actually the very *last* thing Monroe wanted right now.

And yet, Brendan stood on the sidewalk of the Forever Falls main strip, watching her kiss a man with everything she had. And there had been nothing fake about it.

"Who's that?" Ethan asked as Monroe stepped back out of his grip, almost slipping on the tray she'd dropped. The last little cupcake had toppled onto the footpath and she stepped on it, squashing the frosting and fluffy cake into the ground with her boot. The pretzel stick snapped like a twig.

"Um, no one. Give me a minute." Flustered, she scooped up the tray and stomped her boot against the ground, dislodging the frosting like she did with snow build up. "Sorry, Ethan."

She left him standing there, brow furrowed, as she stalked toward her should-have-been-ex-husband. Brendan looked slick, like always. He was wearing a suit, which seemed ridiculous considering there was no earthly reason to be wearing one in Forever Falls. Even the people from the local accounting firm barely wore a suit to work. But that was Brendan's style—he always had to look like the most important person in the room. His hair was overly styled and he had a bit of a tan, which was weird for February. Fake tan? Possibly. Or maybe he'd taken Amber on vacation.

"What do you want?" she asked coldly, as she stopped in front of him, folding her arms across her chest.

"You *know* what I want." But Brendan's eyes weren't on Monroe. Oh no, they drifted past her to where Ethan stood in front of the diner. There was a hard set to his jaw, almost like he was grinding his back teeth.

Was he…jealous?

"And I told you I've been busy and your needs are not my number one priority anymore."

"Let's be real, my needs were never your number one priority," he snapped. That's when the handsome surface cracked and the ugliness inside him poked out. How had it taken her so long to see below the surface? "You were too busy dropping everything for your father and your sisters."

"I love my family." She rolled her eyes. "What a *horrible* wife that must have made me."

"*Makes* you. We're still married remember?"

In true form, Monroe had the complete inability to hide her emotions and she automatically tensed when he spoke. That wasn't good, because Brendan was perceptive—it was how he'd managed to hide the affair for so long.

"He doesn't know?" The bastard had the audacity to laugh.

"I never said that."

"Didn't need to, cupcake." He grinned and Monroe cringed at the nickname. "Like always, your face tells a thousand words. Good to see some things haven't changed. You know, I'd heard from folks around town that you were chronically single, so I have to admit this is quite the surprise…and good timing."

"What's *that* supposed to mean?"

Brendan lifted one suited shoulder into a shrug. "I'm not saying that you got some schmuck to play the part around the time you figured out I'd be coming back to this shit-hole of a town, but it seems mighty coincidental is all."

"Only if you put yourself at the center of the universe… speaking of things that haven't changed," she replied tartly. "And my relationship status is none of your business. I can't imagine why you'd care to follow up on me after you left town. You had everything you wanted, so why would you give a crap what I'm doing?"

Brendan's expression faltered for a bit, but his icy re-solve slid back into place in a second. "I don't care. People talk of their own volition, that's all."

At that moment, Monroe felt a presence behind her and judging by the smug smile morphing on Brendan's lips, she knew exactly what was about to happen. There was no way to get around it. Ethan came up beside Monroe, his hand protectively at her back and his blue eyes narrowed in concern.

She had two choices: let Brendan get one over her again, thus remaining passive in her life…or take control back and start living.

Brendan stuck his hand out. "Hi, there, I'm—"

"Ethan, I'd like you to meet Brendan…" She sucked in a

breath. "My husband."

"Husband?" Ethan raised an eyebrow, his gaze remained locked on Brendan. "This is the guy who ran off with your cousin?"

Brendan's jaw tightened. His hand hung in the air for several more beats, but it was clear that Ethan had no intention of returning the gesture. Eventually, he dropped his arm limply by his side.

"She didn't tell you, huh?" Brendan asked, smug arrogance splashed all over his tone. "Paperwork mix-up, we're still married and for some reason Monroe has been reluctant to make it official. I'm not trying to say it's a reflection on your relationship of course, but..."

He let the implication hang in the air.

"If you have something to say, why don't you say it?" Ethan looked down on Brendan, who's runner-lean frame looked even slighter next to Ethan's muscular bulk. Not that Monroe thought Ethan was the type to let things come to blows—he was a teddy bear in a grizzly's body.

"You want me to be blunt?" Brendan said with a cold laugh. "Fine. Your girlfriend has been lying to you and it's clear she still harbors feelings for me, otherwise why delay the paperwork?"

Despite the guilt and anxiety churning in her gut, Monroe burst out laughing. "*That's* what you think? That I still love you? Good Lord, the ego on this man."

"Maybe she delayed the paperwork because she was sick of being bossed around by an asshole like yourself," Ethan replied, his demeanor cool, calm, and collected. But his hand had dropped from its place at her lower back and Monroe sensed a tightness in him.

This was not good at all.

Ethan had been lied to by his own mother, so this would *have* to come as a blow. And if it didn't, then that would be confirmation that he didn't see the special thing they shared like she did. Either way, no matter which outcome occurred, it was bad news.

Shouldn't that be good news? He got what he wanted and you got what you wanted. Your ex saw you making out with someone hot and your family finally got off your back about being single.

But it felt like a hollow victory. A meaningless victory.

Please give me a chance to explain.

"You're in denial, Thor," Brendan said with a sneer. "Nice costume, by the way. Do you do kids' parties?"

Monroe glared at her ex. "It must seem so strange to you to see a man supporting his partner."

"A partner he can't even trust," Brendan returned.

"People in glass houses shouldn't throw stones," Monroe replied. "But if getting the paperwork done means I never have to see you again, then I'll do it. I'll do it on my time, however, and on my terms. You can turn up here as much as you like, but your actions don't have any impact on me at all anymore."

Brendan's neck turned red. "You're a bitch, Monroe. You're trying to make my life difficult on purpose."

"The world *doesn't* revolve around you and your needs. If you expect the person you betrayed to drop everything simply because you asked, then your ego *is* out of control." Monroe drew her shoulders back and looked him right in the eye the way she couldn't bring herself to the first time they met with their lawyers.

Something had shifted inside her; she wasn't passive anymore. She wasn't ashamed of her marriage breaking down. She wasn't worried what people would think of her. The question she'd asked before — *what if I fail?* — was simply that, a question. It wasn't a prediction of the future, and she could answer that question however she pleased.

I won't fail. I may stumble, but if I do I will pick myself up like I've done all my life.

"Goodbye Brendan," she said, feeling a strange sense of calm wash over her. It was almost as if she was releasing the past and the last vestiges of control her ex had over her. "I hope I never see you again."

His mouth hung open as Monroe turned to Ethan, her heart pounding like she'd run a hundred-yard dash. She had no idea how he was going to react, but she owed him the truth. The whole truth this time — not just the truth she used to shield herself against the world, but the uglier bits underneath.

The bits she'd been ashamed of for far too long.

"Can we talk?" she asked. "Please."

Ethan nodded. But the light had dimmed in his eyes and she felt him closing himself off. No matter the outcome, Monroe would lay everything on the table.

Including telling Ethan how she felt about him.

· · ·

Within fifteen minutes, they were back at Monroe's place. Ethan had changed out of his Thor costume and into a pair of jeans and black hoodie, which felt necessary. He really didn't want to have this conversation dressed as a superhero.

Because frankly, he felt anything but super right now.

Monroe was technically still married and she hadn't told him. The second part of that equation mattered more to him than the first. And it hurt like a sucker-punch, which made him mad because that meant he cared about her... which was *not* part of the plan. It wasn't even adjacent to the plan. It was a whole stratosphere away from the plan.

He watched as Monroe made them some tea in the kitchen. She'd insisted, and Ethan figured it was her way of buying a little extra time to gather her thoughts. Her hair was pulled back into a pretty braid that hung down her back and it flicked as she moved with less grace than normal.

She was anxious about their chat. It radiated off her in waves.

"Here," she said, carrying two mugs to the coffee table. "Green tea with lemon."

"Thanks."

She dropped down onto the couch across from him. He'd taken the single chair to keep his distance, because his head was a messy mélange of emotions right now and he didn't want to be breathing in Monroe's sweet scent, lest it muddle his thoughts further.

"So you're married." He didn't touch the tea on the table in front of him. The steam curled upward, disappearing into the air.

"Technically, yes." She nodded. "After Brendan and Amber left town, we started divorce proceedings. At that time, I thought everything went ahead as it was supposed to and that I was officially divorced. I never followed up on it, though, because it wasn't like I had plans to ever get married again. If it wasn't for Brendan wanting to marry Amber we might not have found out for a long time. Especially since I never took his name, there was nothing to change back and I had my head buried so far into the sand after the last meeting I tried never to think about it again."

"When did you find out you were still married?" *This* was the question he wanted answered most of all—how long had she known?

"Before we started dating...pretending to date..." She shook her head, like neither one of those options was quite correct. "Long enough that I should have told you."

"Then why didn't you?"

She let out a long sigh and looked at the mug of tea cradled in her hands. Her braid hung over one shoulder and her eyes were fixed on something he couldn't see. Despite the hurt coursing through his veins, he still had the urge to reach out to her. To touch her. To comfort her.

She lied to you, just like your mother lied to you. Just like your adoptive father lied to you. Just like Sarah lied when she said she would always be there to support you.

He swallowed back the swirling dark thoughts. He and Monroe were adults, and he wasn't going to let this devolve into a finger-pointing match. The truth needed to be aired and then after that he would figure out how to proceed.

He would be cool and calm and he would *not* let her see how much it hurt.

"Honestly, at first I felt like it was none of your business. Not in a bad way, but more like...it didn't even occur to me that I should tell you. We were pretending to be together for selfish reasons and my past didn't factor into that." Her lip quivered, but she drew her shoulders back and met his gaze without wavering. "Then after we started being more than a fake relationship I was scared, honestly."

"Why?"

"Because I had started to feel things for you. I worried that if I told you I was still married and that I'd kept that information from you, it would drive you away. I was worried you'd think I was just another person who'd lied to you."

"You are just another person who's lied to me."

Monroe winced. "I know. I'm very sorry about that, Ethan. I know what it feels like to be in the dark. The fact that I've done the same thing to you makes me feel incredibly guilty."

Tears sparkled in her eyes and despite his pain, Ethan believed she was telling the truth. Monroe was a good person. Anybody could see that. And underneath her tough exterior there was a very tender heart bearing a lot of scars. Her confidence had been shaken to its core. God, her *world* had been shaken to its core.

And he knew a thing or two about that.

"I *don't* love him anymore," she said fiercely, almost sloshing some of her tea over the edge of the mug. "I did love him at one point and I think that made me blind to who he was, because I was young and he was the only man I'd been with. But him leaving me was a good thing, even though it caused my family and me a lot of pain. There's nothing left in my heart for him."

Ethan didn't quite understand the rush of relief that flooded through him. He wasn't supposed to care about any of this. He wasn't supposed to feel a bloody thing.

"I wish you'd given me a chance to understand, Monroe," he said, raking a hand through his hair. "I understand there's a big difference between a legal technicality and a real-life marriage. It's not like you'd seen him in years and if you believed you were divorced, then that would have been all I needed to know on the situation."

"I know, I know." She shook her head. "It was stupid not to say anything but…"

"But?"

"That afternoon when we were laying here on the couch," she said, pausing to bite down on her lip as a tear plopped onto her cheek. She shook her head and let her gaze drift over to the window for a second as she gathered herself. "I was wondering why the thought of telling you was so damn scary. Because being scared meant I felt like there was something to lose and how can you have something to lose in a fake relationship?"

She'd voiced the very problem swirling around his head. A problem for which he did not have a solution.

"And I *do* feel like I have something to lose." She set her mug down and knotted her hands in her lap. "I *do* feel like there's something here that isn't fake. I mean, I lied to you about something huge and you still stood up for me in front of my ex. I get a buzz every day that I know you're coming over after work. I *think* about you during the day, I plan the things we're going to have for dinner. I wonder about how you're going to touch me when we go to bed."

Ethan felt a deep push and pull inside him. Because he experienced all those things, too—thoughts of Monroe's cooking and her smile and her body and her laugh kept him going through a day of work at the inn. When he walked through her front door it was the closest thing he felt to coming home ever since he'd found out the truth about his father.

She centered him. Grounded him. Made him feel like maybe he could build a life again.

But he wasn't sure that was what he needed in his life right now. It was a commitment he wasn't sure he could honor, a prize he didn't think was his to claim.

"Ethan, I'm so sorry." Monroe brushed the tear away with the back of her hand, blinking so that no more followed. She squared her shoulders, warrior-like, ready to face the consequences of her actions. "I should have been up front about my situation. It was a cowardly thing to do and I promise that's not the kind of person I am usually."

"I know," he said softly, nodding.

"My mom and dad raised me better than to lie." She let out a harsh laugh. "They also probably raised me better than to drag my heels on contacting the lawyer simply because I hate being told what to do."

"Frankly, after meeting the guy, I understand why you did it. That is an arrogant bastard if I've ever met one." Ethan wrinkled his nose and Monroe let out a watery laugh. "First he cheats on you, then he wants to bully you into jumping when he says so? Uh no, that's not how it works."

"Truth." She let out a sigh. "I know it needs to be done, of course. I don't *want* to stay married to him. But during the divorce I was so…"

She twisted her face into a look of pure disgust.

"I don't think I realized how bad it was at the time because I was still in shock, but he demeaned me every chance he got. He'd say things in front of the lawyers to embarrass me so I'd clam up and stop arguing with him." She shook her head. "I had no voice then. I didn't know how to stick up for myself."

"You do now."

"Yes, but it makes me shut people out," she admitted. "I think I went too far in the other direction. To think I lied to you even after we were sleeping together…"

She looked like she was in emotional agony and Ethan gripped the edge of the chair, forcing himself not to go to her. "As much as I would have preferred you tell me the truth, I don't think you're a terrible person because you lied to me. I understand why."

She looked up. "Really?"

"Really." He nodded.

"I appreciate that not many people would be so understanding. I won't take it for granted, though," she said with an almost shy smile. "Lesson learned."

"That's my girl."

Her breath stuttered. "Is that true? Am I still your girl?"

Was Monroe ever his? This wasn't a line they'd talked about, and it certainly wasn't something either of them had wanted at first. Was Ethan even sure he wanted it now? All he knew for certain was that the roaring urge to wipe away the stress on Monroe's face was stronger than anything else in his body right now. Maybe he wasn't ready for a new label, but he was willing to admit that they could drop the fake one.

If only life were black and white. Ethan hated the murky gray, but that was exactly where he'd planted his feet.

"Why don't we worry about what to call it later?" he

said, pushing up from his chair and holding his arm out. Monroe came to him quickly, wrapping her arms around his waist and burying her face against his chest. "For now, we can say that I forgive you."

"I still want to make it up to you," she said, tilting her face up and letting some of her usual cheekiness shine through. "Let me show you how sorry I am."

The saucy tone of her voice sent something hot and needy through him. It was like a spear of lust, driving through his body and laying a blanket of quiet over the rest of his emotions. He had no idea *how* to feel on the inside. But one thing that couldn't be denied was how much holding her felt right.

"You ready to do a little groveling?" he asked, his voice turning smoky.

"Sure am." She intertwined her fingers with his and pulled him toward her bedroom. "And don't go easy on me, either."

Ethan chuckled, unable to stop himself following. Whatever might come tomorrow, tonight he was going to free himself of the burden of trying to figure everything out. Tonight, he only wanted to feel the good things.

CHAPTER NINETEEN

When Monroe woke the next morning she felt like she'd been born a new woman. Maybe it was because there were no more secrets to carry on her shoulders—or maybe it was because she'd started to see what was important in life again.

Ethan had to leave early, because he was supposed to be on site to take delivery of something for the inn. Monroe kissed him goodbye at the door, lingering until the very last moment when he laughed and jogged down the stairs, stopping every few steps to look back at her.

When she closed the door, she leaned back against it with a sigh. Restlessness filled her entire body and it felt like she was almost vibrating with it. A day off stretched ahead of her. Usually on her day off, she would still check in with the diner—sad, right? Or she'd pop by and visit her dad or go to Loren's and pay a visit to her nieces.

She never did anything just for herself because…well, what was the point?

The day she found out about the affair, she'd stopped living for herself. She'd allowed her sadness and regret to overwhelm her to the point that her life wasn't really her own anymore. That she had no direction or drive or thirst for achievement.

She wandered into the kitchen and found herself crouching down in front of her small appliance cupboard. Maybe she could bake something for her dad? He loved chocolate cake, especially if she made a berry compote to go with it. Pulling out the pans and bowls and other tools, she felt the restlessness ease out of her body. It was almost like she went into a state of meditation when she baked — her mind and body found a flow that ignored time so she could lose herself in the process for hours on end.

Monroe set about making some rich, chocolate cake batter with a touch of coffee and cardamom, which had been her signature cake back in the day and the one that had scored her a place on *Sugar Coated*. Then she made a ganache and a chocolate Swiss buttercream to go between the layers, along with the berry compote her father loved. After the cakes cooled, she carefully put it all together — piping the buttercream between each perfect layer in circles like a bullseye, filling the gaps with the compote.

On top, she drizzled the warm ganache, letting it spread and drip over the edge until it hardened into a perfect dripped design. She piped the last of the buttercream in soft, artful peaks around the edge of the cake and shaved a little chocolate over the top and stuck some berries in the middle for good measure.

Then, boxing everything up, she went to visit her father.

When Olly Roberts opened the door, a huge smile lit his face. "This is a nice surprise!"

"Me or the cake?" She laughed. Luckily, she'd easily found the cake carrier she used for whenever she did baking for her sisters' life occasions, like Taylor's engagement or Harlow's first birthday a few months back.

"The cake, of course. It's never a surprise that you come to take care of your father, because you're so good like that." He held the door open for her and she leaned in to brush a kiss against his whiskery cheek as she walked past.

Olly was using his walking stick today and she saw the AFO propped up by the door. "Having some trouble with the brace again?"

"We're still adjusting the fit of this one. It's rubbing in one spot and giving me a blister, so I've got to go and see the specialist again to see what they can do about it."

"I'll take you," Monroe offered automatically.

"No need, Taylor has already taken the day off work. It's about time that stopped falling only to you."

"You know I'm happy to help." Monroe walked into the kitchen and set the cake down on the countertop, carefully unclipping the lid and sliding it off to reveal the treat inside.

His smile grew even wider. "I'll put the coffeepot on so we can have a slice together. Do you have time to stay?"

"Sure."

The two of them worked quietly together, Monroe slicing the cake up and her father making coffee. Eventually they sat at the table, her father's walking stick resting next to him, two very generous slices of chocolate cake in front of them.

"You know, I almost feel a little guilty every time I eat one of your creations," her father said.

"I'm not going to claim they're healthy," she replied. "But everything in moderation, right?"

"No, not everything." Her father drove his fork into the fluffy slice and carved a bit off the end. "Ambition, excitement, love...those things should never be in moderation."

"You don't think?" Monroe pondered the thought for a

second. "You don't think it's possible to dream too big?"

Her father chewed, momentarily lost in the joy of the dessert. When he came back down to earth, he reached out for his daughter's hand. "I know what you're really asking, Monroe."

"You do?" She wasn't even sure *she* knew exactly what she was asking—but her father must have picked up on the messy swirl of things in her head. Her responsibility to Jacob and the people at the Sunshine Diner, her messy feelings for Ethan, the slow return of her joy for baking.

"You want to know what happens if you achieve everything you set out to achieve." He speared a raspberry with his fork. "When you've climbed to the top of one ladder, the only way is down right?"

Huh. Yeah, Monroe guessed that she *did* think that in the back of her mind. If you shot for the moon and actually made connection, what then?

"Wrong," he said, before she had a chance to open her mouth. He punctuated the word with a thrust of his fork in Monroe's direction. "You find another ladder. There is always more to learn, more to conquer. You think I would have gotten bored with your mother if she had still been alive? We could have had fifty years of marriage and never grown bored with one another, because there is always more to explore."

Monroe smiled. She loved how passionate her father was. How *open* he was about his love for his daughters and his late wife. And while Olly might have grown up a dirt-under-the-nails kinda guy, he was never short on expressing his feelings, even the mushy ones. She could see that influence in all of them—in Loren's fierce mama bear tendencies and Taylor's desire to always speak up when she thought it might help people.

And Monroe could see it in herself, too. In her responsibility to the people around her and to this town. At one point, she'd seen it in her passion for her creative process and her drive to push herself to be the best she could be at her chosen craft.

"I feel like I've stalled these last couple of years," Monroe admitted.

"You have. But everybody needs time to find themselves after a curveball like that. You thought your life was one thing and it turned out to be something else. That hurts."

"Yeah, it does." She bobbed her head. "But I've also been wallowing. I guess self-pity is one of those things that *should* have a limit and maybe I overindulged."

"Now you know." Her father shrugged. "And you can move on."

"I don't know where to move on *to*." She stared at the cake, looking at the perfectly even layers. She could still hear the judges' voices in her head.

An exceptional talent for flavor and texture...big things ahead...you can do anything.

But could she? What if she tried again and it all came crumbling down around her a second time?

"Yes, you do." Her father carved off another forkful of the cake. "In your heart you know exactly what you want."

Monroe might have been expecting an image of a bakery or a kitchen to flash across her mind, but instead she got something else entirely. Ethan's face flickered, his smile. His blue eyes. She felt warm on the inside, intuition glowing bright and strong.

He was what she wanted.

Not the only thing, because no person's life should only ever be about their partner and nothing else. But right now, with everything that was going on, *he* was the thing she wanted most. Not a fake relationship, but a real one.

A forever one.

It felt scary to even think about saying it out loud, but...

You told him about the divorce mix-up and you shared what happened to you after the affair. If you can do that, you can tell him this.

The way they'd left things last night was open, to say the least. She'd edged toward the discussion about labeling what they had and Ethan had shied away. Was that because he was still processing her marital situation? Or because of something else?

All Monroe knew was that there was one thing in her control right now, and that was the next step she took.

"Sorry, Dad. I have to make a quick phone call." She pushed back on the chair and bent down to kiss her father on the cheek. "I'll be back in a minute."

Her father knew better than to ask, so he simply shrugged and reached for his coffee, more than happy to be left alone with his treat. Monroe pulled her phone out of her purse and quickly looked up the name of the law firm who'd been in contact with her about the divorce. Getting this finalized was no longer about Brendan's desires, but about her own. About doing what *she* needed to do to move on with her life and start being active, rather than passive.

It was about a clean slate. A chance to start fresh.

And as soon as Ethan was done with his day, she was going to tell him that she wanted that fresh start with him.

• • •

Ethan spent the morning working around the inn. Lottie had ordered a new stove for the kitchen, and while that was being installed Ethan had continued to refinish the railing and balustrades of the staircase. It was fiddly work, but he enjoyed it because it allowed his mind to wander.

There were so many questions, right now.

Like whether or not he'd ever find out the true identity of his father. What would happen if he did? Would there be any point to this whole exercise? Did his life back in Australia still exist? What should he do about the Monroe situation?

That question was the toughest of them all.

Not because she'd lied. He understood why and he believed her when she told him why…but that was exactly it. They were developing feelings for one another when neither of them had any business doing so. Ethan didn't know if he'd be moving on in a week or two. Maybe in a month. Hell, maybe he'd find out tomorrow that this Matthew Brewer wasn't his father…and then what? The idea of walking away from Monroe hurt like a nasty spider bite. Which was exactly why he needed to deal with this situation.

He had *not* come looking for forever in Forever Falls.

Ethan's phone rang, and he picked up the call. "Hello?"

"Hi, is this Ethan Hammersmith?" a gruff male voice asked.

"Yes, it is."

"This is Mike from Coastal Metalwork. My assistant left

a message saying you'd called to speak to me. Anything I can help you with?"

"Yes, actually there is. Thanks so much for calling." Ethan pushed up and dusted his free hand down the front of his jeans. "Any chance I could come by now and talk with you in person?"

"Sure thing. I'm around all afternoon. You know where we're located?"

"I do. I'll be there in twenty minutes."

Ethan felt something churning in his stomach — something told him that he was on the verge of finding out an important piece of information. By the time he made it to the Coastal Metalwork workshop, he was so wound up that he was worried he'd lose his lunch all over the ground. He hadn't felt like this in *all* the places he'd been in the past year.

Something here was different.

He walked up to the small glass door that led to a modest-looking reception area, and an electronic beep announced his arrival. Ethan got the impression this wasn't a large operation, since all their tech seemed quite out-of-date. A picture hanging on the wall showed a young man and two older gentlemen in black and white, standing next to a very large piece of what appeared to be an industrial air duct of some kind.

A minute later, a man walked through from a back room. He was tall and lean, with a black and gray beard and thick hair peppered with more silver strands, and he wiped his hands on a red handkerchief.

"You must be Ethan," he said without asking.

"You can tell that from the way I look?"

The man chuckled. "I know all my clients by name, so it wasn't hard to make the guess. Anyway, I'm Mike. What can I do for you?"

"I'm actually looking for some information about a man named Matthew Brewer."

The friendly smile dropped right off Mike's face. In its place was cold surprise. "What about him?"

At that moment, Ethan was too tired to keep up the pretense of the letters anymore. After a year of spinning stories and skirting the truth, he was done with it all. "I think he might be my father."

"No kidding?" Mike came closer, squinting his eyes as if trying to see some resemblance.

Ethan told Mike the whole story about his mother spending time in the U.S., including a summer in Cape Cod and how she'd told him on her deathbed that his father's name was Matthew Brewer. The older man leaned back against the reception desk, shaking his head.

"Family, eh." He let out a dry laugh. "Can't live with 'em, can't live without 'em."

"Do you know anything that might help me?"

Mike scrubbed a hand over his face, like he really didn't want to get involved. But when he looked at Ethan, he let out a long sigh. "He knocked up a woman he met on vacation. That much I know."

Ethan's heart jolted. "Really?"

"Yeah." Mike nodded. "He came home and we got drunk on his first night back. He let it all out—how he loved this woman and she was going to have his kid and that he had no business being a father because he was terrible at everything."

"Did he say anything about the woman?"

"I wish I could remember, but it was so long ago. But she wasn't American, I know that, because she left and went back to the place where she'd grown up. Matt told her to leave, broke both their hearts. But his own father had been a drunk and a bully and, in all honesty, Matt was a lot like him. I think he knew he wasn't fit to be a dad." Mike bobbed his head. "He swore me to secrecy. Far as I know, me and his mom were the only ones who knew about it. Matt and I were tight, back in the day 'fore I got straightened out."

"I heard from someone that Lottie might know something. Do you think that holds any weight?"

"Who told you that?" Mike's face darkened.

"I can't say. I'm sorry but I promised." He held up both hands. No matter how much he wanted to know, he wasn't going to betray Monroe's trust.

"Lottie May is a good woman."

"I know, I've been helping her around the inn while I was staying here."

"Oh? You're *that* kid."

Ethan wanted to laugh at being called a kid, but he supposed to someone in their mid-sixties he probably looked like one. "I guess so."

"Then she tells me you're good people."

"She said that?" Ethan wasn't sure whether Lottie hated him or felt nothing about him. But he'd never thought she liked him.

"She did. She might seem like a tough old nut—and trust me, she is—but she has a heart of gold that woman. Looked after Matt's mom while she was sick, nursed her into the afterlife, rest her soul." Mike bowed his head for a minute. "There were always rumors, you know."

"Rumors?"

"About her and Mrs. Brewer…"

Suddenly a piece of the puzzle clicked into Ethan's brain. Lottie and Mrs. Brewer weren't only friends. Given Brian said the only time he ever saw her cry was when she came to pick up the sentimental bits they were clearing out of Mrs. Brewer's house and yet Ethan had seen her crying over a letter in her office…

Could it be? Were they in a relationship?

"Course it wasn't confirmed, or anything," Mike said, frowning. "Folks are generally good 'round here, but there's still plenty who are living in the past. Personally, I think you should be with whoever you want to be with, so long as they treat you right. Love is love and all that."

"I totally agree."

"You didn't hear anything from me, okay? Lottie helped me out when I was having a rough time and she gave me somewhere to sleep when I didn't have a place to put my boots, if you know what I mean. I owe her a lot. But if you really *are* Matthew Brewer's son and if his mother knew anything about it, likely she told Lottie."

Everything seemed to circle right back to her and the inn. He needed to find out what she knew. And if she didn't know anything, then Ethan was at a dead end. But Matthew Brewer had been to Cape Cod around the time his mother was there, he'd supposedly gotten a girl pregnant and sent her back home overseas…that was too many coincidences.

This *had* to be it.

"I really appreciate your transparency." Ethan stuck his hand out and Mike returned the gesture, his eyes locked onto Ethan's face.

"I don't know if it's my mind playing tricks on me, but you do look a bit like him," the older man said. "Not what he was like in his later years, but when he was younger. I wish I had an old photo to show you."

"It's okay. I'll see what else I can find out."

"I hope you find what you're looking for." Mike bid him farewell and Ethan walked about in the breezy early-spring air.

He could hear the sound of the ocean from here, and it filled him with a sense of finality. Like the end was coming. Like the truth would be revealed. Like this chapter was almost over.

But at least he would know the truth, and that had to count for something right?

Something told him that he was looking in the right place, but that the right place might turn out to be a hollow victory. A man with no family and a dark past wasn't exactly closure. And Ethan might go home with nothing more in hand than when he arrived.

He couldn't shake the seed of doubt that had started to take root in his mind. What if this had all been for nothing?

CHAPTER TWENTY

Monroe took the rest of the afternoon and evening to prepare herself for what was to come. She'd texted Ethan asking him to come over for dinner and gotten Loren to help her style her hair. She'd bought fresh flowers from the florist and popped them into a vase, had cooked up a storm making her famous "easy but delicious" mushroom and pesto pasta with a homemade vanilla creme brulee for dessert.

Then she'd riffled through her closet, looking for something to wear, and had found the dress she'd worn to the semi-final of *Sugar Coated*. The grand finale dress had belonged to the show's wardrobe team and it had been a grand princess-y thing. But the semi-final dress was all hers—a floral wrap dress in three pretty shades of green that she hadn't worn since the filming. It had been kept in a garment bag, forgotten in the back of her closet.

Shaking the nervous energy out of her hands, she stared at herself in the mirror. It was like peering into a magical time-shifting object and seeing the Monroe from three years ago…though with a few extra little lines and a couple extra pounds. But the flush in her cheeks and the budding smile on her lips…well, that was *all* old Monroe.

The old Monroe who dreamed big. The old Monroe who didn't keep her feelings to herself. The old Monroe who still had a stinging sense of humor, but who only got her spikes out when something called for it, not as her *modus operandi*.

Most importantly, she was like the old Monroe who wouldn't hesitate to put herself out into the world by asking for what she wanted.

"You can do this," she said to her reflection, drawing her shoulders back. She tried to smile at herself, but that just felt weird, so she stuck her tongue out instead.

Okay, so she wasn't going to turn into the kind of person who chanted positivity mantras in the mirror or anything like that. And that was okay. Monroe was going to let herself be whoever she was naturally—no pressure, no expectations. A mix of the old and the new—taking the best parts of who she used to be and who she was now.

Some days that would probably mean pie-in-the-sky dreams. Other days that might mean being scared and doubting herself. Both of those things were part of her, like two sides of the same coin, and she was going to embrace them both.

A knock at the front door made her jump and she raced to answer it, excitement skittering through her veins like a pebble skipping over a pond. When she yanked the door open, her heart almost leaped out of her chest.

"Wow." Ethan shook his head, a smile blossoming on his lips. He had a bottle of wine in one hand and, as usual, looked like every fantasy she'd ever had.

"Wow yourself," she said. "That leather jacket really does it for me, you know."

"Like the bad boy image, huh? A little James Dean get you going?" He walked into her apartment, pressing the bottle into her hands and leaning down to capture her lips in a kiss.

Only something didn't feel right.

Usually when Ethan kissed her it felt like the world was melting away. Like they were both losing themselves in the kiss. But he felt...detached. Almost like he was holding something back.

You're just being paranoid because you're planning to open up tonight. That's all you, not him.

But she couldn't shake the feeling that something was off.

"How was your day?" she asked, walking over to her tiny dining table where she'd set up some wineglasses and the flowers. Ethan's eyes were tracking over the scene, like he was cataloguing every little detail.

"Uh good." He raked a hand through his hair. "Wow, you've gone to so much trouble. I wasn't expecting this."

"It's not that much trouble." She smiled and opened the wine, pouring some into each glass. "Honestly, it never felt like it was worth the effort cooking proper meals when it was just for me. Is that weird?"

"Nah, I lived on my own when I first moved to Melbourne, so I totally understand that feeling." He nodded. "I used to get sushi or tacos most nights."

Monroe laughed. Ethan did *not* look like a guy who lived on takeout.

"But I don't expect you to wait on me, you know," he said.

"I wanted to do this." She blinked. "And trust me, as much as I like you, cooking this pasta was as much for me as it was for you."

Ethan laughed. "Okay, so long as you don't feel pressured."

"Is everything okay?" She set the wine bottle down and

went to him, touching his arm. "You're acting weird."

"Sorry." He blew out a long breath and shook himself off. "It's nothing to do with you. I had an…interesting afternoon."

"Tell me everything." Monroe had planned to dish up as soon as he arrived, but she figured it was more important to let Ethan clear his mind than worry about whether the pasta felt a bit overdone. She pressed a wineglass into his hand and motioned for him to follow her to the couch. "What happened?"

He sat next to her, taking a long draw from his glass. The red liquid sloshed back into place as he set it down on a coaster on the coffee table. "I went to see Mike."

Butterflies congregated in Monroe's stomach. He must have heard something about his father.

"I uh…" He looked down at his hands. "Mike confirmed that Matthew Brewer got a woman pregnant while he was on holiday and that she wasn't American."

"Whoa. That's big."

"It's not anything until it's something," he said. "But it would be a huge coincidence, right?"

"Yeah, massive." She couldn't help the excited bubble building in her stomach—did this mean that Ethan might stay in Forever Falls a while? Maybe…long-term? "How do you feel about that?"

"I don't know, honestly." He looked at her and she could see the turmoil in his eyes. The indecision. The fear. The hope. "I mean, finally finding out who my father is was the entire point of coming to America. But I guess…I don't know what I was hoping to find."

"Family?" she offered.

"Maybe," he admitted. "But if this guy *is* my father then I don't get any of that. There are no relatives left that I can tell. It's not exactly like he left behind any kind of legacy I could connect with. From all accounts he was a deadbeat who didn't do anything but get people into trouble. Did I really go through all of this for *that*?"

Monroe's heart split clean in two. The pain in his voice was like running herself through with a knife. "Just because we get the truth doesn't always mean it's the answer we want."

"Truer words have never been spoken." He sighed. "I've got one more lead to chase up, but I think this is it."

Monroe's blood ran cold at the finality in his tone. "It?"

"The end of the road."

You knew this was coming.

Ethan had never made any promises about sticking around and he'd never shared what his plans were beyond the hunt for information. But Monroe had hoped there'd be something worth staying for. That maybe she could contribute to that.

"Well, I mean you've still got a lead to chase up and…" Her mind was whirring, like she was trying to find the right thing to say, *and* let him know that she wanted him around. "If it turns out he *was* your father then there might be more relatives to find?"

"I don't think so. Nothing in my research so far has pointed to there being anyone else around."

Monroe felt a mild sense of panic stirring in her gut. "But what about the inn?"

"The inn?" He looked at her strangely.

"You're helping Lottie fix it up, right?"

"That was a trade for my accommodation. I was never planning to stay until the whole place was done. Frankly, that's a long-term project." He shook his head. "I don't know why she doesn't sell it to a developer or something."

"That's not how we do things here," Monroe said, shaking her head. "There's a reason we don't have big condo buildings or concrete cubes. We don't pass the buck because something is hard work."

Ethan looked at her, his blue eyes searching her face. "Who's acting weird now?"

"Sorry." She dropped her gaze and shook her head, feeling the waves her sister had spent a good thirty minutes styling fall around her shoulders. What the hell was she doing anyway, getting dressed up like this meant a damn thing? "I feel strongly about that. Same goes for the diner, I don't want to see it sold off to someone from outside the town. Especially a developer who'll just knock it down and put something ugly in its place."

"You really care about this town."

"I do." She nodded. "It's where my family chose to make a life and it's where my sisters and I chose to stay. Any of us could have left, but Forever Falls needs people who are going to keep this place going, you know? We need people who care to keep small businesses around and keep us from getting overrun by McDonald's and Starbucks."

"Maybe it also needs people who are going to build something new?" he said softly. "Maybe the diner has run its course."

Monroe gaped. "How can you say that when you agree that Big Frank's eggs are the best on the coast?"

"Oh they are, no denying that. But what I guess I mean

is that things have a natural lifecycle to them." He clasped his hands together, leaning his forearms against his thighs. "Some things must end so other things can begin, because nothing lasts forever."

Monroe's heart sank. This was precisely the opposite of the sentiment she was hoping to achieve tonight—because forever was exactly what she wanted. After three years of living only in the present, because she hated the past and feared the future had made for a very stagnant, lackluster existence.

"But it's my responsibility to—"

"Is it your business?" Ethan turned to her.

"Well, no."

"Then it's not your responsibility. It's not your job to save something that isn't yours in the first place...unless you're thinking of buying your boss out?"

Monroe frowned. She hadn't thought of that, actually. Mr. Sullivan would likely sell to her and probably even put some kind of payment plan in place. Hell, if she asked her sisters to chip in the three of them could buy it and Monroe could keep on running it like she was now.

It was actually a possibility. A very attainable possibility.

But if she thought about owning the diner and making that her future...a resounding *no* echoed through her body. It wasn't what she wanted. It wasn't the future she saw for herself—waiting tables and trying to manage the endlessly changing staff and having other people in the kitchen.

"I can see by the look on your face that it's not what you want, Monroe." Ethan reached for her hand. "So if you wouldn't buy him out—assuming you had the means to— then why are you so worried about making sure your boss doesn't sell?"

Because she hated change. Change had caused her nothing but pain in the past—the change of her marital status, the change in her family. And yet, the security of keeping everything the same had done nothing but form a protective bubble of nothingness around her, holding her in place like her feet were stuck in concrete blocks.

"I worry about people's jobs," she admitted. "But…I guess I wasn't ready for things to change."

"Hmm." Ethan nodded. "How old is your boss?"

"He'll be eighty-one very soon."

"Maybe he's done running a business," Ethan said gently. "Maybe he's hung onto it longer than he wanted because he's also worried about people's jobs."

Guilt struck her in the chest. This wasn't the first time Mr. Sullivan had talked about selling, and every time Monroe convinced him to keep the business. It was out of selfishness, in part. Out of fear. But Ethan was right. The man deserved to spend the rest of his time on this earth just relaxing and enjoying himself. And if she didn't want to buy him out then what right was it of hers to push him to keep things the same?

"You're right." She nodded. Monroe made a note to drop by Mr. Sullivan's house tomorrow and sit him down for a chat—she would support him in whatever he wanted to do and stop putting her own demons first. "And I could help Big Frank and Darlene find new jobs. They're both great workers and good people."

"And what about you?" he asked.

"Me? I'm just wondering how you managed to turn this whole conversation around to me without me even noticing until right now." She raised an eyebrow. "That's quite a talent."

"You're more interesting than I am," he teased with a smile.

"That's smooth, but complete bullshit." She turned on the couch, propping her elbow up on the back of it so she could take in every part of Ethan. From the coiled energy in his stance to the crease between his eyes, to the way he fidgeted with a tiny hole in her couch. "Can we stop dancing around things, Ethan? We're both grown-ass adults who've been in relationships before and yet I feel like we're being cagier than a bunch of teenagers at a spin-the-bottle party."

For a moment he let out a genuine laugh and all the tension momentarily disappeared from his face. "You know what, that sounds really good to me."

Silence settled over the apartment and Monroe briefly thought about her poor pasta getting gloopier by the minute. But that wasn't important. *This* was important. Talking honestly about her feelings for this man who'd stumbled into her life and not knowing if those feelings were reciprocated.

Not knowing if forever was on the table.

Forever is on the table. Forever for you, because your life has to go on.

That's when Monroe knew that forever wasn't only about love with another person, it was about self-love and she hadn't loved herself in a very long time. But looking back over the time she'd spent with Ethan, he'd helped her find that again. She'd started baking again, regained her love of dressing up, stopped fearing the future quite so much and found herself dreaming again. Planning. Wishing.

That was his influence.

"I like you a lot, Ethan. You…" She ran her tongue along her bottom lip as she gathered herself. "Before you came into my diner I was in a really miserable place. I was floating through life without any ambition or hope or purpose other than to get through the day. You helped me turn that around."

"*You* turned it around, Monroe." He reached out and tucked her hair behind her ears, the back of his finger grazing her skin in the most tender way. "You have that power inside you. I didn't do anything."

"Yes, you did. I was so closed off to the world and to people that I never let anybody get close to me anymore. I stopped making new friends, I hadn't been intimate with anyone…hell, I hadn't even been intimate with myself. Because there was no spark in me, no joy." It hurt even thinking about how she had been just a month ago. "I honestly believed that I was going to live the same day over and over and over until I died. I never thought I would find love or passion again."

"And you did."

"Because of you." She placed her hand over his, pressing his palm to her cheek. "You helped me see that I was cutting myself off from so many things. Your search for your father, that focus and drive you had, it inspired me."

"No one should be inspired by this." His expression went cold. "I have a horrible feeling it's going to be a fruitless exercise in the end and that I came here searching for something, only to go home empty-handed."

Go home…

"What if…" She steeled herself. "What if you didn't go home? What if you made a new home here with me?"

For a moment Ethan was deathly still. He looked like a stone monument, hard and impenetrable and reverent. But Monroe could hear the whirr in his brain, and the cooling of the air around him. He was withdrawing.

"That's not what we agreed to." He shook his head. "This was supposed to be an arrangement to help us both out and I think we achieved that."

"It's not an arrangement to me anymore." Monroe was proud of how her voice didn't shake, of how she didn't stumble over her words—because she was speaking her truth. "It may have started out that way, but I have *real* feelings for you, Ethan. I…"

Say it. You are not that woman who's afraid anymore.

"I love you."

"*How* can you love me?" He pushed up off the couch and raked a hand through his hair, the movement agitated and jerky. "*I* don't even know who I am, so how the hell can you know me enough to love me?"

"What?" Monroe pushed up, her dress falling around her legs. "Do you want to replay that question back so you can hear how ridiculous that sounds? I know plenty about you. I know that you've got a brilliant sense of humor, that you're good with people and that you're not a stranger to hard work. I know you've got baggage just like I do, but that you're strong enough to work through it."

"You don't know that because *I* don't know that."

Tears pricked the backs of Monroe's eyes—she hated hearing him speak like this, like he didn't see what he had to offer the world. Like he didn't understand that he was valuable in spite of his perceived shortcomings.

This must be how he felt talking to you.

"Yes, you do." Monroe went to him, grabbing both his hands and looking right up into his eyes. "I know you're worried about what you might find out and that the end to this exercise might not be exactly what you wanted. But family is…family is what you make it. Blood relatives don't always treat you the way they should and friends are sometimes the missing piece of that puzzle. I consider Big Frank and Darlene and Mr. Sullivan part of my family, and I've lost people that share my blood. That's sad, but just because we don't have the family we *think* we should have, doesn't mean we don't have a family at all."

"And you think you don't have power in you," he replied softly. "You could have changed all on your own."

"Maybe I could have, but I *wouldn't* have." She shook her head. "Sometimes it takes the right person to shine a light on us so we can see who we've become."

He searched her eyes. "And what if I find out my father was a horrible person?"

"Ethan…whatever happens with your dad, it doesn't change who you are inside."

"All this time I thought I wanted to know no matter what, but now that I think I'm on the verge of actually finding out I'm…I'm fucking terrified."

Monroe pulled Ethan to her, wrapping her arms around his waist and burying her face against his chest. She forced herself to hold back her tears, because no matter what he decided, Monroe was going to be there for him. She wasn't going to walk away like his ex did, simply because his actions didn't align with her desires.

She wasn't going to hurt him like Brendan did to her when she wouldn't comply with his wishes.

She was going to be the kind of person they both deserved.

They stood like that for a moment, her arms holding him tight and his hand absently stroking her hair. When she looked up, he was staring into space. She was losing him, and it hurt like hell.

CHAPTER TWENTY-ONE

Ethan had always been a guy in control of his emotions *and* he'd always been a guy with a plan. Two things he believed had held him in good stead. But in this very moment, he was neither of those things.

Holding Monroe was like clutching a buoy in the middle of the ocean during a storm—he had something to hold onto, but it was slipping through his fingers and there was no point pretending that the inevitable moment where he lost his grip altogether and was flung into the waves wasn't hurtling toward him.

"It's only information," Monroe said softly. "Whether you know who he was or if you never find out…it makes no difference to the person *you* are."

"But I'm untethered," he said, his voice cracked with pain. "I have an adoptive father who always treated me like I was odd, a half brother I don't get along with, two dead biological parents and…nothing else."

"That's not true. Nobody is defined by their relationship to others. Trust me, I made that mistake for *way* too long." She squeezed him as if it might strengthen her statement. "And maybe this is a chance for you to build what you've always wanted. Start fresh, choose the people to be your family based on the kind of people you want in your life. You have that control."

"I left everything behind to come here. *Everything*. And for what? To be forced to start over because I put all my money on black, hoping it would pay off?"

He stepped out of her grip, the dark swirling thoughts consuming him. Why had he walked away from his life for this? He'd walked away from every relationship he had to chase a dead man.

But you found Monroe.

Against all the odds and everything he wanted, he found the one woman who *spoke* to him on a level no one else ever had. Because if this was anyone else standing before him, he wouldn't even be having this conversation now. He wouldn't be letting someone see him in pain. He would have simply walked right back out that door and hidden himself away like he'd been doing for the past twelve months.

And what does staying here achieve? She said she loves you and you're just going to hurt her.

Forever Falls was not his home. Yet Melbourne wasn't his home, either. And going back to the small town where he grew up in Australia…well that reminded him of lies and bad memories.

He didn't belong anywhere.

"I thought finding him would magically fix things." How naive he'd been. How pathetic. "Like it would help me to stop being angry at my mother for holding such a secret my whole life."

"You're jumping the gun, aren't you?" she said gently. "Get confirmation first and then spiral."

In spite of the sensation sucking him down into despair, he laughed. "I appreciate you not telling me to quit spiraling, just to delay it."

She shrugged and looked up at him with her warm,

brown eyes. "Bottling it up is worse. Ask me how I know."

He looked at Monroe long and hard. In these few weeks they'd spent together, she'd blossomed. The woman he saw standing before him tonight was lightyears ahead of the woman who came by his table at the diner on that first day.

She was a vision tonight. Her hair gleamed and her eyes sparkled and he recognized the dress she wore from an episode of *Sugar Coated*. He knew instinctively that her wearing something from that time in her life was a big deal, almost like she was finally acknowledging the part of her that had chased goals and dreamed big.

And he loved every version of Monroe—dressed up and made up, sweats and T-shirt and no makeup, just woken up with messy hair, half-asleep and reaching for him in the dark. When she was excited, nervous, teasing, relaxed.

He loved it all, because behind every look was the same thing: a heart of gold.

He'd never met a person with raw goodness inside of them like her. Playing the corporate game back home, he'd met a lot of climbers. A lot of people who'd be ready to smile to your face so they could step over you the second you took your eyes off them. He'd been surrounded by people with an agenda of some kind his whole life.

But Monroe had no agenda. Despite her not telling him about the failed divorce—which he genuinely *had* forgiven her for—she let him in wholly and completely.

Her telling him that she loved him…

That must have taken guts. More so for her to be standing here right now when he hadn't said it back.

You can't love her. You don't have room for that right now.

"Monroe..." He lowered his head. "I appreciate everything you're doing. The nice table, the dinner, the kind words, the..."

He shook his head as he looked at her.

"All of this." He waved his hand in her direction.

"All of what?"

"Looking so good it's hard for me to keep my wits straight." He scrubbed a hand over his face. "You deserve someone who's in it for the long haul. Someone worthy of all this."

"You don't get to determine who's worthy of me," she replied steadily. "That's my decision and my decision only."

"Then find that person, find them and cherish them."

"I already did."

The way she looked up at him, eyes brimming with hope and sincerity and not even the tiniest prickle...it was too much. He was going to bring her down at a time when she'd finally gotten her feet back on the ground. When she'd finally seen what she could do with her life.

He would *not* allow his issues to affect her.

"Not me, Monroe." He shook his head, backing away from her. The hurt splashed across her face was like ice in his veins, but he knew that a little pain now was saving a whole lotta pain later.

"Yes, you." She came toward him, fierce and beautiful. "I don't care if you're not sure what's happening next. I don't care if you don't have a conventional family. I don't care that you're still figuring things out. All of those things are fine by me."

"I'm not staying here."

The words shot out of him, more defense than anything else, but she looked like he'd slapped her. Her eyes sparkled but she blinked, not letting her posture drop or her determined look soften.

"At least tell me if you feel something for me," she said. "If you have to walk away, fine. But it won't be without me laying all my cards on the table and I hope you'll do the same. This isn't fake, Ethan. Even if it ends now, it *meant* something."

It might be easier to lie, to walk away and keep that secret tucked close to his heart in the hopes that she'd get on with her life and forget all about him. But lies had brought him to this point. Lies had brought her here, too.

And the only chance that he had to rebuild things was to stop that cycle.

"You're unlike anybody I have ever met before," he said. "I wish I were here in another time, because whoever ends up with your heart should consider themselves the luckiest man alive."

Her bottom lip quivered for just a second, but she didn't budge. Didn't flinch. She held herself like the queen she was.

"I hope you find what you're looking for," she said softly. "You *do* deserve to be happy."

He reached for his coat, emotion tearing him up inside. Every cell in his body screamed at him to stay, to be with her, to forget all about his past and start over right this bloody second.

But there were loose ends that had to be tied up. Truth that had to be uncovered. And then Ethan needed to start figuring out how to put his life back together.

Alone.

. . .

He walked into the inn ten minutes later, feeling like there was a black cloud inside him. For a moment, he thought about packing his bags right then and there and making the drive to the nearest airport to catch whatever flight had a spare seat just to get out of the country.

Maybe pulling the ripcord on this whole crazy plan was the smartest thing he could do.

There was nothing to be gained. Nothing to be achieved.

"Lottie." The name popped out of his lips the second he saw her sitting in her office, the door wide open like she'd been waiting for him.

A glass of something amber-toned was sitting on her desk, the light from the lamp casting a warm glow over her features. She seemed smaller than he remembered, hunched almost as if the life had been sucked out of her.

"Come here," she said, motioning with one work-worn hand. "Sit."

He hesitated. Ethan wasn't sure he wanted to go down this rabbit hole anymore. What if he found the truth he'd wanted so badly when he boarded an international flight last year and it was nothing but more unanswered questions and disappointment? Whoever said ignorance was bliss was smarter than they sounded.

"I don't want to argue with you," she said, her voice

sharp like a whip. "Now hurry up."

She was a crotchety old woman, he'd give her that. But there was something in him that responded to it—maybe he liked that she wasn't what people thought she should be. That she marched to the beat of her own drum, that she was resilient.

Like Monroe. Like his mother had been, despite her flaws.

"I know you went and spoke with Mike," she said, as he walked into her office. He always felt like a bear in an enclosure in the tiny space, like the walls were pressing in.

"Does nobody mind their business in this town?" he grumbled.

"Never have, never will. Here." She shoved a second glass of what smelled like a peaty Scotch toward him. He hadn't even noticed the second glass until now.

"How long have you been waiting?" he asked.

"Since Mike called me. Seems he ran his mouth a bit and then felt bad about it." She sighed. "So before you can go poking your nose into my business, yes...I was in a relationship with Mary Brewer."

"That's none of my business."

Lottie held up her hand. "Let me finish."

Ethan leaned back, nursing the Scotch in one hand and swirling it so the liquid clung to the edges and let out a smoky aroma into the air. He forced himself not to knock the whole thing back in one go out of self-pity.

"Mary and I, we..." Lottie sighed. Suddenly she seemed very old and very tired, like the past had finally caught up with her. "I loved her so much."

Ethan swallowed, a lump blocking his throat.

"She was my first and only love, but back then folks weren't quite ready for two women to be together. Not here, anyway. So we kept things secret, but I was troubled back then. Unsure of myself. We…we broke up. Her parents pressured her to get married and she did, then she had Matthew a few years later." She sipped her drink. "Her husband ended up leaving Mary to raise Matthew by herself. He was a handful, that boy. But Mary and I started seeing each other again and I felt like my life was back in one piece."

The way Lottie spoke about it—the soft, dreamy quality of her voice—was surprising, but he supposed that given she'd had to keep her relationship a secret for so many years hiding her romantic side must have become habit.

"Those were the happiest days of my life and we were together for the rest of her time on this earth." She swirled the glass, her eyes fixed on the way the liquid moved. "It was tough, sneaking around, and Mary often left Matthew by himself, so she could be with me. That boy didn't really know what a family looked like growing up. His father was never around, even before he officially left, and his mother was always torn between two worlds—wanting to fit in and wanting to be true to herself."

Lottie reached into the top drawer on her desk and pulled out a letter. She slid it across the table toward Ethan. He stared at it for a moment, unsure that he wanted to know what information it contained.

He was at a crossroads now.

"If you want to know for sure, then read it," she said.

His mouth was dry. The whole year had been pushing

him to this point and now he was here it felt like…fuck. He was scared. The tumbler shook in his hand and he placed it down on the desk with an unsteady *thunk*.

Then he snatched up the letter without giving himself a chance to overthink it anymore and started reading.

> *Dear Mom,*
>
> *I know what you told me, that people like us don't make for good family. But I love Marcie. I shouldn't have sent her away when I knew she was going to have my baby. I let the fear get to me and your words, as well. But I'm going to be a dad and I want my child to have a father, unlike what I had growing up.*
>
> *I'm leaving for Australia in three days and Marcie is meeting me at the airport in Melbourne.*
>
> *I love you, Mom. Please be happy.*
>
> *Mattie.*
>
> *ps. Marcie tells me the little boy is going to be called Ethan, after her great-grandfather. I like that name.*

The letter was dated five months before Ethan's birthday. For a moment, he felt nothing but ice-cold numbness filtering through his body. It wasn't a legal document to prove anything, but in his mind this was the closest he would get. Proof in the only form that likely existed.

He'd finally found his father.

"There are more letters," she said. "I've had them in a box for years in my bedroom closet, along with other things that belonged to Mary. Some photo albums and such. It's all I have left of her."

Ethan was still staring at the letter. "Do you know

whether he made it to Australia?"

"He got thrown into lockup the night before he was supposed to leave—drunk and disorderly. Far as I know, he never made the flight."

Ethan let out a breath. He could imagine his mother standing around the Tullamarine airport, waiting and waiting. Back then they didn't have cell phones—at least his mother wouldn't have, because they wouldn't have been commonplace yet. Did she know Matthew wasn't coming after all?

"When did you know it was me?" he asked.

"The day you mentioned the letters something clicked. I went digging around in those old boxes. Funny thing was, I was pretty sure the story about the letters was bullshit... but then I found 'em." The older woman's steely gaze met his. "Your mom told you the truth before she died?"

"Some of it. She was pretty drugged up by then, so I'm sure some parts of the story are lost forever. All I knew was that my family was not what I thought it was. And so I came looking—to find my father, to see if I had any real family left..."

Lottie looked sad for a moment, a crease deepening between her brows. "I'm sorry to tell you, there's no one from that family left. Mary was an only child and so was her husband. There's some cousins out West, but...nobody they ever spent time with, you know."

So that was it. Mystery solved.

His father couldn't stay sober long enough to hop on a flight and be there for his girlfriend and future son. And there was nobody left to grieve his loss.

Ethan bobbed his head, feeling utterly hollowed out.

"Well, I guess that's it then. Looks like I can head home."

"What about the girl you've been seeing?" She narrowed her eyes at him. "You're just going to up and leave without saying goodbye?"

"I already said goodbye." He pushed back on his chair and bumped right into the wall. Cursing under his breath, he stood for a minute, unsure what to do next.

It was like the entire driving force that had propelled him the past year was suddenly stolen away and now he didn't know how to keep himself moving. Lottie watched him, as if waiting for something to happen. When he stood there, rooted to the spot like an old tree, she sighed.

"I'll dig out anything I can find that might help you," she said, standing and coming around the side of the desk. "I don't know that there's much, but if I think it might help then you can have it."

"Thank you," he said. "I'm sorry that you lost Mary."

"I didn't lose her, boy. We came back to each other before it was too late, and I'll always be grateful for that. We had twenty good years together."

She placed a hand on his shoulder for a brief moment, before leaving him alone in the office. For the first time in as long as Ethan could remember, he had nothing in front of him. No dreams, no purpose, no future.

Heading home felt like his only option…but where *was* home? That was a problem he needed to figure out.

CHAPTER TWENTY-TWO

The following week…

Monroe sucked in a deep breath as she walked through the door of the Sunshine Diner. Darlene waved as she served a couple at one of the booths, and Monroe quickly scanned the room. It was about 30 percent full, not bad for a Tuesday morning given it was barely eight thirty. She was confident that more people would roll in across the next hour, filling up even more tables.

But did that keep each step from feeling like she was dragging a concrete block behind her? Nope. Every day she waited for the pain to ease, for the great chasm in her heart to start closing over, and every day it was even worse than the one before it.

Darlene came over and placed a motherly hand on her arm. Today she was wearing bright yellow, which looked great against her brown skin, and Monroe was thankful for the little bit of brightness. And for Darlene's support. She needed it.

"You look like hell," Darlene said.

"Gee, thanks." Monroe tried to laugh but it came out more like a wheeze.

"I could hunt that boy down for hurting you." She pulled Monroe into a hug and squeezed. "Nobody messes with my boss."

"Thanks, but don't think badly of Ethan." She pulled

back. "It was nothing to do with me. He…"

Ethan's parentage and history were still a secret in Forever Falls. Monroe suspected she and Lottie may be the only two people who knew for certain that Matthew Brewer was his father—and it would likely stay that way.

"He had things back home to deal with," she finished.

Darlene raised an eyebrow. "You're far more understanding than most people, Monroe. I could see how much you cared about him and I saw that he cared about you, too."

Tears pricked the backs of Monroe's eyes, but she blinked them away. "Yeah, I know he did."

At least Ethan had called her right before he left for Australia and told her everything he found out. She'd hoped it would feel like closure…but it didn't. Saying goodbye had been brutal. The pain in his voice was etched into her memory, and it echoed whenever she had a quiet moment. It was hard seeing him so broken down, when she knew he deserved so much more. So much love, so much support, so much belonging. But no amount of rationalizing had convinced him to stay.

He needed to be alone and figure out what was next.

Monroe respected that, even if she'd cried and he'd sounded as though he felt sick with guilt over it. Fact was, he was a good person, through and through. He just wasn't *her* person. And she wasn't his.

Ethan is gone. You need to get over it.

"If we'd met at another time…" She scrubbed a hand over her face, willing herself to feel better. But there was no point thinking this way—she could drown herself in an ocean of what-if's.

"Oh, honey." Darlene's eyes watered. "I wish I could make it better. You deserve someone who's going to stick around."

How did the saying go? Fool me once, shame on you. Fool me twice...

Well, Monroe had gotten herself into this mess. She knew from the start Ethan had an agenda and it was one that she could empathize with—the truth was important. Family meant everything to her. Maybe the healing process would have been easier if she could hate him for leaving, but the fact was she couldn't. It wasn't his fault she'd fallen for him.

Fallen head over heels right off the edge of a cliff.

Deep down she knew that no other man would come close to what she'd shared with him. *That* was love. Real love. And knowing what she had lost was like wearing rocks on her back.

But life had to go on, even if she had about as much enthusiasm for it as she did a plate of over-boiled Brussels sprouts.

"Monroe, get your butt back here," Big Frank called from the kitchen.

Shaking herself, she sucked in a breath and tried to put her game face on. Today was her check-in with Mr. Sullivan regarding the health and future of the diner, where she would present that her campaign with Ethan had worked to bring in more people to the diner *and* increase the spend per table. His tech skills had also helped them implement a better inventory tracking system, with much less manual work thereby reducing the hours she spent doing that each month.

Blowing out a long breath and shaking her hands, she made her way through the diner and into the kitchen out back. Mr. Sullivan was chatting with Big Frank, a smile on his face, though he looked tired.

Ethan's words swam back into her mind, about the older man perhaps being ready for life to slow down a bit.

"Hello, dear," Mr. Sullivan said as she walked into the kitchen. "Shall we go for a walk while we have our meeting? It's lovely outside."

"Sure." She held her arm out and helped him through the kitchen and out the back door, which was a bit unstable and in need of repair.

They wandered down the narrow street behind the back of the diner and out onto the side road. There was a park a block down the street, and they headed in that direction. Spring had well and truly sprung, and bright green leaves filled the trees, some also blossoming with tiny white buds. The air was still crisp, but the sun was out in full force.

"So, I hear you've achieved quite a lot this past month," he said, looking up at her. His eyes crinkled at their edges as he smiled. "Big Frank said you've been working very hard to make positive changes."

"That's right." Monroe ran him through some of the activities they'd tried and the results—mostly improvements, although a few things hadn't shifted the needle as much as she'd hoped. "Overall, I think the business will be more profitable for everything we've done. And there are still more things we can try. I'm sure Big Frank told you that we keep a list in the office for anyone who has an idea for improvements, and if that idea is implemented and it makes a good saving then we reward that person with a small bonus in their next pay."

"That's a very good idea." Mr. Sullivan bobbed his head. "Anything that encourages innovation is always good for the workplace."

"I agree."

"That's great, Monroe. You've done a wonderful job and you should be very proud of yourself."

"Thanks." She tried to feel excited about it—*this* was what she wanted, right? To make an improvement and see the diner performing better and to have job security and...

To stay the same.

Funny how that didn't sound as appealing as it once did.

"You don't look like someone who just achieved their goal," Mr. Sullivan said as she helped him down to one of the benches at the edge of the park. Ahead of them, a few children were playing on some equipment, hanging upside down and racing around with seemingly boundless energy.

"I don't feel like it, either," she replied quietly.

"Talk to me." He reached for her hand and she stared at it, how weathered and wrinkled the skin was and yet how strong his grip felt. "I never had the chance to build a family of my own and you're the closest thing I have to a granddaughter."

"Are you saying you have two generations of advice and wisdom saved up?" She smiled.

"I do."

"I'm sad." Her voice wavered and she tried to fight the rush of resistance up the back of her throat. Being vulnerable, even with those she trusted, didn't come easy. And that voice that told her no one would care was only a reflection of her doubt, not the truth. "I lost someone important and I don't know what to do."

"Ah." Jacob nodded. "Thor."

Monroe laughed. "How did you know about us?"

"You can't put a man in a superhero costume outside my restaurant and expect me not to hear about it." He chuckled. "I got notified by at least ten different people."

"Really?" She snorted. "Slow news day, huh?"

"Something like that. So, tell me about Thor."

"Ethan," she corrected with a sigh. "He was…"

How was she even supposed to describe him? Everything felt too raw, too soon. Too damn *much*.

"You know I never dated anyone after my marriage broke down. I didn't think I wanted to fall in love again, because the first time had been such a monumental disaster and I was afraid to get hurt like that a second time." She scrubbed her hands over her face. "But there was something about him that made me wonder if…"

"What?"

"He made me wonder if I might be able to be my old self again. If maybe I was only bruised instead of broken."

"Of course you aren't broken. My dear, I knew your grandfather when he was alive, God rest his soul, and that man was one of the strongest people I ever knew. There is no way someone who shares his blood would be weak."

A cool breeze brushed past them, and the sun shined bright overhead. Spring was in the air, and yet Monroe had none of the hope budding in her heart that she should.

"I felt weak," she admitted.

"No, you felt afraid. It's different." He looked at her and for a moment, she saw all his history in his eyes. All his experience. "Feeling emotions does not make you weak, it makes you human. Getting out of bed every day and facing the world when you would rather not—taking action even when you are afraid—is the epitome of strength. You have a warrior's spirit, my girl, and the heart of a lion."

A tear dropped onto her cheek and she brushed it away with the back of her hand. "I wish I could believe it."

"Those who have the capacity for great things are often plagued by doubt and those who boast the loudest often have little substance underneath the noise. It's a funny thing." He shook his head. "But in one month, you've managed to keep a dying business from going under. You've done that all while supporting your father and your sisters and while falling in love."

"And it wasn't enough," she whispered.

"No, it wasn't," Jacob replied, surprising Monroe. "It wasn't enough because, as usual, you were focused on other people and not yourself."

"What do you mean?"

"You're worried about letting me down and you're worried about what might happen to Darlene and Frank. You worry about your father's needs and even when this man walked away, you're worried for his well-being." He held up a hand when she opened her mouth to protest. "I ran into Loren yesterday and she told me everything."

Dammit, Loren.

"She's got a big mouth." Her sister had been devastated by the breakup, convinced Monroe and Ethan were meant to be together. Of course, Monroe had tried to act nonchalant about the breakup, as was her plan all along, but her big sister saw right through it.

"It's *your* time, Monroe, to be your own top priority. And I don't mean protecting yourself by hiding away in the shadows, either. I mean, it's time for you to be who you were meant to be." He sighed. "Tell me, if you think about that version of yourself, are you here? At the diner?"

No.

The answer came so sharp and so clear it almost took her back. A month ago, she was terrified at the thought of changing her job. Now the sameness of every day was wearing her down. She had nothing to look forward to, nothing to strive for or drive toward.

"I don't know," she said, even though in her heart of hearts she knew it was a lie.

"Bullshit," Jacob said sharply. "I can see it in your face. Don't lie to me."

"But I don't know what else there is, beside this. The diner has been a huge part of my life since I was in high school and I'm…scared." The truth of it was like ice in her chest. Monroe wasn't just scared of what would come next, she was terrified.

Yet there was a voice in the back of her head, asking her how long before doing the same thing day in and day out would wear her down completely.

Jacob nodded his head, like he fully understood her situation. "By the way, you're fired and I'm going to sell the diner."

"Wait, what?" Monroe shook her head and looked at her boss. "Fired?"

"Your work this past month has been phenomenal and it will mean I can get a much better price for the business. I'm also going to make it a condition of sale that my longstanding employees are given the option to stay on, if they so wish."

"Your longtime employees except me, because you're firing me?"

"That's right."

She waited for the anxiety and fear to settle deeper into her chest and yet, it didn't. Strangely, she felt lighter than she had in a long time.

"You don't belong here anymore, Monroe." Jacob shook his head. "If I sell and you stay on as manager, thirty years will pass before you know it and you'll wonder what the heck happened to your life. Trust me."

"How do you know I'll feel like that?"

"Close your eyes," he said and Monroe raised an eyebrow. "Just do it, girl."

"Fine," she huffed, following his orders.

"I want you to think about what your life would have looked like if you'd ended up being with Ethan instead of Brendan? If you'd never married him or gotten divorced?"

An image floated up clearly in Monroe's mind—she was wearing her green dress from the semifinal of *Sugar Coated* and she was pouring two glasses of wine. Ethan came through the front door. It looked almost the same as the night they'd broken up, only this time she'd served dinner. But there was something in fridge, a white box with a business logo on the side.

Her business logo.

In her mind, she pulled the box out to show off the cake.

It was a birthday cake for someone—topped with strawberries and cream. It was beautiful, professional. Then she saw the mixer in her kitchen, the bags of flour and dyes and piping bags.

"What can you see?" Jacob asked.

"I'm running a dessert catering business out of my kitchen," she said. "Ethan is there. I'm dressed up and... happy."

That was her dream life. Doing what she loved with the man she loved—building something for herself. Pushing herself to work hard and improve. Trying. Being out in the world. Being in love with life.

"Excellent. I'll be looking for a business to invest in after I sell the diner." Mr. Sullivan nodded.

"No."

"Why not?" He looked insulted.

"Because it's a huge risk. Do you know how many small businesses fail in the first five years?"

"A lot. But you won't." His conviction warmed Monroe's heart. "My girl, you work harder and more diligently than anyone I know. You *care* about doing the right thing and being responsible. Plus, I have tasted your cake and anyone who doesn't buy from you is a fool."

"Thank you," she whispered, feeling emotional all of a sudden.

"It has been a privilege to watch you and your sisters grow up. I know life hasn't always been kind to you, Monroe, but you are strong and you are resilient and you can make this work."

"You sound so confident."

"I am. In you, I can only be confident."

Monroe threw her arms around her boss's neck and squeezed him. The thought of striking out on her own was terrifying, but for the first time in over three years she finally felt like it was *worth* taking the risk. That failure was only a possibility, not an inevitability.

And striking out on her own felt really, truly right.

The only thing that would have made the future look even sweeter was a big hunky Australian Thor-doppelgänger by her side.

You can't have it all. But maybe you can build it all and when the time is right, everything will fall into place.

She had to trust, because the future was unknown. All she could control were the steps she took toward it. And for the first time in a long time, she *was* going to take a step.

• • •

Ethan strolled barefoot along the beach. It was blisteringly hot and damply humid, and the smell of warm air and ocean and tropical flowers should have been relaxing. But paradise had yet to uncoil him. A week ago, he'd packed his meager possessions and had driven his rental out of Forever Falls. After making it all the way to the Boston airport, he'd gotten himself a flight.

Somewhere hot. Somewhere…far away. Those were his only criteria.

Denarau Island, Fiji.

It was a beautiful place. Ironically, where he and Sarah had talked about having their honeymoon. He didn't remember that until he'd stepped off the plane and it was too late to turn around. But maybe that was an important lesson—if you kept running, eventually you'd be without a place to run *to*.

That was how he'd found himself at a fancy resort, no longer worrying whether he burned through the money in his bank account. Why? Because what was the point of planning for the future when anything could happen?

He wandered along the beach until he found his way back to the resort he was staying at, hot and desperately in need of a beer. There was a casual catery near one of the pools and within minutes, Ethan was sitting at the bar, a foamy beverage in front of him. He sat and stared, almost oblivious to the natural beauty around him. It was a crime not to appreciate it, but he felt so disconnected from himself. Disengaged.

He thought about Monroe constantly. About the way she'd bloomed in front of him while they were together. About the way she never hesitated to help someone she cared about. About how she'd sounded over the phone when he'd called to say he was leaving town—the soft sniffles, the wobble in her voice, the way she tried so damn hard to be strong and supportive, even when he knew it was hurting her.

Fuck.

That woman. That passionate, kind, resilient woman.

She deserved a man who knew who he was and what he wanted. A man with solid ground beneath his feet. A man who could give her all of himself without doubt or reservation or fear. And right now, he wasn't that man.

"Ethan Hammersmith?"

Ethan blinked, turning around to find a man striding

toward him, a big smile on his face. He recognized him instantly—an old school mate named Trent Walters. He was shirtless, like most people lounging around the pool, and wearing a pair of brightly colored boardshorts.

"It *is* you!" Trent smiled and came over to him, hand outstretched. "Of all places to bump into someone from home."

"Hey man, it's been a long time."

"Mind if I join?" Trent gestured to the empty seat and Ethan nodded.

"What are you doing here?"

"Got married last week." Trent held up a hand, which had a thick gold band wrapped around his ring finger. "My lovely wife is currently getting a massage or a pedicure or some girlie shit like that."

He tried to hide his surprise. Trent had always been a guy who didn't take life—or dating—too seriously. Back when Ethan had been in Patterson's Bluff, taking care of his mother before she died, they'd gone out for drinks a few times and women flocked to Trent wherever he was. That hadn't changed since they were in high school.

"Congratulations, that's great news."

"I shocked my whole family." Trent laughed good-naturedly. "I swear, they thought I would be the last one of us to get hitched."

"I *do* remember a surfer guy who once proclaimed that settling down had the word 'settling' in it for a reason." Ethan chuckled and took a sip of his beer, pausing while Trent ordered a drink for himself.

"I said that, huh?" He raked a hand through his overlong blond hair. After his beer was poured, he held it up to cheers with Ethan. "I was young and stupid then."

"I don't know about that. I guess we all want different things."

Trent took a long gulp of his beer and then set the pint glass back down on the bar. He looked like he was turning something over in his head. "So long as you wanting something is *actually* wanting it and not using it as a cover."

"What do you mean?"

"I said I was happier being single for years. Truth was it was *easier* being single, less risky…but I wasn't happier. I'd mixed up security and certainty with happiness." He lifted one shoulder into a shrug. "And yeah, certainty is good but it can also be a sinkhole, you know?"

"I'd kill for some certainty right now." Ethan blew out a long breath.

"I heard about your mum." Trent lowered his eyes. "I'm so sorry."

Ethan had been in the same grade as Trent's older brother, so they'd spent time at each other's houses. The two families weren't super close, but they were friendly and Trent's parents had come to pay their respects at the funeral. But nobody had any idea about what was going on underneath the surface — only Ethan's half brother, adoptive father, and his ex knew and they'd all promised his mother they'd keep it secret.

It was precisely why he couldn't go home. Why it was no longer home. Because he would have to live a lie in order to keep his mother's dying wish.

"It's not only that." Ethan shook his head. "I found some stuff out about my family and it messed me up. I don't know where my future is anymore. I don't know... anything."

He swore under his breath. Why was he spilling his guts about this? The poor guy was on his honeymoon and probably trying to unwind. He wasn't here to listen to Ethan's bullshit.

"You have no idea how much I understand that." Trent slapped a hand down on Ethan's back. "Seriously. On *so* many levels."

"Really?"

"Yeah. Family is complicated, even the good ones. I don't want to overstep by doling out advice you're not looking for, but..." Trent paused to take another long draw on his beer. "You don't need to let the family stuff define you. You are your own person separate to all that and you get to decide what kind of person you want to be. Each day is a fresh start."

The words hit Ethan square in the chest. He had no idea what Trent had been through—because on the outside the Walters family looked perfect. But Trent probably would have said the same thing about the Hammersmiths. Outside appearances could be deceiving like that.

"It's hard to know who I want to be when I feel like everything I understood was wrong."

"Of course you know." Trent gestured with the hand not holding his drink. "In the moments where you're acting and not thinking about it, *that's* who you are."

The moments like when he'd lost himself in Monroe— kissing her against the wall of the haunted house and seeing her joy when she baked and binging old episodes of *Sugar Coated* and pretending to be Thor just to make her happy. All those times he'd felt like the man he was before his mother's death. He'd felt…free. Authentic.

"See, you *know*," Trent replied with a grin. "I can see it in your face."

"Did you fuck up along the way?" Ethan asked.

"Hell yeah." Trent laughed. "I shut people out and I kept a big secret from the world and I denied what I wanted at every turn. It made me into someone who floated through life never planning and never striving. It was lucky I finally pulled my head out of the sand and saw what was going on before I lost anyone else."

Trent's gaze drifted to a woman walking toward them. She was willowy, with long light brown hair that looked like it had seen some sun. Her limbs were tanned and she had a small tattoo on her upper thigh, which could be seen through the gauzy fabric of the white sarong covering the lower half of her bikini. The smile on her lips was pure bliss.

"I promised Cora we'd go for a boat ride this afternoon." Trent's smile was almost goofy with happiness. "It was great to see you, anyway. If you spot us at breakfast tomorrow, come say hi."

"I will. Congrats again."

Trent chugged the rest of his beer and then hopped down from the bar stool, heading off with a wave. The woman's smile grew bigger as he got close, and when he pulled her into a warm embrace, her face tilted up to his without any reservation. They were utterly in love.

You don't need to let the family stuff define you. You are your own person separate to all that and you get to decide what kind of person you want to be.

Trent's words circled in his head as he sat, watching people frolic and relax around him. He drank his beer slowly, then ordered another. And another. At some point he couldn't seem to taste it anymore, so he shoved the half-consumed drink away and stared out into the ocean.

He *had* been defining himself by his family's actions. He *had* been looking to be further defined by figuring out who his father was, which was why the reality of Matthew Brewer had hurt him so much. There was no "plug and play" new family at the end of his journey, no open arms or welcoming smiles. Only hurt and broken promises.

But what if he didn't let that define him? What if he thought about all of this as a clean slate? A do-over? A fresh start?

What would he choose?

Monroe.

Her name came to him in a rush, like a welcome breeze on an arid summer day. The time he'd spent with Monroe laughing, kissing, dreaming, planning…all those things had made him feel like the person he was deep inside. The person under the weight of his parents' lies and deception. Was it possible he would regret leaving Monroe for the rest of his life? Absolutely.

And with so much regret already settled on his shoulders, the only way to move forward was to start healing. His life back in Australia would never be what it was, but that didn't mean Ethan couldn't build something for himself *now*. Something new. Something that was exactly as he wanted it to be. Something that supported the values he cared about—honesty, hard work, family.

He couldn't drift forever.

While he was still tied to a life that was gone, he could never be happy. Did he know what the future held? No. But did he want to waste his life looking backward instead of forward? Definitely not.

Pulling his phone out of his pocket, he navigated to his usual travel website and booked a flight home to Australia. It was time to make a clean break with the past.

CHAPTER TWENTY-THREE

One month later…

"Cheers!" Monroe raised her wineglass toward her sisters and it was clinked on both sides. To her left, Taylor sat perched on a bar stool wearing a sleeveless black leather top and red lipstick. To her right, Loren looked the polar-opposite in a pale yellow and green gauzy maxi-dress and gold strappy sandals.

Monroe had come from her first full day of work in her new business, and she'd barely had time to throw on some lip gloss. But she'd piled her curls up onto her head and speared the bun with a decorative pin and had quickly changed out of her jeans and T-shirt into something that *wasn't* dusted with flour.

"Here's to the grand opening of *Some Like it Sweet*," Loren said. "May your business blossom and your customer base grow."

"And your bank account get nice and fat." Taylor grinned.

"Thank you." Monroe sighed, a mixture of excitement and exhaustion creeping into her veins. Everything had come together quickly after Jacob "fired" her. Once she launched the website and started spreading the word, events came rolling in. She was catering a dessert buffet for a baby shower next weekend, baking a birthday cake for her dad's next-door neighbor *and* she already had two engagement parties booked for the following month.

It wasn't huge, but it was more than she could have hoped for…and her inbox had several queries in it from that afternoon alone. It turned out that Loren's husband was quite the photographer and he'd helped her snap a bunch of pictures for the website's portfolio section… which had resulted in Monroe making *a lot* of cakes and then foisting them on her family members.

"What did you do today?" Loren asked.

Monroe sipped her wine. "I did practice runs of a few of my old recipes from the *Sugar Coated* competition that I want to make part of my standard offerings. The high school is having a bake sale tomorrow, so I contacted them and I'm going to donate what I made today and frost it fresh in the morning."

"That's nice of you. So you're going to put it on your website then? *Sugar Coated Winning Baker!* And make sure you include some photos from the show, too, leverage that for all it's worth," Taylor said. "And we can revive your old Instagram account as well."

"It feels crazy to mention it, since it was so long ago." Monroe looked down into her wine, already feeling that Taylor was going to jump in with a protest. "But I know it's a good idea. I *did* win, after all."

"That's right. No sense hiding your achievements away out of modesty." Loren nodded. "Toot your own horn as much as you can."

"It all feels like it's happening so quickly." In only a month, she'd started getting business even without some of the infrastructure in place—like a proper portfolio, business cards, or some of the professional tools that would make things easier. She could already see how she was going to outgrow her little kitchen, even with the option to impose on Loren's house for the big gigs.

"I'm so proud of you." Loren reached out and pulled Monroe into a hug.

"Thank you both." Monroe reached out for Taylor and brought her into the group hug. "I couldn't have made this leap without you guys."

"Liar." Loren pulled back. "We have been bugging you for ages to make this leap, so don't think we didn't notice that the time you made your decision coincided with the arrival of a handsome and strapping Australian man."

Monroe looked to Taylor for support, but her sister simply shrugged. "Okay, fine. Ethan may have had something to do with it."

"It's okay." Taylor patted her shoulder. "Sometimes it takes hearing advice from the right person at the right time delivered in the right way."

Maybe that's exactly what it was—a weird snap of cosmic timing and circumstance that had been everything Monroe needed. A hollow ache yawned in her chest. But that thinking would mean that they only connected to serve a purpose…and she couldn't buy that.

She loved him.

As scary as it had been to say it out loud, with all her years of baggage behind her and all the doubts swirling in her mind, she felt the truth of it deep in her soul. Their relationship wasn't just about helping her move on. It was more than that.

"How are you doing anyway? Has he called?"

Monroe had downplayed the "breakup," saying Ethan

had left for Australia to deal with some personal family things back home, which wasn't a lie. Part of her didn't want to admit out loud that they'd split, almost as if wishing might bring him back.

You know that's a fool's game. Wishing does nothing.

"Uh no." Monroe shook her head, and her sisters exchanged a glance. "But in other good news, it looks like I'm officially divorced…again."

"Well that *is* good news!" Taylor signaled to the bartender to bring them another round. "Good riddance to that dumpster fire."

Monroe snorted. "He's probably happy he got his way. Now he can go off and marry Amber."

"They deserve each other," Loren said, leaning her head on Monroe's shoulder.

"Yeah, they do."

And for the first time since it had all happened, Monroe really didn't feel anything bad in her heart. No regret, no sadness, just…peace. She'd finally moved on.

The girls continued to drink and pick at bar snacks for another hour, before Rudy came to pick up Loren. Taylor was meeting Tim at a music venue to listen to a band they both liked, and Monroe waited out front with her until the cab came.

"You sure you don't want me to drop you home first?" Taylor asked.

"Nah, a walk will do me good." Forever Falls was the kind of place where she could walk home safely at nine o'clock at night, and for that she was grateful.

Besides, there was one last thing she needed to do to complete her transformation into Monroe 2.0. She waved her sister off as the cab pulled into the street and then she set about walking down Main Street toward her apartment. Usually, at this point, she would peel off down a side street and continue in her zig-zag path, all so she could avoid the yoga studio Amber used to own.

Not anymore.

She walked straight, skipping her usual turn off and even the "emergency turn off" one street down that she'd used a few times to chicken out at the last minute. The studio came into view. It was a small but cute place, with a glass window and door. Sucking in a breath, Monroe walked right over to it and peered in the window.

It was empty—had been for a little while, which wasn't uncommon through the colder months. Businesses couldn't last through the quiet season, and it was sometimes hard to get new tenants in, especially in this economy. The person who'd taken on the lease after Amber had kept the yoga studio going for a while, but this past winter it had shut down.

At one point even walking up to this place would have sent her into a spiral, but now she felt…relief.

That part of her life was behind her. She was facing the opposite direction and putting one foot in front of the other toward her goals. She took out her phone and snapped a picture of the "for lease" sign, telling herself it was to capture the moment but a little voice inside her whispered: *call the number*.

Tomorrow. In the morning she would call and make a casual inquiry and just see what happened. But even as she walked home, Monroe was crunching the numbers in her head.

• • •

Ethan walked through the empty apartment in Melbourne that had once been his home. Over the last month the furniture had all been either sold or donated, and the rest of the items picked over by family and friends. Even Sarah had come by to pick up some things she wanted.

It had been hard seeing her, but there was a sense of closure between them. The spark they'd once nurtured was no longer there and Sarah was dating someone new. She seemed happy and that made Ethan happy. He was surprised at how little it hurt to hear she'd moved on, and he'd found himself saying that he had someone, too.

Monroe.

The woman who haunted his dreams on the nightly. The woman he couldn't get out of his head, no matter how much he tried.

Ethan stood at the large window that overlooked the city. The Yarra River cut through Melbourne, dividing north and south. The glowing spire of the Arts Centre shifted colors against an inky night sky and the flash and brilliance of the Crown Casino and Southbank lit up like pure gold. He'd loved this place, though it had never truly felt like home.

To be honest, the glitz and glamour of city life wasn't really him.

At some point he'd been chasing all this—the fancy apartment, the career accolades, the big salary—more to prove a point than because he wanted it for himself. He'd felt this need to prove himself to his father, because deep down he knew something was wrong. But Ethan had felt more at home hauling firewood at Lottie's inn than he did suiting up like a monkey every day to work in an office.

"Ethan."

At the sound of his name in a very familiar voice, he turned. Ivan Hammersmith, the man who'd raised him, stood in the doorway of the apartment. Ethan had left the door unlocked because he hadn't planned to stay long. Ivan looked the same as he always did, jeans and steel-capped boots, a utility jacket, cap pulled down low on his brow, a gray-flecked goatee which remained on his face regardless of whether it was in or out of fashion.

"Hi uh…" He didn't even know what to call the man.

"You can use my name," Ivan said gruffly, walking through the apartment, the sound of his heavy boots echoing in the empty space. "You don't have to call me Dad anymore."

They hadn't spoken about this since Ethan's mother revealed the truth. Not after she died, nor in the time since Ethan had returned home. After leaving Fiji, he'd returned to Australia to tie up loose ends. That involved clearing out the apartment and getting a real estate agent to put it up for sale. The new owners wouldn't be moving in for another month, but Ethan wasn't sticking around for that. It was nothing the real estate agent couldn't handle and frankly, he knew there was nothing here for him anymore.

"What are you doing here?" Ethan asked.

"Sarah called me." He took his cap off. The top of his head was thinning even more than Ethan remembered and Ivan rubbed his hand over it, as if self-conscious. "She said you were packing up and that she'd been by. She thought I might want the chance to speak with you before you leave again."

Oh Sarah. Ethan sighed. His ex was always quite fond of Ivan, since her own father lived overseas.

"Funny how they can still meddle in your life even after they're not in it anymore," Ivan said gruffly.

"That's the bloody truth."

"But she was right, though. I did want the chance to talk to you."

What could Ivan possibly have to say? They'd never seen eye-to-eye, never been close or had any kind of real connection. But Ethan could readily admit that Ivan had loved Marcie and they'd had a good marriage. And he worked hard to provide for their family, put food on the table, and he'd been tender with his wife when he thought no one was looking.

He was a decent man. Just not the father Ethan had hoped for.

"So talk," Ethan said.

Ivan toyed with his cap. "You know I loved your mother more than anything on this earth, right? She was my sunshine."

"I know."

"I knew her before she went overseas and came back pregnant. I'd always loved her, ever since we were kids in high school. When she came back from the States, she was..." His eyes were haunted for a moment. "She was broken. There was no sunshine in her smile anymore."

Ethan didn't want to imagine his mother like that. Even after the lies she'd told, he still loved her.

"She told me about the pregnancy and I said I'd marry

her. We could pretend we'd been dating and we'd lie about how far along she was so people didn't know, since she was only seven or eight weeks pregnant at that point." He sighed. "Then a few months later, I hear the man who got her pregnant suddenly wanted to come back. She told me that she couldn't marry me because she still loved this bloke who'd…"

Ivan bit back a curse.

"She still loved him," he said. "Anyway, she left to go and meet him at the airport."

"But he never showed." The words popped out of Ethan's mouth.

"That's right." Ivan looked at him curiously but didn't question how Ethan knew that detail. "She waited there overnight. Some security guard found her sleeping on a bench. She was dehydrated. Hadn't eaten. I drove all the way to Melbourne to convince her to come back to Patterson's Bluff. I forgave her, and we agreed never to talk about it."

"That seems to be the Hammersmith MO," Ethan said bitterly.

"When you were born, she wanted to put all that pain behind her," Ivan explained. "And I said I would do whatever she felt was right. If she wanted to raise you knowing I wasn't your dad, then fine. If she wanted me to be your dad, then I was also willing to do that. I just wanted her to have her sunshine again."

Ivan's voice caught. Grief flashed across his face like lightning, but he took a moment to compose himself and fought it down.

"As you got older I asked her if we should say something,

but she was always too afraid. She worried that you would want to go and find your father and that you'd end up like him—a troublemaker."

"Did he ever try to contact her? Or me?" Ethan asked.

"Yes. But after the airport incident, your mother changed the home phone number and put his letters straight in the rubbish without opening them. I would find them in there sometimes and frankly, that made me happy." He shrugged. "I know it probably makes me sound like a prick, but it's the truth."

"I can't blame you for that," Ethan replied. He certainly wouldn't want to be in Ivan's position.

"It was hard to know what role I had to play. Especially since you were the smartest little ankle biter I'd ever met. Always asking questions, always wanting to know everything, getting into stuff and running circles around everyone." Ivan shook his head. "I knew you didn't get that from me and...I always wondered how much of your real father you had in you. You didn't look like me, of course, and you didn't think like me. It was like being reminded every day that this man who hurt your mother still lived in our house in some form."

That would explain the resentment Ethan had always felt underneath everything. He'd been a very empathetic person, even as a kid, picking up on things that no one else could see.

"That wasn't my fault," Ethan said.

"No, it wasn't. I'm not proud that I felt that way." Ivan looked down at his boots. "I'm not proud that we lied to you, either. But I promised I would love and support your mother no matter what, and I didn't break that promise the entire time she was alive."

"She was lucky to have you," Ethan said, and he believed it. For the first time he saw Ivan for who he was—a man who was deeply in love with a scarred woman, who likely wasn't equipped with the emotional tools to handle it all. But he had tried his best.

"I'm sorry about all the lies, Ethan. I knew it was wrong."

Ethan opened his mouth to say that he wished they'd told him before Matthew Brewer died, but…*did* he wish that? From all accounts, the man wasn't the kind of father Ethan would have wanted. And going through every single bit of paperwork Lottie had given him—a few more letters, some photographs, legal documents—didn't do anything to prove otherwise.

"I forgive you," Ethan said, realizing that for the first time since it all happened that he didn't blame Ivan. Or his mother. They did the best with what they had—and Ethan *had* been raised in a home with love and without chaos, even if there were a few skeletons buried in the closet.

In a very uncharacteristic gesture, Ivan pulled Ethan into a hug and squeezed him tight. A second later he released him, stepping back as though he wanted to make sure the moment was over.

"Your mother loved you very much," Ivan said. "You were her whole world."

"No, *we* were her whole world. She loved you, too."

Ivan's eyes grew misty, but the muscles in his jaw moved as if he was trying to grind the feeling away. "Did you find him over there? I mean, we knew he was dead, but…"

"Yeah. I found him." Ethan sighed. "And yet, it feels like I found nothing."

"What are you doing next?"

"I wanted to get rid of this place, since I knew I wouldn't be moving back here but beyond that…"

He was drifting. Aimless. Going through the motions one day after the next without any real goals in sight.

"Don't waste all this," Ivan said, gesturing to the empty apartment around them. "You've always had a bright future ahead of you and none of this information changes that. You can *do* things, Ethan. Things a lot of other people can't."

Ethan made a scoffing sound.

"Really." Ivan looked him dead in the eye. "If I learned one thing from loving your mother it was that sometimes you have to set your ego to one side. I could have very easily *not* have gone to the airport that day, stroking my wounded pride at home. I could have walked out on her anytime I found her pining over him. But I didn't, because loving her was more important than my ego."

This was the first time Ivan had ever given Ethan any sort of fatherly advice. Growing up, Ethan had always gone to his mother when he had an issue to talk through, but now he saw that perhaps the rift between him and the man who raised him wasn't *only* Ivan's doing. Ethan had played a role in it, too.

"Don't let your bruised ego stand in the way of the life you want." Ivan clamped a hand down on his shoulder and Ethan felt, for the very first time, the true strength of a father-son bond. "I know you're angry and hurt. You have every right to be. But don't let that hold you back from the things you *really* want."

As soon as Ivan said that, Ethan's mind flashed to

Monroe. To standing in her bedroom doorway, watching her bake. To holding her hand as she dragged him into her bedroom. To sitting around her sister's table, delighting in how close and kind her family was. They were the same images that bubbled up when he'd talked to Trent.

And there was part of him that thought about Lottie, too. How satisfied he'd felt helping her bring the inn back to its former glory, even if that end state was a long way off. How he'd felt seeing the appreciation in her eyes as she appraised his work, even if she didn't always have the words to speak her praise out loud.

He'd felt an inkling of a life in Forever Falls. Like a glimmer of a dream he was trying to remember, that flickered in and out of his consciousness. There might not be any more blood relatives alive there for him to call family, but he'd always wanted to build one of his own. Monroe's words echoed in his head:

Maybe this is a chance for you to build what you've always wanted. Start fresh, choose the people to be your family based on the kind of people you want in your life. You have that control.

He did. And he could.

"I wondered if you might tell me it was time to come home, to Patterson's Bluff," Ethan said.

Ivan shook his head. "That's not for me to tell you. Now you have all the information you wanted, it's *your* decision what to do next."

"I have a clean slate," he said, almost to himself.

"That's right. But I will ask one thing. If you go back there or off to somewhere new, will you come visit every so often? I know that maybe I wasn't the best father for you growing up, but I still consider you my son."

"Yeah, I'll come visit." For a moment, Ethan was a little choked up. "Hey uh, since you're in the city I assume you're not driving all the way back home tonight? Maybe we should go to the pub and get a beer."

"I'd really like that." Ivan smiled.

As Ethan locked up his former home in Melbourne for the very last time, it was like something clicked into place. Like a string had been cut, or a shackle had been unlocked. The mystery of his father had been solved, and yet a hollowness had been following him around these past weeks.

That was because Ethan had been looking for something that might fill the hole his mother had left behind—not only in her passing, but in his assumption that she'd denied him his true family. Only she hadn't. She'd *given* him a family in the best way she knew how, by finding a man who loved and provided and tried to love him back.

Was it perfect? No.

But that was life—making mistakes and then making amends, trying something and failing and then trying again. Ethan walked down the apartment hallway, his steps falling in time with Ivan's, and both of them lost in deep contemplation.

The ball was in Ethan's court, now. Would he continue on like a wounded bull, angry at what could have been? Or would he take that bull by the horns and make sure that what was to come fulfilled him in every way?

He *could* have the family he desired—one of his own making, one that might span multiple countries, one that might not be perfect but was full of love. And that all started with putting his ego to one side, like Ivan said.

The very next thing would be telling the woman who'd stolen his heart exactly how he felt about her.

• • •

When Ethan pulled into Forever Falls a week later, he almost didn't recognize the place. Gone were the dirty snow drifts and bare trees and people huddling in their coats to protect themselves from the gusty coastal wind. In spring, Forever Falls transformed into a postcard. Trees full of bright green leaves lined Main Street. The sky was blue, but it must have rained overnight, because the pavement was wet in patches and a few people were wearing brightly colored gumboots over their jeans and carrying equally bright umbrellas at their sides.

There were more people around and the town had lost some of its sleepy vibe, matching the vibrancy of the sky and the flora. He parked his rental car along the side of the road and got out in front of the Sunshine Diner. A sign in the window told him that new management had taken over.

Monroe's boss must have sold after all.

He pushed through the front door and a familiar face greeted him. Darlene broke into a big smile. "Now that is a face we haven't seen in some time!"

Big Frank emerged from the kitchen and also smiled, carrying a load of fresh baked rolls that he was distributing to the tables. "Hey, nice to see you."

At the table closest to him, two women stared with their mouths hanging open. "Wait a minute. Is that Chris—?"

"No!" Big Frank and Darlene said at the same time and Ethan burst out laughing.

"I'm sorry to come in and not order anything, but I was hoping to speak to Monroe if she's around." He hoped they wouldn't go too hard on him, but neither one of them seemed to hold any animosity.

"I'm afraid Monroe doesn't work here anymore," Darlene said.

The wind was knocked out of him, and Ethan's shoulders sagged. What if he'd lost her? What if she'd gone somewhere else and—

"You'll need to head down to her cake shop."

"Her cake shop?" Joy spread through him like sunshine, and he couldn't help the beaming smile spreading across his lips. "Really? She did it?"

"She sure did. If you want, I can give you the address?"

But a penny dropped that made him smile even harder. "You know what, don't worry about that. I know exactly where she is."

He waved goodbye to the confused faces of the Sunshine Diner employees and customers, and then he headed back out into the fresh air. He had *one* chance to make an impression on Monroe—one chance to make things up to her and to show her that she'd made an impact not only on his life, but on *him* as a person.

For the entire duration of the flight from Australia, he'd thought about her. Perhaps Monroe was the point of his year-long journey after all—because he'd been looking for family and he'd found it. Only, it wasn't his father who'd given him that family. It was Monroe.

And he loved her.

He'd thought about it as he sat awake staring into the darkened cabin of the QANTAS Boeing 747 while his neighbors slept. Of course he loved her. She was everything that he believed love should be—resilient, tough but kind, protective, loyal. Add to that a physical attraction that burned brightly between them and he'd fallen so quick he didn't even know he was over the edge of the cliff until he hit the rocky bottom below.

She surprised him in the best ways possible and she'd proven to be the kind of person who was invested in her own growth and betterment, which was something Ethan believed in.

He loved her.

And she'd finally taken the plunge to realize her own talents and potential. A simple "I'm sorry" wasn't going to cut it.

CHAPTER TWENTY-FOUR

The next day…

Monroe had been in her new shop for a week now. No longer a place of bad memories, the space had been turned into a sweet-tooth's dreams. With the help of some investment from Mr. Sullivan, a forthcoming small business grant *and* plenty of hours of elbow grease over the last month from her sisters, their partners, Darlene *and* Big Frank's entire family, *Some Like it Sweet's* brick and mortar store was officially open for business.

Early morning sunlight streamed in through the front windows, casting a buttery light over the cake cabinet and register. Monroe flipped the sign on the door to say they were open and made her way behind the counter to get back to work on her current commission.

Loren breezed in from the back room, a pink apron tied over a blue and yellow floral dress. The customized aprons had been a gift from Loren, on the proviso that she be able to work a few shifts a week while Harlow and Jesse were in daycare, and the other girls were at school. Monroe was more than happy for the help.

"Looking good. The pink really suits you," Monroe said.

"Thanks. I'm glad you decided to go with pink in the logo instead of purple. It suits my skin tone much better." Loren grinned.

"Yeah, that's *totally* why I chose it." Monroe rolled her

eyes, but laughed as she worked.

The front door opened and two women in their twenties strolled in, ooh-ing and aahh-ing over the desserts in the front counter. Monroe had decided to expand beyond making event cakes to have a small selection of "single serve" cakes and confections, too. Today they had her "cupcakes for breakfast" cupcakes, which were a healthier cake chock full of nuts, raisins and honey topped with a maple coconut creme. It was one of her most popular recipes from *Sugar Coated*.

Alongside those were chunky white chocolate and sea salt cookies, birthday cake cookie balls and mini cupcakes in her three standard flavors—vanilla, chocolate, and choc mint.

"This stuff looks amazing!" one of the girls said.

Loren served them with her usual friendly style, leaving Monroe to work on her birthday cake order. They'd set the cake making station up with a big open window between the kitchen and the front, so on days where Monroe worked alone, she could easily see into the front of the shop to go out and help people.

The front door swung open and two more people came in, then another woman with a small child holding her hand. In minutes, the line for the counter was three deep.

Huh?

Monroe abandoned her cake and went out front to help Loren, busying herself with chatting to the customers as more poured through the door. In the first half hour of opening, they'd sold through half their daily inventory.

"What is going on?" Monroe said as it finally slowed for a minute.

Loren shrugged, looking equally perplexed. "Apparently

you hit on the *exact* thing Forever Falls was missing?"

"I wish. A business doesn't boom like this without reason." She went out the back to thaw out some extra cookie dough, so even if they ran out of some of the fiddlier items at least she could keep throwing cookies in the oven.

More people came into the store and Monroe worked at twice her usual speed, getting more treats into the ovens and even whipping up another batch of mini cupcakes in between helping people. Thankfully the birthday cake needed to sit in the fridge for a while anyway, to let the layers set.

By lunchtime, she and Loren were run off their feet and the cake display was barren. Another batch of cookies was coming up, but it needed to cool for a few minutes to firm up so they wouldn't crumble in being transported out of the kitchen.

Yet another customer wandered into the store. "Wow, are you guys sold out of everything already?"

"We've got some white chocolate cookies coming in a few minutes if you're willing to wait," Monroe offered with a smile.

"Sure." The woman, who was dressed like she worked in an office and who looked vaguely familiar, peered into the glass cabinet containing the premade six- and ten-inch cakes. "Actually, I'll grab one of the smaller vanilla strawberry layer cakes if they're not on hold for another customer."

"Of course! Good choice, too," Loren said with a wink. "That's my favorite one."

"A colleague of mine is having her birthday tomorrow,

so I thought it might be nice to surprise her. She's a *huge* Chris Hemsworth fan, so knowing that she's getting a cake from a bakery he recommended will be a huge kick."

Monroe stopped in her tracks, almost screeching to a halt. "Say that again?"

"Chris Hemsworth, you know the Australian actor? Blond hair, dreamy blue eyes—"

"Oh, I know who he is." Monroe nodded. "He recommended my bakery?"

"Uh-huh." The woman smiled.

"Holy crap." Loren blinked and then clamped a hand over her mouth. Wow, if Loren said a word like "crap" she must have been shocked. Only, it wasn't shock over the likelihood of an actual celebrity recommending her bakery. More likely it was that a certain doppelgänger had something to do with it.

"Here, I'll show you." The woman dug her phone out of her bag and turned it toward Monroe.

There was a picture with the woman, a friend, and what appeared to be Chris Hemsworth dressed in a very familiar Thor outfit.

"That's not the real Chris Hemsworth, I'm sorry to say." Monroe handed the phone back.

"Oh, I know." The woman winked. "But how you found someone who looks *exactly* like him—with the accent and everything—to dress up and hand out flyers is wild. It was enough to have me coming down here right away to check out your bakery. I work in marketing, actually, and this plan is genius!"

Monroe blinked. Ethan was dressed up and handing out flyers?

"Where did you say you saw him?" Monroe asked, already taking off her apron.

"Oh, he was down by the town square."

"Think you can manage if I duck out for a few minutes?" Monroe asked Loren, who nodded. "Just take the cookies out when the timer goes off and give them at least five minutes to cool before you bag them up. Throw in an extra one on the house as well."

The customer's face lit up. "Thank you."

Monroe whipped off her apron and grabbed her purse, then she headed outside. The town square was a small space paved with cobblestones, and was flanked by a local government office, the Forever Falls tourism center, and a small office building. In the middle stood a large tree and the Goldie statue that Monroe had shared with Ethan on their day out together.

Sure enough, he was standing next to it in full Thor getup and there was a crowd of people around him. He was taking photos and handing out colorful pieces of paper, smiling and chatting with the townsfolk. For a moment, she could only watch. His broad frame filled out the costume to perfection and this time he had his muscular arms out which, even now, made her mouth run dry.

But it wasn't his handsome face, intense blue eyes, or cut physique that held her attention beyond the initial glance. No, it was his energy. He seemed…lighter, somehow. Happier.

Monroe walked over to the group with her hands on her hips. "What exactly is going on here?"

Ethan looked over to her and if he was surprised to see her, he didn't show it one bit. When he smiled, Monroe had to stop her knees from going weak. "Making sure the good folks of Forever Falls know where to indulge their sweet tooth."

"Oh you're the *Sugar Coated* lady!" One girl, who looked to be about sixteen, turned to Monroe. "That's so cool. I used to watch that show every night with my mom."

"Here." Ethan thrust a flyer into her hand. "You and your mother should go visit Monroe at her store and then you'll get to see how great her baking is in person."

"I will!" The girl scampered off.

"Did you…make these on your own?" Monroe plucked a flyer from his hand. It was gorgeously designed, featuring *Some Like It Sweet*'s logo and all the correct information, including opening hours and their website.

"I may have had a little help from a friend back home who's a graphic designer, but we printed them up at the inn."

"We?" Monroe raised an eyebrow.

"Lottie and me."

Monroe shook her head, words escaping her. "Why?"

"Because I realized that I made a grave mistake." Ethan took a step toward her. "And that was letting my ego and my pride get in the way of my decision-making."

"And how did you come to that conclusion?"

"I spoke with my dad, back home. We cleared the air over some beers and I got the full story about how everything happened from his side. It put a lot of things into perspective. Namely, that the very thing I'd been looking for all this time was family." He bobbed his head. There were a few people standing by, watching curiously, but that didn't deter Ethan. "And you were right, family isn't just blood. It's the people you choose to bring into your life, the relationships you build because they lift you up and make you a better person."

"What does that have to do with my bakery?"

"Nothing. But it has *everything* to do with you, Monroe. You're that person for me—the person who lifts me up and makes me a better man. You're the person I want to bring into my life."

For a moment, there was a whirring in Monroe's mind so loud she was sure this whole thing was a dream. Or a hallucination. Maybe she'd gone too long without eating and the sugar fumes from making buckets of frosting was getting to her.

"But, I thought…"

"That I was stubborn and pig-headed and maybe a little bit of a dickhead?"

"I mean, I wouldn't use that word but…yeah." She laughed, and shook her head. "I knew you were hurting and you had a lot of things to work through. Trust me, I get that. I've *been* there."

"Past tense." Ethan reached for her hand. "That's good to hear."

"It feels good, too," she said softly.

"I still have a lot of things to work through and yeah, I'll probably be hurting a while. But when I went back to Australia and looked at what my life used to be, I realized I had been chasing all the wrong things, even before my mother's bombshell. I spent my whole adult life clawing my way up the corporate ladder to prove something to my dad, and I was chasing career accolades and a big shiny house to prove something to *myself*."

"There's nothing wrong with dreams," she replied.

"True, but dreams should come from within. They shouldn't be about making other people think highly of you." Ethan tugged her closer, his blue eyes boring right into her. "When I came here and spent time with you, I felt like for the first time in my whole life I could just be myself. I wasn't trying to prove anything to you, or Lottie, or anyone else here. I've never had so much fun as the time I spent with you, learning about you and your family and this town, and helping Lottie fix up the inn."

Her heart skipped a beat, hope gathering steam like a flame drawing oxygen to grow. "You're back? For good?"

"I want to get to know the place my birth father called home." He nodded. "And I want to make a family of my own. I want to take control of the thing that's always been missing, and I can't see any other future but the one with you in it."

Monroe wasn't sure what to say—her heart was thumping like a rabbit's foot and her brain was waving red flags. Conflicted didn't even begin to cover it, but not because she was unsure of her feelings for Ethan—*those* were rock solid—but her fear of being discarded still lurked below the surface. What if he left again? What if he decided he wanted to go back to Australia and she had the same issues as before?

He's worth the risk.

"Monroe, the entire time I was on my flight out of here I knew something was wrong. I could feel it in my gut. I missed you the second I boarded the plane. I thought about nothing but you for hours as everyone slept around me." He brought one hand up to her face and brushed his thumb over her cheek. "I messed up in leaving you but I had to close that loop."

"Even though it hurt like hell, I understand why you did it. I guess I closed my own loop too," she said. "I am now officially divorced. For real, this time."

"That's wonderful. Everything is out in the open now. No more lies, no more secrets, no more searching."

Could she really believe him? "How can you be sure?"

"Because I found that piece of my life that was missing. I found it here in this town, with you. I want to build a life, Monroe. A life with all the right things and that's full of love and…" He sucked in a breath. "I want it to have meaning. I don't just want to be some guy in a suit chasing the next bonus, you know? I want to build something with people I care about and provide for future generations. I want to learn from the mistakes my parents made and I want to forgive them, too."

"That sounds wonderful." Tears pricked her eyes hot and sharp, but she blinked them away.

"And that all starts with coming back here and support-ing the woman I love." He lowered his forehead down to hers. "I wasn't ready to say it before I left because I needed to figure things out, but that didn't mean the feeling wasn't there already. Because I did love you then, Monroe, even if I didn't have the guts to say it."

"Then say it now," she whispered.

"I love you, Monroe. More than anything."

• • •

Was he mad? This whole thing—the costume, standing in the town square declaring his love in front of strangers, laying *everything* on the line…who was he right now?

A new and improved Ethan.

A man who knew love, who knew the power of truth, who knew that life was what you made it. A man who knew that mistakes could be overcome and that forgiveness was golden.

Monroe looked up at him, her beautiful brown eyes wide and glimmering, her curly ginger hair ruffled by the wind, and her freckles standing out loud and proud and pretty as always.

"I love you, too, Ethan." She ran her tongue along her lips. "But how do I know that you won't get bored here? How do I know that you won't want to go back home?"

"Because I *am* home," he said. "Will I want to go back to Australia to visit people there? Yeah, of course. But can I see myself growing old with you and having babies and dogs and setting down roots in Forever Falls? Hell yeah I can."

Putting his wishes out into the world was like a weight being lifted off his chest. He felt unshackled. Free. Ready.

"Are you sure?" she whispered.

"Monroe, I have never been more certain of anything in my whole life. Even when the rest of my world felt like it was crumbling, being with you was the only thing that felt right. You're my safe harbor."

"And you're my superhero," she said, a grin spreading across her lips. "Literally."

"You like the costume, huh?"

"It's very sexy, especially when you get your guns out." She laughed.

"I'll see if the costume place will let me keep it." He

waggled his eyebrows.

"Will you just kiss her already!" someone yelled from the crowd.

And what a crowd they'd drawn. People were standing around waiting to see what happened. Ethan looked at Monroe and she nodded, a flush spreading across her cheeks that filled his heart with joy.

And when he lowered his head to hers, Monroe melted into him. Her hands clutched at the fake armor of his costume and she tilted her head back, lips parting. Their kiss was sugary sweet, and he swept his tongue into her mouth, holding her so tight it was a miracle she didn't gasp for air. But he never wanted to let her go, because this woman had seen him through his darkest times.

Her light and gold heart had been an anchor when he'd felt like the universe was ripping everything from him. The crowd around them cheered and Monroe pulled back, laughing, her face that adorable shade of deep rose-red that he loved so much.

"And you all lived happily ever after," a little girl said, scurrying up to them. "Can I have a photo now? We've been waiting *aaaaages*."

Laughing, Monroe stepped back and motioned for him to keep the people happy. But he shot her a look. "This isn't over yet," he said.

"No, it's not." She grinned. "But I have to get back to work. I'm running a very successful business, you know."

"That's my girl."

"I am your girl." This time it wasn't a question.

"And I'm your Thor."

"Forever?" she asked.

"And always."

As Ethan crouched down to take a picture with the curly-haired little girl, he looked at her chubby face and eager smile, and he knew that there was so much more that life had to offer.

Love. Family. Hope. Truth.

And everything else good in the world.

EPILOGUE

One year later…

The grand reopening of the Forever Falls Inn had come quicker than Monroe could believe. It felt like yesterday that she'd made a deal with a handsome stranger on a secret mission. And now here they were, standing in the event space at the newly renovated inn.

The room was filled with people, dressed in Forever Falls's version of fancy clothing. Ethan was in all black, from the sweater hugging his broad chest, to the dress pants making his long legs look even longer. Next to him was Lottie, who wore black pants of her own and a checkered button down, never one to put on airs and graces even for the grand re-opening of her own business.

But Monroe had never seen the older woman smile the way she was now, beaming like actual rays of sunshine were coming out of her.

"Monroe, these cupcakes are *unreal*." One of the guests approached, a woman that used to frequent the diner when Monroe worked there. "Tell me I can book you for my daughter's birthday party later this year."

"Give me a call and we'll see what we can work out." Monroe slipped her a business card. "But I'm almost booked out for about the next six months, so call me this week okay?"

"I will. Thanks." The woman pocketed the card and

headed back into the crowd.

Monroe let her staff member look after the dessert bar which was filled with all manner of treats—mini cupcakes, truffles, neat squares of cake decorated with a tiny fondant version of Lottie's business logo, cake pops, and more. Monroe was half working, half playing a supporting role tonight.

Since his return to Forever Falls, Ethan has struck up a relationship with Lottie. It was a rather unexpected friendship as well as working partnership. Lottie had hired him on to help her finish the renovations on the inn but to also do all the tech stuff she hated, like building a website and figuring out how to implement a proper booking and payment system from this century.

In turn, she'd told him more about the woman who would have been his grandmother and had shed light on questions that Ethan still had. In many ways, Lottie had almost filled that grandmother role for him, and Ethan became the grandson she never had. Seeing the two of them together could warm even the coldest of hearts, because the love they had for one another was about the most beautiful thing Monroe had ever seen.

"Hey, it's our resident sugar pusher!" Ethan laughed and held out his hand, motioning for her to join him and Lottie as they chatted with some of the local business owners they were hoping to partner with for the inn. Monroe recognized a local artist and one of the men who ran a furniture restoration company. "I hope you've all had a chance to taste something from the dessert bar."

"Oh yes, the chocolate cake is delicious," one of the men piped up. "I bought one of your cakes for my wife's birthday last month and I swear we devoured the whole thing in a single sitting."

"I'm so glad to hear that." Monroe grinned. Ethan slung his arm around her shoulders and squeezed, his pride radiating.

Despite her fears that Ethan might one day change his mind about his life in Forever Falls, the two of them had grown closer every day. She'd never felt so loved and supported by a partner as she did now. He was her biggest fan—even if she was jealous that he could seemingly eat endless amounts of cake without putting on a pound—he was her best brainstorming partner, her cheerleader, and her shoulder to cry on after a tough day.

Whatever fears she might have from time to time, they were certainly getting quieter.

"I'm going to steal Monroe for a minute to show her upstairs," Ethan said to Lottie. "Are you okay down here to keep things going?"

"I'm not used to having quite so many people around here," Lottie grumbled. The grand opening party had been Ethan's idea for drumming up business, and the older woman had needed some cajoling.

"I'll keep you company," Loren said. She'd been standing with her husband off to the side, but clearly keeping an eye on things. "If that's okay with you, Lottie?"

She nodded. "Yeah, that's good by me."

Ethan smiled and grabbed Monroe's hand, intertwining their fingers as he led her toward the stairs. Now that it was all refinished, the polish gleamed, and the old place looked grand and loved once more.

"It's almost like two families coming together," he

said. "I'm honored both your sisters came by and brought some friends."

"Of course! We're all here to support one another." She squeezed his hand. "Loren's friend is getting married next year, and she was thinking the inn might make for a fun 'classy bachelorette party' location."

They ascended the stairs, some of them still squeaking as old buildings were want to do, and when they made it to the top, the hallway was lit with the gentle glow of antique glass lamps. Every bit of this place sparkled.

"You've put so much work into this inn," Monroe said. "I'm proud of you and Lottie for breathing new life into it."

"And to think she wanted to tear it down at one point, even though it had belonged to her family for generations." Ethan shook his head. "I think when she had me working on it the first time, it was just to spruce it up enough to sell it, but after I came back and asked for a job, she changed her mind."

"You've already had a lot of impact on the people in this town." She smiled.

Ethan hadn't only been working with Lottie, but he also taught a computer class at the local community center for older folks who wanted to learn how to use spreadsheets and some more intermediate programs. His students had taken to calling him "Thor" and he leaned into the role, keeping a mini Thor hammer on his key chain and making all his in-class exercises superhero themed.

Everybody loved Ethan, though not quite as much as she did.

"What did you want to show me?" she asked.

"Well, when we were deciding on the themes for each of

the rooms, we uh…decided to call this one Mary's Room." He pushed open the door and inside was a modest, but beautiful guest room decorated in pale blues. "This was her favorite color, apparently."

Monroe couldn't speak for a moment. She knew Ethan had wanted to learn more about the Brewers and Lottie had helped him connect to the more positive parts of his family history. On the wall of the guest room was an old sun-faded photo of a woman and a young boy with blond hair and a cheeky smile.

"That's them isn't it? Mary and Matthew." She walked closer and took in the details. There was something of Ethan in Matthew's smile, an inhibited joy. "This is a lovely tribute."

She turned around, her mouth already open to ask more questions, but her breath halted in her lungs as she saw Ethan down on one knee, a box in his hands.

"I wanted to do it here," he said. "Because I felt like I figured out who I was in this place. I felt like I connected with my past and in doing that found my future, and you're a critical piece of that puzzle."

"Oh my gosh." She pressed a hand to her heart, and it was beating wildly.

"I can't see a future without you in it, Monroe. You've opened my eyes to the important things in life, you've given me hope that I could heal and get past the bad things that happened. I owe you everything for the life you've helped me grasp." He sucked in a breath. "Monroe Roberts, it would make me the happiest man alive if you would say yes to forever. I want you to be my wife, my lifelong partner, the mother to my future children. And I want to stand by you as you soar to new heights and achieve everything your heart desires. What do you say?"

"Yes." The word barely got out of her before the tears did and it was only when a cheer erupted at the door, Loren and Taylor both squeezed into the frame and keeping everyone else behind them, that Monroe realized Ethan had planned every little detail. "I want to be your wife."

He got up and grabbed her, throwing both arms around her, the velvet box in one hand as he kissed her long and deep.

"Show her the damn ring!" Taylor shouted from the door, and there was laughter and cheering behind her.

"Oh yeah." Ethan laughed, momentarily embarrassed. "I was too interested in kissing you that I almost forgot the most important bit."

He opened the velvet box and showed the contents to Monroe. Inside was an old-fashioned ring, with a gold band and a platinum setting nestling three diamonds—the center one slightly larger than the other two.

"It belonged to my grandmother. To Mary," he said, still unsure whether he was supposed to call her by name or not. "Lottie said it was right for you to have it. That it's what she would have wanted. I know the diamonds aren't too big—"

"Stop, it's perfect. You know I don't care about that stuff." She held out her hand and it trembled as he slid the ring onto her finger. "It's precious and beautiful and it means something. *That's* what matters."

"You've made me so happy, Monroe. You have no idea."

"I have some idea, because I imagine it's as happy as you've made me." She pressed up onto her toes, admiring her ring as she slipped her hands over his shoulders and kissed her fiancé with everything she had. "I love you, Ethan. I'm so glad you found your way here."

Lottie pushed her way into the room and without a word wrapped them both into a brief but tight hug. Then she stepped back, looking a little embarrassed at the display of affection. "She would have been proud of you, boy."

"Thanks, Lottie."

The older woman nodded. "All right, well that's enough mushy stuff. And don't go thinking you're going to defile any of my nice rooms now, okay?"

Monroe flushed and Ethan threw his head back, a laugh rushing out of them. "Wouldn't dream of it."

"I would," Monroe said with a wink. "But I guess we can wait until we get home."

"Good thing there's a party already going on downstairs. We need to celebrate."

"We've got our whole lives to celebrate," she said, unable to wipe the smile off her face. "And I tend to treasure every single moment."

When Ethan's lips found hers again, it was like her heart was made of champagne and glitter.

This was love—this giddy, unnamable, irrepressible feeling. Being with the man she cherished, surrounded by family both blood and found, in a place where hope and new life had breathed into the walls and floors. Forever started now, and she would never let herself be closed off to it ever again.

ACKNOWLEDGEMENTS

With each and every book I write, it feels like the list of people to thank grows stronger. To my husband Justin, I couldn't do any of this without you. Thank you for bringing me endless coffees while I'm on crunch, for picking up the slack when the deadlines roll in and for always being ready to help with a brainstorming session.

To my writer friends: Taryn, Amy, Tara, Jen, Heidi, Lauren and Becca, you all make doing my dream job even better. Thank you for the laughs, for always being ready to share ideas and knowledge, for the craft talks and plot fixing, and for making me feel less alone at my desk. I'm so grateful to have you all in my life.

To my mum and dad, thank you for always fostering my love of books. To Sami, Albie, Melissa, Michael, and Violet—I'm grateful to be surrounded by such creative people. You all inspire me!

Thank you to the Ladies Supper Club, to the "…Station" group, to the friends I've made through Strengths and the wonderful people I met through the RAGT. You all make my world brighter.

Thank you to my agent Jill Marsal and to Liz Pelletier, Lydia Sharp, and the rest of the team at Entangled Publishing for helping me bring this story to life. There are so many hands that touch a story before it ends up on shelves, and I am grateful to every single person who works on my books.

Most important of all, thank you to my readers. I am grateful for each and every person who picks up one of my stories, for all the people who write to me letting me know they enjoy the worlds I create and to all the people who love romance as much as I do. You're all amazing.

*Don't miss the new sweet rom-com about
returning a sleepy beach town B&B to its former
tourist-destination glory.*

A Lot Like
LOVE

JENNIFER
USA TODAY BESTSELLING AUTHOR
SNOW

When Sarah Lewis inherits a run-down B&B from her late grandmother in coastal Blue Moon Bay, the logical thing to do is sell it and focus on her life in L.A. Her career is on the rise, and this setback could cost her the opportunities she's worked hard for. But when she learns that interested buyers will only tear it down in its current state, she feels a sense of obligation to her grandmother to get it back to the landmark tourist destination it once was...even if that means hiring the best contractor for the job, which happens to be her old high school crush.

Wes Sharrun's life has continued to unravel since the death of his wife three years before. Now with a struggling construction company and a nine-year-old daughter, he sees the B&B as an opportunity to get back on his feet. Unfortunately, despite trying to keep his distance, his daughter has taken a liking to Sarah, and his own feelings are tough to deny.

As they spend more time together painting, exploring a forgotten treasure trove of wine in a basement cellar, and arguing over balcony placement, the more the spark between them ignites. But will saving the B&B be enough to convince them both to take a second chance at love?

Hilarity ensues when the wrong brother arrives to play wingman at her sister's wedding.

the
wedding
date
disaster

AVERY FLYNN
USA TODAY BESTSELLING AUTHOR

Hadley Donavan can't believe she has to go home to Nebraska for her sister's wedding. She's gonna need a wingman and a whole lot of vodka for this level of family interaction. At least her bestie agreed he'd man up and help. But then instead of her best friend, his evil twin strolls out of the airport.

If you looked up doesn't-deserve-to-be-that-confident, way-too-hot-for-his-own-good billionaire in the dictionary, you'd find a picture of Will Holt. He's awful. Horrible. The worst—even if his butt looks phenomenal in those jeans.

Ten times worse? Hadley's buffer was supposed to be there to keep her away from the million and one family events. But Satan's spawn just grins and signs them up for every. Single. Thing.

Fine. "Cutthroat" Scrabble? She's in. She can't wait to take this guy down a notch. But somewhere between Pictionary and the teasing glint in his eyes, their bickering starts to feel like more than just a game…

Find out what happens when a woman shows up on his doorstep with a cowboy's baby all grown up…

Wishing for a *Cowboy*

VICTORIA
NEW YORK TIMES BESTSELLING AUTHOR
JAMES

Janie Adams has been a single parent to her nephew since he was a baby. Fifteen years later, she's finally found out who his father might be, so the two of them travel across the country to find him. She'd do *anything* for this kid. But when they arrive in the small town of Wishing River, Montana, and Janie finally meets the ruggedly handsome cowboy she'd been told had abandoned his son, his shocked response changes everything.

Aiden Rivers can't dispute this is his kid when he sees his own features staring back at him, but he had no idea Janie's sister was pregnant when she left him. He didn't even know she had a sister—clearly they'd *all* been lied to. Now he has fifteen years of fatherhood to make up for and no idea how to be a dad. This was never in his plans.

Janie sticks around to help him ease into parenting, everything from showing him how to lure a sulky kid out of his bedroom to keeping up with the latest teen-speak. Together, they surprisingly make a good team, this city girl and country boy. But when the past catches up with them, Aiden and Janie must decide what's best for the boy who's connecting them, not only for each other…which could mean splitting them apart.

AMARA
an imprint of Entangled Publishing LLC